# The Karma Suture

# The Karma Suture

Rosamund Kendal

*This is a work of fiction and all the characters, institutions and events described in it are fictional and the products of the author's imagination.*

First published by Jacana Media (Pty) Ltd in 2008

10 Orange Street
Sunnyside
Auckland Park 2092
South Africa
+2711 628 3200
www.jacana.co.za

© Rosamund Kendal, 2008

ISBN 978-1-77009-543-4

Set in Sabon 10.5/14
Printed by CTP Book Printers, Cape Town
Job No. 000608

See a complete list of Jacana titles at www.jacana.co.za

# Chapter One

## The beginning

A black man in his early thirties stumbles into the emergency room, clutching his chest. Blood oozes from between his fingers, stains his sweater, seeps red into his white sneakers. 'Help, I've been shot!' he yells, then collapses to the floor.

A nurse rushes to his side, feels his wrist for a pulse and then shakes her head. 'Code red! Code red!' she shouts as she pulls on latex gloves. With considerable effort she lifts the man up onto a trolley and begins chest compressions. Another sister and two doctors run to the scene and start helping her.

'You take charge,' Dr Greenblatt commands the newly qualified Dr Jude as they push the patient to the resuscitation room. Panic clouds the intern's face.

'Are you sure, Dr Greenblatt? You're much more experienced.'

Dr Greenblatt grasps the younger doctor's hand across the trolley. 'This is your chance to prove yourself. Show us that you are worth the degree that we have given you.'

Dr Jude nods, obviously inspired by his mentor's words. 'Sister Linda, please attach the leads,' he instructs the nurse. His voice breaks with tension.

The sister swiftly sticks the electrocardiogram probes onto the patient's chest. Miraculously, the bleeding seems to have abated. Dr Jude looks at the wriggly green line on the screen of the bleeping monitor and his face drops in consternation.

'Oh no, we're losing him! We're going to have to shock. Get the paddles ready.'

Paddles appear in the hands of the efficient Sister Linda and she hands them to Dr Jude. He places them on the patient's chest. Mentally, I will him to turn on the defibrillator. My telepathy works. He turns his muscular torso and flips up the obvious on/off switch, then leans over the patient, stress creasing his otherwise perfect face. 'Everybody clear!' he shouts. 'I'm shocking on three. One! Two! Three!' He presses the flashing red buttons on the sides of the paddles and the patient's body convulses.

God, what bullshit. I turn off the television and take my empty pizza box through to the kitchen, squashing it so that it fits into the already full rubbish bin. In real life a resuscitation would never look like that, especially not in a South African government hospital. And in real life the good-looking doctor would turn out to be an arsehole.

## Introductions

I am late for my first Practical Philosophy workshop, not so much because I got distracted watching *Emergency in New York General*, but because I have lost the piece of paper on which I previously scribbled the address for the course. Eventually I give up trying to find the building using only instinct and phone Leah to get her to reread the advert to me. She answers our shared home phone immediately, so I know that she has been sitting on the entrance hall floor next to the telephone waiting for John to call. I can imagine her flicking her carefully straightened black hair over her right shoulder as she listens to my request. *How could you manage to lose the piece of paper?* Flick, flick. *Why didn't you check the map book before you left home?* Flick. But she consents to hunt for the missing address, and I hear the muffled shuffle of her newspaper being shifted aside and then the sharp crack of her fashionable high heels on the wooden floor as she gets up from the telephone and walks to my room. I remember too late the piles of still-to-be-paid bills, unfiled bank statements and hastily stashed journal articles cluttering my desktop. I wonder how long her patience will hold out as she hunts for a torn ten-centimetre by ten-centimetre scrap of paper in the mess and for how long after that I will have to listen to her lecture me on tidy workspaces. But she is waiting for John's call, so I get just a quick 'Please don't shove empty pizza boxes into the rubbish bin when it's already full' before she reads out the address to me and puts down the phone.

The building to which the directions on the scrap of paper lead me is far from the dismal, academic-looking schoolhouse of my imagination. It is an old Victorian-style house with shuttered windows and a great carved wooden door. There is no wall surrounding the property and the unkempt garden is a green and silver landscape in the moonlight. I ring the doorbell and a child who looks about ten takes my hand and leads me to a room with heavy velvet curtains and a worn Persian carpet. A group of people sit in a semicircle in front of the lecturer. I sit down in the only open seat.

'Sorry I'm late. I got a little lost,' I apologise to the lecturer.

'Don't worry. We've only just started. We're still introducing ourselves. If everyone could tell us their name and perhaps a little bit about themselves?' Her red lipstick seeps into the fine smoker's wrinkles above her upper lip.

The man three seats to the left of me stands. 'Hi, my name's Gilbert. I'm married with two boys, and I work as a builder. From Jo'burg originally but I've been here in Cape Town for the past eight years.'

I wonder if I have erroneously walked into an Alcoholics Anonymous meeting instead of the Practical Philosophy class I saw advertised. Grace, perhaps, nudging me in the right direction. I dread the all-too-quick progression of the introductions. A Mexican wave of embarrassment travels round the group. Mentally I rehearse a few opening lines.

*Hi, I'm Sue, a disillusioned doctor and unacknowledged alcoholic.*

*Hi, I'm Sue, unattached, no children, and desperately seeking suitable single man, preferably of the Colin Farrell persuasion.*

*Hi, I'm Sue, bordering on depressed and trying to figure out if happy endings exist outside of fairy tales and the* Oprah *show.*

An expectant silence jolts me from my reverie. It's my turn. I stand. Sweat collects in slimy droplets in my armpits.

'Hi, I'm Sue . . .'

'Speak up, dear, we can't hear you here.' The woman who interrupted me is wearing huge gold hooped earrings. Her smile seems to float on her face, dancing between her jewellery.

'My name is Sue.' I coax my reluctant voice from a constricted throat. 'I'm a doctor at Bellville Hospital.'

'Wow, a doctor,' Gilbert the builder says.

'Gosh, you look so young. Are you still studying?' asks the scarlet-lipped guru in the front of the room.

'You must really see a lot,' the woman next to me says, and I want to say to her that she has no idea, but instead I smile sweetly, as a bright young doctor should.

Once again, I am defined by my degree. I have lost my identity to my vocation. I once heard that if you tell someone your true name, the one given to you by the gods at birth, that person has power over you for eternity. Medicine has stolen my soul.

\* \* \*

'So, how was your philosophy class?' Leah wants to know, having waited up for me to get home.

I take a half-empty bottle of red wine from the fridge and pour myself a glass. 'Interesting,' I tell her. 'Not really what I thought it would be.'

'What do you mean?' Leah is eating teaspoons of peanut butter from the jar. She only does this with crunchy peanut butter, so whenever it's my turn to do the shopping I buy smooth.

'I don't know. I thought it would be a proper course with notes and a PowerPoint presentation or at least overhead transparencies. I was expecting to hear all about Socrates and Plato and Descartes. Instead we sit in a semicircle in front of the lecturer like we're in some group therapy session. I think we all spoke more than she did.' The red wine eases comfortably down my throat and I can feel the muscles in my neck relaxing for the first time since I woke up this morning. I follow Leah to the lounge.

'What did you talk about?' she asks.

'Just introductory stuff. The meaning of philosophy, which is the love of wisdom, by the way. What we expect from the workshops, and all that kind of thing. And of course we did the obligatory round-the-circle introductions.'

'Were there any decent guys?' Leah has curled herself up on the worn leather couch in front of the television and is playing with the remote.

I know what she is looking for. 'Channel 36,' I prompt.

'Thanks.' She flips to the *Jerry Springer* show. A little clump of peanut butter has stuck to the corner of her mouth, a thick brown crack when she talks. It irritates me. She irritates me. Actually, her asking me about the guys in the class irritates me. It reminds me of what a failure I am when it comes to forming relationships with men. While she and John have been together for over three years, I haven't managed to keep a boyfriend for longer than a week since my and Kevin's engagement ended. I try to fool myself that I don't want a serious relationship and that my life is too busy to fit in a partner, but I suspect the real reason that I consistently choose to have flings with guys who I know will not phone me the next day is fear. Strangely, it's not so much a fear of being hurt that holds me back, but a fear of failing. The fear that another deficient relationship will prove my inability to form an emotionally mature partnership. I have seen a psychologist, but without much success. The psychologist and I constructed an extensive list of the reasons underlying my emotional detachment (as evidenced by my serial one-night stands), and I had the insight to realise that most of the reasons were not only valid, but also remediable. However, in some ways I think that therapy is like giving up smoking: one needs to want to make the change. I made a conscious decision then that I would rather choose to behave like an emotional cripple than risk having myself proved one.

'So,' Leah persists, 'was there anyone?' She's not just curious. I can see the concern in her eyes.

'There is one decent guy. He's in his early thirties, I guess. He's a sailor or something.'

She turns away from Jerry and looks at me with one neatly plucked eyebrow raised. 'What? Is he Taiwanese?'

'No, you idiot, not that kind of sailor. He owns a yacht.'

'A yacht, eh? He's obviously not struggling financially. What does he look like?'

'Tall, tanned. Kind of Camel-mannish, but not amazingly good-looking.'

'Are you going back next week?'

'I guess so. And no, not because of the guy. I'm hoping that these workshops will give me some direction. What I need is a kind of moral meter, something that tells me what's right and what's wrong.' I down the last sip of my wine. 'I need answers and not just excuses.'

'You're probably expecting a bit much from the workshops,' she says, sighing.

'I know. It's because I'm desperate. So often life just seems to make no sense.'

I want to explain to Leah how difficult it is for me to reconcile my working and my personal lives, but I can't find the right words without sounding arrogant or condescending. The time that I spend in the hospital is so dauntingly real that it makes my activities and emotions outside of working hours feel childish and superficial, like a sitcom, a half-hour television comedy. I wonder whether dealing all day with sickness and death and the decisions that they entail has made me devalue other emotions. I am petrified that, in the tide of trauma, pain, injustice and anger that drowns me daily, I have lost the ability to love.

## Chocolate éclair sweets for lunch

It's Friday morning and I'm on call, which means that once I have finished my ward round I will work in casualty for the rest of the day. The call roster is designed so that I am on call every Wednesday, alternate days and nights, and one Sunday and Friday a month. When I work a 'night' Wednesday, I work from Wednesday morning to Thursday evening. Between calls I have normal nine-hour working days, which I spend seeing patients in the out-patient department and sorting out my in-patients in the wards. In addition, I do ward rounds every second weekend and a few extra night calls at other hospitals. The latter is not part of my registrar job at Bellville Hospital but is necessary in order to pay off the rather large student loan that I accumulated over my six years at medical school. At the moment the extra calls cover the interest on the loan.

As usual, I have misjudged the morning traffic and my intern, Justine, is already waiting for me when I arrive at the ward. Justine is a strange girl, perhaps best described as obsessive-compulsive bordering on paranoid. Her perfectionism is debilitating, so that in the time that it takes her to see one patient, I see ten. She drives a brand-new Volvo, a graduation gift from her doctor-parents, because it's the safest car on the road. It gets washed once a week, on Wednesday at six in the evening. I once asked her once how many kilometres she can drive after the light for the reserve petrol tank comes on. She didn't know because she always fills up with petrol before the warning light appears. Perhaps I'm just jealous: all I got from my parents for graduation was a bottle of Bolls cherry liqueur, most of which ended up disappearing into one of Leah's creative desserts.

Justine is holding a plastic-covered green file in which she writes down my instructions from the ward round. The file is an appendage to her neat orderliness. She asks me where I would like to start the ward round.

'Let's start with Mr Nomdoe,' I say. 'Have the students arrived yet?'

'No, I don't think so. I haven't seen them.'

I have been allocated two fourth-year and two sixth-year medical students to whom I am supposed to pass on my superior knowledge and skills. They learnt after the first week that I seldom arrive before eight fifteen and, unlike the conscientious Justine, they take full advantage of my poor punctuality.

Usually the students spend their days drawing blood specimens and acting as porters for patients who need to be transported to and from special examinations. There is a joke popular among medical students: *What does MBChB stand for? Messenger Boy and Carrier of Human Blood.* I hope that in the breaks from acting as unpaid employment in an understaffed institution they will learn a bit more than how to push a wheelchair and which is the quickest route to the haematology lab. When I'm not too busy, I try to teach them something that is actually part of their syllabus.

Justine and I walk down the hospital corridor to Mr Nomdoe's room. The grey vinyl is peeling from the walls in thick strips, revealing large scars of discoloured concrete reminiscent of post-Communist Eastern Bloc decor. I don't know which is worse: the fake-marble seventies vinyl or the rough glue-stained cement. Cigarettes stubbed out on the linoleum floor have left it pock-marked with melted black punctures that are impossible to clean off. Many years ago, somebody stuck a handwritten copy of the Lord's Prayer on the door of what now serves as Mr Nomdoe's room. The putty has seeped through the corners of the page, leaving four greasy blotches.

'Mr Nomdoe, how are you this morning?' I reach around my neck for my stethoscope. Not there. I search in my bag, even though I know that I have left it on the table next to the front door where I deliberately placed it so that I wouldn't forget it. I wonder whether I can conjure it up if I concentrate hard enough.

I am waxing superstitious. This is a bad omen, a sign that I am going to have a horrible call.

'Justine, can I use your stethoscope, please?' She hesitates. I know that sharing an intimate thing like a stethoscope goes against the grain of her obsessive-compulsiveness. All too often borrowed stethoscopes are returned to the owner with small flakes of wax dangling from the earpieces. But perhaps my desperation is evident on my face: she relents and hands it to me. It is an expensive stethoscope, bought for her by her parents. Much nicer than mine.

'Mr Nomdoe, can you sit forward, please.' I place the diaphragm of the stethoscope against his chest. His breath sounds are strangely harsh, amplified more than I am used to by the superior German technology.

'Sounds fine. Have you coughed up any more blood?'

'No, Doctor.'

'Good. Justine, please contact radiology again and find out when they are going to do the embolisation.'

Mr Nomdoe has been waiting for the radiologist to block off the bleeding vessel in his chest for over two weeks. His case is an emergency. I panic each morning before I get to his room, anxious that someone else will be in his bed, that the artery will have started bleeding again overnight and that he will have bled to death. I've seen it happen: it takes less than fifteen minutes. Thus far he has been lucky, and I have been lucky, because each morning he has been in his bed reading the scrappy Gideon Bible that he found in the drawer of his bedside table. Perhaps I will call the radiologist later on but I know that it won't make much difference. He is willing to do the embolisation but there is a list of emergency patients waiting in front of Mr Nomdoe. I suspect that his reading the Bible will do more good than I am able to.

One of my students, Matthew, has arrived and he slips quietly into Mr Nomdoe's room, as though an inconspicuous entry will fail to remind me of his tardiness. I ask him to draw a full blood count and clotting profile on Mr Nomdoe.

'I drew bloods three days ago,' he complains. 'Must I do them again so soon?'

'Yes. If he actually does get called for the embolisation and there are no recent blood results, he will be cancelled. If he gets cancelled, he will slip right down to the bottom of the list and we will have to start all over again. So, if you want to save yourself from having to draw bloods on him for the next three months, I suggest you make sure that his most recent results are no older than seventy-two hours.'

The other students arrive and we speed through the ward round. We finish early, by eleven thirty, but the casualty staff have already started plaguing me with pages. The medical officer that is supposed to help out with the work in casualty has not turned up this morning and there are six patients waiting. I will not have time for coffee. I ask Justine and the students to finish off the ward work and then to meet me in casualty at one o'clock, after they have had some lunch. I know already that it is going to be a busy call and I will need as many hands as possible.

I make a small detour and take the D-block steps down to the casualty unit because they go past the benevolent society tuckshop that sells chocolate éclair toffees. Benevolent indeed. I buy twenty and shove them into the front pouch of the bag slung over my shoulder. Lunch on the go.

* * *

When referred or unbooked patients arrive at the hospital they go to admissions, where they are triaged into surgical, medical or gynaecological emergencies. Depending on their classification, they are pointed in different directions. Casualty, for medical emergencies, is on the first floor, around the corner from trauma. It is divided into a high-care unit for the very unstable patients who are waiting for beds in intensive care, a ward for the more stable patients who are waiting for beds in the normal wards, and an overnight ward for those patients whom we plan to discharge within twenty-four hours. In addition there is a patients' waiting room (which usually functions as an unofficial ward), a sisters' office and a doctors' office. The doctors' office is fitted out with a sagging bed, an old green chair and a television that has reception for a single channel specialising in Xhosa soap operas and reruns of eighties movies that never made it to the big screen.

Sister Lilly is waiting to pounce on me as I enter the unit. 'Doctor, where have you been? There are ten patients waiting for you already.'

Her accusatory look makes me defensive. I know that she thinks I have been sitting drinking coffee in the cafeteria for the whole morning. 'I was doing my round. I've got forty patients in the ward. Do you have a problem with that?'

Sister Lilly snorts. After years of practice she has perfected the disbelieving snort. It is pointless responding. I skim the list of names written up on the whiteboard. Ten of the names have been ticked off. These are the patients who are in the waiting room already, waiting to be seen by me. The other seven have been referred by general practitioners or day hospitals and are on their way in. I glance over names and diagnoses. The list contains only one piece of important information: where each patient has been referred from. Stellenbosch; Elsies River; Caledon (too far and one down: I will already be off duty by the time the ambulance brings the patient in); Paarl; Ravensmead; Bishop Lavis; Durbanville. I have managed to whittle the list down to five but already my bleeper is going off almost continuously. I go to the telephone in the sisters' office to answer it. It is a doctor from outside Bellville Hospital calling in to refer a patient. He asks for the registrar on call for internal medicine.

'Speaking,' I say, making my voice as hostile-sounding and abrupt as possible.

'It's Doctor Loubscher from Ravensmead day hospital. I've got a fifty-year-old lady here with congestive heart failure who I would like to refer in.'

I'm attending carefully to what he is saying, listening for any gaps that will allow me to refuse the patient. I don't have the time or space to pick up more than ten patients today.

'She's very short of breath at rest and quite distressed,' he adds.

'Blood pressure?'

'Our blood-pressure cuff was stolen last week and we haven't got a new one yet so I can't tell you, but she feels quite shocked.'

I have worked at the day hospitals, so I know he isn't making up excuses. As unlikely as it may seem, since it is useless without the whole machine, the blood-pressure cuff probably was stolen. Perhaps it has another use of which I know nothing.

'How much furosemide have you given her?' I ask.

'A hundred and twenty milligrams intravenous infusion.'

It's a bad sign that she is not responding to the diuretic, especially if it was given intravenously.

'Sats?' I query.

'We don't have a saturation monitor.'

I will have to accept the patient. I give the doctor what he has been waiting for.

'Okay, send her through.'

* * *

Justine arrives in casualty at ten to one. She has brought a packet of apples with her for lunch.

'They're great for calls,' she tells me, polishing one with a tissue, 'so nice and clean and low fat.' My chocolate éclair toffee sticks to my back molar. Guiltily working the sugary mass free with my tongue, I wonder whether she is going to eat the whole packet of apples.

The students arrive late, at two o'clock. I'm too busy to scold them. Besides, were I a student, I would also have arrived an hour late. Perhaps I'm too young to be in charge of students, too close to their age. I tell them to start seeing patients and to call me when they are ready to present them to me.

The first time I get an opportunity to sit down is at four thirty in the afternoon. Two minutes to down a Coke and check through the list of new admissions, already up to seventeen. I will be forced to discharge any patient in the ward who has shown the smallest sign of recovery. Justine comes into the doctors' office, eating another apple. She glances at my Coke.

'You should drink Coke Lite. It tastes the same.'

'It doesn't. It tastes awful. I can't stand the taste of artificial sweetener; it leaves a bitter aftertaste in my mouth. Did you manage to get a pus swab from that woman's peri-anal abscess?'

Justine nods. 'I've already sent it off. The abscess has burst open and it's leaking this thick brown pus everywhere. It was definitely anaerobic, it really stank. Coke Lite doesn't leave a bitter taste in my mouth. I think it's just in your mind. You could learn to like it if you tried. When I was growing up, my mom only kept artificial sweetener in the house, so we got used to it.'

Justine's incessant apple-crunching is starting to irritate me. 'Peri-anal abscesses always stink,' I tell her, probably too shortly. 'Please refer her to the surgeons. They can take her over. Just don't admit her into one of our beds, otherwise we'll never get her into a surgery ward. How many beds have you got?'

As the intern, Justine has the unofficial job of finding ward beds for all the new patients. No matter how many new wards are opened, Bellville has a permanent shortage of beds.

'I've got three,' she says.

'Three beds?'

I hope that I haven't heard her properly, that she will correct me, but she nods.

'So we still have to sort out beds for fourteen patients?' I ask by way of confirmation.

'Yes. No, thirteen. The peri-anal abscess is going to surgery.'

The bed deficit means at least another hour added onto my call. An hour of pleading and arguing and bargaining for beds for my patients, for which I do not have the energy.

'Have you tried all the wards?'

'Yes.'

'Dermatology?'

'Yes.'

'Okay, phone neurology and see if we can use any ...'

'Already done. They have one spare bed but they're expecting an elective admission this evening.'

'Shit. Have you phoned the matron for the bed status?'

'It will only be ready at six o'clock.'

I'm tired. My back tooth is aching from too many chocolate éclairs. I can't handle this right now. 'Okay,' I force myself to sound in control. 'I want you to go up to each of the wards and search for any open beds. If you see an unused bed, look for a sister and interrogate her. Find out who is sleeping in the bed.'

Sometimes when you phone the wards the nursing sisters lie about the bed status. They're not lazy, just too few in number.

My Coke is finished, my two minutes of respite are up. I walk back into the unit.

'Zahira,' I call out to a young Muslim woman, one of my best students, 'where is that patient that you wanted to present to me?' I turn to Matthew and hand him an X-ray request form that is blank except for my signature. 'Please organise a chest X-ray for the woman with the pneumonia. I'll be with you as soon as I have finished with Zahira.'

* * *

I get home at nine o'clock in the evening, although my call officially finished at six. Leah is out, watching *Queen at the Ballet,* and the house is wonderfully dark and quiet. I revel in the silence, in the loneliness. I have had enough of people. I leave the lights off, get into the shower and drown away the hospital dirt. A tin of Pringles, salt and vinegar flavour, is good enough for supper; I'm way too tired to cook. By my third glass of wine the day is fading and the prospect of fitting fifty-seven patients into tomorrow's shift seems slightly less daunting. I lie down on the couch and turn on the television. Dr Phil advises me on the essential pointers for establishing good communication with my partner. Perhaps that is where I failed in my relationship with Kevin. I want to phone in and ask Dr Phil how I am supposed to communicate with someone when I am too tired to talk, when he cannot possibly understand what my day has consisted of, when he thinks that a major problem at work is a new computer virus.

I wake up at ten past one shivering and with a sore neck. Leah is still not home. I brush the stale taste of slept-in red wine from my mouth and collapse into bed. Tomorrow is a new day. Tomorrow I will be a better doctor. Tomorrow I will care.

# Chapter Two

## Justine and the chest drain

Boxing classes (suggested by my ex-psychologist and multiple women's magazines) are my attempt at managing my stress more healthily. I know that I have become addicted to the red-bag endorphin high, but boxing carries fewer health risks than smoking, so I consider it a good substitution. My boxing class starts at half past five and I am still in the ward at four thirty, trying to sort out my last patient. I look at my watch again, hoping that somehow I have misread the time.

'Justine, I want to ask you a huge favour. I need to be somewhere at five thirty. Would you mind putting in a chest drain for Mrs Mboya?'

She freezes in panic, like a deer caught in the headlights.

'I've helped you with the last three drains that you've put in,' I remind her. 'You need to learn how to do them alone. Next year, for your community service you'll be in some rural place on your own with nobody to help you.'

Probably not the most sensitive thing I could have said. Justine gulps, and I relent somewhat.

'I'll have my cellphone with me and you can call me if you have any problems. I'll be five minutes away.'

'Okay.' She succumbs to my pleading. 'I'll try. I'll call you if I get stuck.'

'Thank you, thank you, thank you! There shouldn't be

any problems. Mrs Mboya is nice and thin, you can feel her rib spaces easily.'

I grab my bag and rush out of the ward before Justine loses her nerve, then take the steps two at a time and down to my car. It's ten past five. I should make it to the gym in time for the boxing class. Tenderly I coerce my fifteen-year-old hatchback to start and say a quick prayer of thanks as I hear the splutter of the ignition. I accelerate into peak-hour traffic leaving a cloud of white smoke behind me. Somehow I must have inadvertently pleased the gods, for they are conspiring with me: the traffic is free-flowing and all the robots are green. I screech into the gym parking lot at twenty-five past five. I have five minutes to change and get to the boxing studio. My car boot is full of bags of newspaper and glass and tins that have yet to be delivered to the recycling depot. I scrabble for my gym bag between the good intentions, and my phone starts ringing. Shit. I don't want to answer it. I hesitate for a moment but my conscience pushes my finger onto the 'answer' button.

'Hello.'

'Dr Carey, it's Sister Booyse here from ward D9. Dr Minelli needs your help.'

'Can I speak to her?'

'She's sterile.'

'Put the phone up against her ear.'

'Hello, Sue.' Justine's voice.

'Justine, is everything okay?' I know that everything is not okay or Sister B would not be calling me.

'I need your help. I can't get the drain in. I've infiltrated with local anaesthetic and made the incision but I can't seem to get the chest-drain tube between the ribs.'

'Have you used the dissecting forceps?'

'Yes, it doesn't help.' Her voice is quavering.

'And the trochar?'

I can hear her swallow. 'No, we were taught not to,' she says. 'I'm a bit scared to use it.'

'Justine, I know that at med school you are taught not to use the trochar because it can pierce into the heart and all that crap, but I've used it hundreds of times and it's safe. Just control it. Don't stab it into the chest. You aren't a fool. Besides, we are putting the drain into the *right* side of the chest.'

I am being unfairly harsh, pissed off with her caution. I know that I will have to go back to the hospital. I know that I will not be doing tonight's boxing class.

'I'll be there now,' I say, resigned to the situation. 'Just keep your hand over the incision. Whatever you do, don't let the wound suck in air.'

I get back into my car and punch the steering wheel with the palms of my hands. The car guard disappears, probably thinking that it is safer not to hover around waiting for a tip. I open the dashboard ashtray and feel between empty sweet wrappers for the emergency cigarette that I keep there since I gave up smoking. It has been replaced numerous times. I light it and inhale deeply to keep myself from screaming. It's too strong and makes me nauseous. I roll the window down and drive away playing Guns N' Roses at top volume. All you need is just a little patience.

\* \* \*

I can't shout at her. When I reach the ward Justine is standing with bloody gloved hands jammed against Mrs Mboya's chest wall and tears streaming down her cheeks. Mrs Mboya is crying. The pink-frocked patient next to her is crying. Even stalwart Sister B looks on the brink of tears.

'Okay, let's see what's going on.' I put on some gloves and, with my fingers, explore the incision that Justine has made. She leans over me to see what I am doing.

'Justine, you haven't gone deep enough. You're not even in the pleural space yet. Pass me the dissecting forceps.'

I gently tease the flesh between the ribs apart and then, when I am deep enough, lean on the closed dissecting forceps with almost all my weight. The pleura is thick and difficult to penetrate and my hands are shaking by the time I hear the pop and then hiss of expelled air that I have been waiting for. I stick my finger into the incision and carefully break away any adhesions that are present on the inner aspect of the chest wall.

'Justine, feel here.' I remove my hand to make space for her to feel. She stares at me and the wound begins to suck air. 'Quickly!' I snap and she wakes up.

'Can you feel how much deeper in I am than you?' I ask. Her smudged face nods back at me. 'Now, give me the chest-drain tube.' I ease the tube into the chest cavity and stitch it into place.

'Please organise a chest X-ray to check that the tube is positioned correctly,' I instruct her. Justine is looking at me hopelessly. I don't know what to say to make her feel better. She is nearly halfway through her internship; she should be able to insert chest drains. Eventually I manage a few words.

'Don't be so gentle. In future you need to use more force. Next time you put a drain in I'll stand behind you and guide you through it step by step.'

Fresh tears well up in her eyes. I know that she is thinking the same thing as I am, that I have already shown her three times how to insert a chest drain step by step. Three times is twice more than the usual 'See one, do one, teach one'.

I soften a bit. 'Sometimes when you don't get a procedure right the first time you try it, you develop a mental block about it. If you stop stressing about it, it'll be much easier, I promise. It took me more than three times before I could intubate.'

It is six thirty and I have missed the entire boxing class. I am not angry as I drive home. I am not frustrated or disappointed. I don't even feel bad about the fact that, yet again, I have made Justine cry. All that I feel is a gaping emptiness. It's as though I have used up my quota of passion for this life. I wonder if, when I die and the pathologists do an autopsy, there will be only a big hole in the left side of my chest. They could even write it up for the *South African Medical Journal*: 'Case report of a young doctor with no visible evidence of a heart'.

## The loneliness of an intern away from home

This Friday night, for the first time in four weeks, I am not on call, pre-call or post-call, which means I can actually attend the dinner party that Leah has been planning for the past month.

Miraculously, during the course of the morning I manage to discharge eight patients and the ward round proceeds without the usual hitches. By three o'clock the end is in sight.

'I'm glad that we're actually getting somewhere today,' I say to Justine, touching the fake wooden veneer on the sister's desk just to be safe. 'And no one is really unstable so we should be out by four.'

Justine glances at her watch. 'Something special happening tonight?' she asks.

'No, not really. Just a girls' evening. It's a tradition. We try to do something at least once a month, but everyone has been so busy lately we haven't been able to meet. We're all friends from high school.'

'I've also got a group of friends like that, from high school, I mean. In Johannesburg. I miss them. It's not the same talking over the phone. I'm worried that when I get back they will have moved on with their lives and I won't really be a part of the group any more.' Justine looks away for a moment. 'I wish I could have got an intern position closer to home. I suppose I shouldn't complain though; at least I'm at a decent hospital.'

I wonder why Justine has chosen to confide in me, of all people. I don't really consider myself the type who inspires tête-à-têtes. The only time I've been called a good listener is when my awkward unresponsiveness has been mistaken for silent compassion.

I did my internship year in a small hospital outside Springbok. It was a tired grey building of unfulfilled promises on the edge of the desert, a present from the 'new government' to its people, complete with two freshly packaged white female doctors. After three days of working, any illusions of knowledge that I may have had on leaving medical school were smashed. I still wonder how many lives I took through ineptitude. The woman working with me, a twenty-four-year-old *cum laude* graduate from Wits University, crumbled after her tenth failed resuscitation and tried to take an overdose of morphine. She was unsuccessful in killing herself but developed a certain fondness for the drug and spent most of her internship in a distant dream-world completely inaccessible to me. It was a lonely year.

'What are you doing tonight?' The words are out of my mouth before I remember how much Justine's perfectionism irritates me.

'Nothing planned,' she says. 'Probably a date with my television.'

'Well, you're welcome to join us if you want to. It won't be anything special, just dinner at our house.'

'Thanks, that will be so awesome. It's so sweet of you to invite me.' Her excitement embarrasses me and I avoid eye contact. 'Can I bring anything?' she asks.

'No, it's fine. Maybe just a bottle of wine or some snacks.'

\* \* \*

Leah has already started cooking by the time I get home. She is an infrequent cook, but she seems to forget this when she chooses her recipes. Most of them a professional chef would find challenging. This makes for interesting dinners.

'Hello. You're going to kill me.'

'Don't tell me you're working, because I promise you I'll never cook dinner for you again.'

I consider the proposal for a moment before answering.

'No, I'm not working. I invited my intern to join us. I know it messes up the numbers. Sorry.'

Leah opens the oven and smoke billows out. 'Shit, the aubergine soufflé has burnt. What? The paranoid one who irritates you?'

'Yep, the very same.' I struggle to answer between coughs. Our kitchen, like the rest of the semi-detached rental house, is old, built well before the era of extractor fans. I open one of the windows while Leah tries to fan away the smoke with a dishcloth.

'Why?' she asks.

I don't know whether she is asking me why I invited Justine or asking an unknown power why her meals always flop. I opt for the answer that will keep our friendship intact. 'I don't know. I felt sorry for her. She's from Jo'burg and doesn't have any friends here. She's actually not that bad. To be completely honest, I think that the real reason she irritates me is because she's so perfect that I feel like a fat, lazy slob next to her.'

But Leah isn't listening. She's concentrating on scraping black cinders from the sides of the soufflé dish.

Justine arrives early, before I have even had time to pour my first glass of champagne. She is carrying a platter of vegetarian spring rolls and miniature goat-cheese pies that she baked herself. She must have been baking since she left the hospital. I wish that she hadn't brought them, or at least that she hadn't baked them herself. It's too much effort. I suppose I don't like the hard evidence of her loneliness. I try to convince myself that maybe she simply loves to bake.

'Champagne?' I ask, easing the cork from the top of the bottle.

'Please.'

I pour the champagne down the side of a glass and hand it to her.

'Cheers,' I say, 'and thanks for coming.'

'No, thank *you*. If you hadn't invited me I'd be sitting at home all on my lonesome ownsome.'

The champagne has a delicious palate of yeast and grass.

## The birth of an unwanted baby

It's Sunday morning and I'm still recovering from Friday night. My throat feels as though someone has grated it and I wonder if I'm getting sick. I have a theory that doctors are permanently tired because they are always fighting off some new virus to which they have been exposed. (I take vitamin C and ginseng to try to combat this.) But then again, the tiredness could also be caused by the sleep deficit that builds up when one works eight nights a month as well as most days.

The roads are quiet on a Sunday morning. Even the devout are still asleep. It seems to me that only doctors and runners are up this early. The world feels lonely, too big for so few people. I imagine that I can see through the curtained suburban windows; I picture loving couples snuggling together in bed, children waking up and running to their parents' bedrooms, the *Sunday Times* and the kettle on for coffee, the life that I can't have.

I arrive at Goodwood Hospital and realise that I cannot remember the last ten minutes of my journey. I hope that I didn't jump any red robots. I get out of my car and try to shake myself awake. I'm exhausted and I somehow have to get through twenty-four hours and then the whole of Monday. At least I'm doing a paediatrics call. I prefer treating children rather than the intoxicated adults that are the usual weekend fare when I do trauma calls at Paarl Hospital. There is only one aspect to the paediatrics calls that I do not enjoy: the parents.

The day is busy. I am covering not only paediatric casualty but also the paediatric and neonatal wards. Casualty is on the ground floor, the neonatal ward on the third floor and the paediatrics ward on the fourth floor. The lifts are not working and I have to use the stairs, so eight hours into my call I feel as though I have completed an endurance event. I try to convince myself that at least I'm getting fit. I wonder when maintenance will get around to fixing the lifts.

I have just sat down in the doctors' office to eat the microwave-heated spaghetti bolognaise that I have brought for supper when my name crackles over the intercom.

'Dr Carey, baby room, please. Dr Carey, baby room, please.'

Because I am not part of the permanent staff at Goodwood, I don't have a pager. When I'm needed in one of the wards, the sister contacts the operator in the radio room, who in turn announces over the intercom for me to call the ward. The result is that everybody in the hospital is able to track my every move. I dial up to the neonatal ward. I hope that whatever it is I am needed for can wait for half an hour, or at least until I have eaten my dinner. My stair training has given me the appetite of an endurance athlete.

'Babasaal.'

'Sister, it's Dr Carey. Were you looking for me?'

'Yes, Doctor. Baby Peters is gasping.'

I jump up, supper suddenly irrelevant. Gasping is pre-terminal. Baby Peters I know well. We have a long history together, in neonatal terms: we've known each other for a month, Baby Peters's entire lifetime. He was born far too early, weighed seven hundred and fifty grams when he was expelled from his reluctant mother's vagina. He was not meant to live, but when he refused to stop breathing the sister on duty in the labour ward called me. He was well under the magic one thousand grams that would qualify him for life. Babies over one thousand grams can be actively resuscitated, intubated, ventilated, sent to Bellville Hospital neonatal intensive-care unit. The euphemism is 'for active management', so that the babies who weigh less than one thousand grams and are therefore left to die can be labelled 'not for active management'. The first instruction on Baby Peters's prescription chart is 'Not for active management'. This doesn't have quite the same ring as 'Leave to die'. So, those mites below one thousand grams who manage to survive the trauma of a too-early birth are thrown out on their own. We are allowed to give them oxygen, to put up a drip and run in intravenous fluids, to give them antibiotics, but beyond that they must fight for themselves.

Baby Peters was indomitable. I expected him to die that first night. His tiny chest of prominent elastic ribs caved in with the effort of each breath. His whole being was concentrated on surviving. I sat with him for a while, waiting for him to tire and stop breathing. But he carried on, determined to live. He was still struggling for life at eight o'clock the next morning when I finished my call.

I stopped in at Goodwood Hospital on my way home from Bellville Hospital that evening to see whether he had survived the day. Reason told me that I was being stupid, that he would surely be dead, that I was wasting my time. But somehow Baby Peters was still breathing. And in my post-call exhaustion I managed to convince myself that he recognised my voice.

Now, one month later, at eight hundred grams, Baby Peters is gasping and I am called to his bedside. When I reach him, I know it is too late. He is still two hundred grams away from active resuscitation. A few quiet breaths shudder through his body. His pulse has slowed to twenty beats per minute. There is adrenaline a few metres away from me, an endotracheal tube at my side, a ventilator standing open, but I am forbidden by budget to touch them. Not for him. And so I stand next to his incubator and stroke his almost transparent skin. I spill tears. I hold his tiny hand in mine and try to coerce him back to life. His knitted yellow cap has slipped down over one eye and I lift it up so that he can see.

'Come on. You've held on for so long. Not now. Don't go now. Just two hundred grams more. Please, little one, not yet.' But he is slipping away. There is no palpable pulse and only a flicker of movement over his chest wall. He has struggled long enough. Born to a rape victim who didn't want him, in a hospital that couldn't afford him, at last he has given up. What a fighter, what a Churchill he would have made had he been given the chance to live.

My spaghetti is cold by the time that I get back to the doctors' office. I don't want it anyway. My appetite has disappeared. I can't get the vision of Baby Peters's perfect eight-hundred-gram baby fingernails out of my mind. He never even got his own name. Just the surname of the mother he never knew.

When I get home on Monday evening I have been awake for over thirty hours, but I cannot sleep. Baby Peters is still haunting me. So I go to the gym and punch the punching bag. I wish that I was punching someone's face, that I had something concrete on which to loose my frustration and anger. But there is nothing tangible to fight against, just a government policy. So I punch and punch, until my arms are shaking and my knuckles are bleeding inside my gloves.

## True beauty

I am back at philosophy class, discussing the nature of beauty. My life is surreal, a living Dalí masterpiece. An hour ago I was wiping coughed-up lung off my shoe and now I'm sitting in a Victorian parlour discussing beauty. I enjoy the conversations though, relish the escape from reality that they provide. I can lose myself in the maze of reasoning. Forget life's ugliness in the elegance of debate.

The Camel-man yacht owner is sitting across from me in the semicircle and I try to see whether he is wearing a wedding ring. His hands are folded and his left ring finger is obscured from my view.

'So Sue, what do you think?' Mrs De Marigny, our lecturer, breaks into my yachting dreams. What do I think about what? I have lost the thread of beauty.

'I'm sorry, I wasn't concentrating,' I admit. 'Could you repeat the question?'

At least Mrs De Marigny has the decency not to show her exasperation with my lack of concentration.

'Do you think that one's perception of beauty externally is a reflection of one's inner state of being?'

'Uh, I've never really thought about it,' I stammer. I hope not. What would it imply about me? Do happier people perceive the world as more beautiful than unhappy people, or is it the other way round: are people who have the ability to see more beauty in the world happier? Perhaps I need to look for beauty more. Mrs De Marigny tells us to think about the question over tea and the group files out of the room and down a narrow passage to a small kitchenette.

Three-quarters of the way through the tea break, I finally pluck up the courage to approach the Camel-man yacht owner. I am taking the first few hesitant steps in his direction when a willowy blond woman approaches me. She is wearing a feathered wooden object, similar to a dream catcher, around her neck. It sits uneasily with the rest of her outfit: a sleek white linen designer suit and high-heeled white sandals. She is holding a cup of black rooibos tea in one hand.

'Am I remembering correctly that you are a doctor?' she says to me. But it is more a statement than a question. I nod, wary of the direction that the conversation is going to take. I am worried that the dream catcher around her neck symbolises a shamanic connection. I have been softly beaten to near death before by well-dressed alternative medicine gurus. But the tirade against modern medicine does not come. We both sip our tea, silence stretching tautly between us.

'I'm Carol,' the woman says. 'I hope I don't sound presumptuous speaking to you like this and please let me know if I'm out of line.' She is looking down, avoiding eye contact. Her voice is even-toned but her restless manicured fingers betray her nervousness. 'A friend of mine has just been diagnosed with cancer. Lymphoma. I don't know anything about it. I've tried to look it up on the Internet, but there's so much conflicting information I don't really know what to make of it. I was wondering if you could tell me anything about lymphomas.'

'I'm definitely not an expert but I could try to answer some of your questions,' I say, hoping I sound both professional and friendly. 'Do you know what kind of lymphoma it is?' I try to dredge up long-forgotten knowledge, but all I can remember at the moment is that there are two different kinds of lymphoma and that one has a better prognosis than the other.

'No, I don't know what kind it is, but I can find out. My friend has an appointment with the oncologist on Monday.'

'Try to find out what kind it is and also what stage. I think that it makes a difference to the prognosis. The oncologist will know a lot more than I do, but if there's anything you are confused about you are more than welcome to ask me next week.' Which will give me time to revise my knowledge of lymphomas.

'Thanks so much.' She looks younger when she smiles.

'How old is she?' I ask. She registers surprise, or confusion, I can't tell which. 'Your friend,' I prompt.

'Oh, almost thirty-four. She's turning thirty-four this May.'

That's six years older than me. Young for a lymphoma. But then, cancer knows no age restrictions.

The philosophy class exercise for the week is to open one's eyes to beauty, to look for unexpected beauty. The beauty in the smile of a woman with cancer.

## Dead man walking

Beauty is difficult to find at Bellville Hospital. Even the building is ugly, fraught with reminders of apartheid: a large, vomit-orange, face-brick monstrosity that hulks on its turf of desolate parking bays and dried yellow grass. Trees grow skew beside it, forced into abnormal giant bonsai shapes by the ubiquitous southeaster. The hospital is a single building, divided in the middle by an imaginary line so that the two halves form a mirror image of each other. Previous government policy decreed that one half of the hospital was reserved for the use of whites, the other for non-whites. Now one half lies empty, ghosts pacing the wards. This is another government decision, this time based on financial resolutions rather than racial policies. Bellville is a hospital tired of conflict.

I am starting my ward round in ward A5. A5 is, in theory, the high-care ward, but I suspect that the reason it has been designated high care has more to do with its proximity to the intensive-care unit than with the rendering of superior patient care. A5 is where my sickest patients are lying, the ones that take up the most of my time. Currently I have three very ill patients: Mr Mohammed, Mr Moloti and Mr Hendricks.

Mr Mohammed has only recently crossed the South African border. He has fled the poverty and bouts of civil war in Somalia and come to the Mecca of Africa. Southwards seeking survival. Unfortunately he brought with him the progeny of a small, deceptively insignificant *Anopheles* mosquito.

He cannot speak English well, and I am hardly proficient in Arabic, Somali or Italian, but it matters little at this stage. Once the cerebral malaria has subsided and his delirium has resolved, I will worry about finding a translator.

I enter his room and he sits up, disturbed by the noise of the door opening. He has the privilege of a single room because his altered perception makes him too disruptive for the general ward. Wide yellow eyes stare at me, or at least at the place where I am standing. I do not know what hallucinations his fever might be precipitating. I could be a dog or a bull or his wife or a long-lost brother. Or perhaps I am an overworked doctor in a bloodstained white coat with smudged mascara rings beneath her eyes.

He does not respond when I greet him. I don't know whether he understands me or even hears me. Is his name different in Arabic? After four days in hospital he is still teetering on the very fine knife-edge between life and death, waiting for one tiny change to upset the balance. His urine remains black, the colour of Coca-Cola. His temperature is still spiking forty degrees and the crumpled hospital sheets on his bed are damp with sweat. When I first admitted him, his sweat smelt foreign, exotic, spicy like day-old curry. But now it is odourless. Bellville has sweated out his culture.

I increase his dose of intravenous quinine to almost toxic levels, hoping the bitterness will chase away the microscopic malarial protozoa that are eating away at his consciousness.

\* \* \*

Mr Hendricks is next. He is fifty-four and dying. I met him for the first time three days ago, when his wife dragged him into the casualty unit because he refused to see a doctor, even though he was suffocating.

'He's not a man who complains,' she told me. 'He's not one to get sick. He hasn't been to a doctor in twenty years.'

His admission three days ago was Mr Hendricks's first time in hospital. Since then I have told him that he has lung cancer, that he probably has less than three months to live and that a fair proportion of that time will be spent within the plastic grey walls of Bellville Hospital.

He is a small-boned man, shrunken even more by the cancer. Only his head and neck are abnormally large, congested with the blood that has pooled there as a result of the tumour occluding his superior vena cava. We have a name for it: superior vena cava syndrome. We treat SVC syndrome not to cure it but to alleviate the pain of the last few steps to death. I tried to explain this to Mr Hendricks yesterday, in my dysfunctional Afrikaans. I could see that he didn't understand what I was telling him. He nodded, but his protruding, red-veined eyes were uncomprehending.

'Mr Hendricks, how are you this morning?' I ask him.

'Much better, thank you, Doctor,' he tells me. But I know that he is no better. And I can predict what will come next.

'Do you think that I can go home soon? I'm running my own business, doing plumbing, and I can't take too much time off.'

I sit down on the edge of Mr Hendricks's bed, then get up again to draw the curtain around us. The other five men in the ward do not need to know that he is dying. I can smell that he has been smoking, using the drawer next to his bed as an ashtray. I let it pass. He will not smoke many more cigarettes. And now they will no longer do him any harm.

'Mr Hendricks, you understand that you have lung cancer?'

He nods. I pick up his chest X-ray and hold it to the light.

'You see that big white thing there?' I point to the cancer that is opacifying one half of his right lung field. 'That is the cancer. It should be black like on this side.' My finger slips across to the relatively normal translucent left lung. 'The cancer is too big for us to cut out. It is pressing on the large vein that carries the blood from your upper body back to your heart. That is why your face and neck are so swollen, because the blood can't get back to your heart and it is pooling in your head and neck. Unfortunately we cannot treat your cancer because it is too advanced. But we can give you radiotherapy that will make it smaller. Shrinking it will allow the blood to flow back to your heart and you will not feel so uncomfortable. Do you understand?'

'But Doctor, why can't you cut it out? Or give me chemotherapy for it?'

I have explained all of this to him before.

'Mr Hendricks, your cancer is too advanced. We cannot cut it out because it has spread too much. We would have to cut out your whole lung and your heart and the blood vessels. You would not survive the operation. Even if we manage to make the cancer smaller with radiotherapy, it will still be too large to cut out. Certain cancers respond to chemotherapy, but unfortunately most lung cancers don't.'

'So how much longer have I got?'

This is the question that I have been dreading. I want to tell him that I don't know, that it is in God's hands, that miracles can happen, but some well-hidden part of me that still retains a hint of decency knows that he deserves an honest answer. I place my hand on his swollen shoulder, the tortuous, congested veins thick like rope beneath my palm.

'Not much longer. With radiotherapy, maybe another two or three months. I'm very sorry. I wish that there was something that I could do for you.'

And I do.

I leave the curtain drawn when I walk away.

\* \* \*

I rush to the bed of my last patient in ward A5: Mr Moloti, who is dying of AIDS. The bed is empty when I reach his room. I wonder if he has died during the night.

'Sister?' I shout into the corridor, too lazy to go and find her.

'Ja, Doctor?' comes the equally lazy response from the sisters' office.

'Where is Mr Moloti?'

'In the bathroom.'

He has survived one more night. I am busy rewriting his prescription chart when he walks into the room. Mr Moloti is skeletal, his skin drawn so tautly over his bones that it is shiny. He leans on the drip stand as he walks, its metal permanency supporting him. His body is covered in the secret tattoos of HIV, visible only to those who know where to look for them. I can pick them out immediately: the white fungal infection on his tongue; the swollen lymph nodes in unusual places; the diffuse itchy rash raked with scratch marks; the fleshy, pigmented swellings of Kaposi's sarcoma. None are individually pathognomonic, but together they are highly suggestive of full-blown AIDS.

He nods at me as he sits down on the bed. I do not ask him how he is feeling. I can see that he doesn't have the energy to talk. I don't know how he has landed up at

Bellville Hospital, a tertiary-care centre. Patients like him are usually seen at the primary-care level, at day hospitals and community health centres. Usually they are brought in under the anonymity of night, their families too ashamed to call the ambulance out during the day. They are seldom referred to a secondary or tertiary hospital because there is so little left to do for them. We can offer an intravenous line and some rehydration fluid for the chronic diarrhoea, a vitamin B injection to try to relieve the unrelenting exhaustion, some drops or a topical cream for the ravaging fungal infections, and then send them home again to fade into the silent shroud of disgrace.

Mr Moloti is dying. There is nothing more that I can do for him. He is thirty-five years old. I wonder whether he has a wife. Is she also dying? Has he any children? Will he leave behind orphans? Nobody has come to visit him. Nobody has sent him flowers or a card or brought him a basket of dried fruit and chocolate wrapped up with a ribbon. He has no toiletry bag neatly packed for him by a loved one at home. He washes himself with the harsh hospital soap. I can smell its astringent scent on his skin as I bend over him to listen to his chest. But it cannot disguise the smell of death.

I have put his name on the waiting list for a hospice, but the AIDS hospices are all overflowing. He will be dead before a place opens up for him. And so he lies in Bellville Hospital, where we can dose him with morphine and perhaps, in his drug-induced delirium, he can forget that he is forgotten.

\* \* \*

I am called back to Mr Hendricks's bedside later in the day. His wife has come to visit him and she wants to talk to me. I dawdle my way up to the ward because I am dreading speaking to her. I don't know what I will say to her. I'm tired of carrying bad news around with me.

I can see that Mrs Hendricks has been crying. Her nose is red and chafed from the stiff hospital tissue paper. I take some tissues from my bag and pass them to her.

'Thank you.' She blows her nose, composes herself. 'Doctor, please can you tell me how my husband is.'

I sense that she already knows that her husband does not have much longer, but I go through what I told her husband that morning. She listens quietly, without moving or saying a word.

'I'm going to check some blood results on the computer in the sisters' office,' I say. 'I'll be back in about ten minutes in case you have any questions.'

There are no results to check, but I need to get away for a few minutes. I've run out of words. Nobody has taught me how to tell a woman that her husband is dying. I keep on picturing my mother's face superimposed on Mrs Hendricks's.

I sit down on the chair in the sisters' office and think of what I have told her. None of the euphemisms that I used would have softened the blow. The implications are the same, no matter how the message was worded. I wonder how long Mr and Mrs Hendricks have been married but then quickly push the thought away. It makes me want to cry and I can't afford to cry, not in the sisters' office in the middle of the afternoon. It would be unprofessional. It seems wrong that the only way I can survive my job is to dehumanise my patients; it feels contrary to the principles of medicine, the very essence of healing that attracted me to this work in the first place. When I enrolled for my medical degree I had a whole array of expectation of what working in the healing professions would be like and of what I would become. I pictured myself as a Florence Nightingale, the epitome of compassion and empathy. I believed, firmly and with utter conviction, that I would be able to help and that I would make a difference. I cannot remember a single, defining moment when that dream disappeared. Rather, it was a gradual fading away. With each situation that I encountered in which I was helpless and in which the problems seemed insurmountable, or in which the emotions that I was feeling threatened to consume me, I closed my heart a tiny bit more and the ideal image moved a little further away. I suppose it was a defensive mechanism. I was protecting myself from feeling helpless, from feeling disillusioned and from feeling like a failure. I was protecting myself from feeling altogether. I wonder, sometimes, where this has left me. I am more than capable in my job but I am not happy. I know that there is something missing.

Ten minutes have passed, so I make my way back to Mr Hendricks's bedside.

'Do you have anything you want to ask me?' My words sound awkward and intrusive, an unwelcome imposition on their mourning.

Mr Hendricks is quiet but for the snorting efforts of his breathing. Mrs Hendricks responds with 'Can Willem come home?' This is a question I was not anticipating. She continues: 'We understand that . . . that . . .,' she stumbles a little over her words but then finds her way again quickly, 'there is not much time left. There are things that we need to sort out at home and with the business. We have two boys, you know, twenty-three and eighteen. Willem doesn't like being in hospital. He wants to be in his own bed. He's in a lot of pain, so maybe if you could give something strong for that?'

Again I don't know what to say. Mr Hendricks needs

radiotherapy; without it he will not live longer than a week, two at most. But even the radiotherapy will only alleviate his symptoms. The pain and shortness of breath will diminish for a while but they will return. And then there will be nothing that we can offer him.

Finally I speak up, mustering as professional a tone as I can. 'I can't make this decision for you; it is something that you must decide as a couple. Whatever decision you do make, I will respect. The radiotherapy will help, and it will prolong your time, but it isn't a cure. I'm going to prescribe some morphine for the pain. It's the strongest thing that I can give you. I'll tell the sister that I've left the decision up to you, and if you do decide that you want to go home, you can take the morphine with you. Please also remember that if you do leave tonight, you can come back at any time if you change your mind. Any time at all.'

'Thank you, Doctor,' they say in unison. I don't really know what they are thanking me for. I can offer them nothing and have given them only bad news.

I see Mr and Mrs Hendricks again in the evening, as I am leaving the hospital. The lift disgorges them as I reach the ground-floor stairwell. He is in a wheelchair and she is pushing him towards the door, packed up to go. He is wearing a small felt hat wedged onto his swollen head. They wave goodbye to me as I slip through the automatic doors ahead of them.

# Chapter Three

## Reasons not to date a doctor

My two best friends are like opposite poles. Occasionally I wonder whether they have become my best friends because they represent the extremes of my personality, the latent aspects of myself that I suppress. Leah is temperance personified; Gina, excess.

I am meeting Temperance and Excess for sundowners at a restaurant in Camps Bay. As usual I leave the hospital later than expected, and I arrive in Camps Bay only as the sun is setting. The wind shakes black silhouettes from the palm trees that line the beachfront. A drunk vagrant leans against a bus shelter and spits onto the scorched pavement. I drive up and down the main road for ten minutes before a parking space becomes available. Gina has parked directly outside the restaurant on a red no-parking line. A pink parking ticket flutters from her windscreen. Cape Town is too full tonight.

Barrazzo's is busy too. Leah and Gina are on their second cocktails by the time I sit down at the table with them. They must have arrived early because they have a prime position, directly in front of one of the large bay windows that overlook the sea.

'Hi, sorry I'm late. Got stuck in the hospital.' They do not comment. It's my usual excuse. I catch the last few strokes of orange as they drown in the grey-blue sea.

'Who's your waitress?' I ask.

Gina looks around and eventually her eyes settle on a young woman with braided blond hair. 'That one. I'll call her.' She waves her arms wildly and the waitress rushes to our table. I think she has misinterpreted Gina's enthusiasm for an emergency.

'Please can we have three more of these?' Gina asks, pointing to her empty glass.

'No, make it two,' Leah interrupts. 'I'll take a break this round. You can bring me a Coke.'

'Don't be such a loser.' Gina is on a mission.

'Some of us actually have proper jobs that require us to be up at six in the morning,' Leah says, then turns to the waitress. 'Two sex-on-the-beaches and one Coke, please.'

I am underdressed and feel drab compared to Gina and Leah. Leah is the fashion editor for a health and beauty magazine and always looks ultra-chic, as though her appearance is a supplement to her magazine. She has come straight from work, wearing clothes that I would never be able to do my job in: flared black miniskirt, cleavage-revealing blouse and stilettos, versus my expendable jeans (so that the stains don't matter), unflattering T-shirt (so that patients don't leer at me) and sensible flat shoes (closed so that I don't get splatters of body fluids on my bare toes). At least I left my shapeless white doctor's coat in the car.

Gina is a model and it is not unusual for me to feel unglamorous next to her. Her father is Lebanese and her mother Norwegian, a consummation that endowed her with six-foot-long legs, blond hair, almost-violet eyes and a dark olive skin. It also left her with a disrupted childhood, parents that are apart for nine months of the year and some shady family connections. Nevertheless, she is far more beautiful than I could ever hope to be. I down my cocktail when it arrives, hoping that the alcohol will blunt my sense of inadequacy.

I order another drink and finish it as quickly as the first, then follow it with some shooters. Leah announces that she will have to drive me home and we'll pick up my car tomorrow. Sounds like a fine plan to me. My hands are sticky from the sugar on the top of the cocktail glasses and my ears throb with the deep bass beats of the African jazz that oozes from the loudspeakers. We order a plate of cheese nachos with sour cream and guacamole. I pick from the platter and leave a stringy cheese cobweb on the table. At last I am relaxing. For the first time today I can forget skeletal Mr Moloti and dying Mr Hendricks and his sad wife.

'Gina, what do you think of that guy over there?' I ask, looking in the direction of a man who, I noticed, had been glancing over at our table.

'Where?'

'At the table next to the door. He's got blue stripes on his sleeves.' I point across the club to where the object of my scrutiny is sitting and Gina cranes her neck.

'Mmm. Not bad. Leah, what do you think?'

'Not really my type but definitely not too shabby. Bit of a wanker friend, though.'

The friend bears a myopic resemblance to Sylvester Stallone. Too many cocktails have made me brave. I call the waitress.

'Please could you take that guy a drink, the one with the blue stripes on his sleeves? Take him another one of whatever he's drinking at the moment. Tell him it's from me. You can put it on our bill.'

The man that I have singled out turns around to look at us when the waitress brings him the drink. Initially he thinks it's from Gina and I see his face fall as the waitress corrects him. I blush, conscious once again of my sensible jeans and tackies. I'm such an idiot. Who wants a girl in shapeless trousers and flat shoes? Who wants a girl that is too tired to put on make-up in the morning, and who comes home splattered in some stranger's vomit? Who wants a girl that survives her job by getting drunk? Rhetorical questions. I know the answers. And tomorrow I will be temporarily carless, hung-over and still a doctor.

## Another murder on the convict's tally

I have a new admission in the ward: a prisoner from Pollsmoor. He was admitted overnight, while I was downing cocktails with Leah and Gina. His conspicuous orange prison overalls have been exchanged for a light-blue hospital gown, and were it not for the khaki-clad guard outside the door of his room and the leg irons chaining him to the bed, he would look like any other patient. Nevertheless, I struggle to see him as just another patient. I cannot, even with the change of outfit, forget that he is a prisoner.

Matthew is interested in what crimes the man has committed and I hear him chatting to the guard as I examine the convict. He asks the guard what the prisoner is in for and the guard replies that he doesn't know but that the man still has thirteen years of his sentence left, which means that it must have been something serious. I am glad that the guard doesn't know what the prisoner has been incarcerated for. I prefer not to know the crimes of those that I am forced to look after, because it makes treating them a bit easier. But sometimes the knowledge is inescapable. It is a custom of gangsters in the prisons to tattoo their own criminal records onto their bodies and I am forced, every time I examine them, to come face to face with their blue-ink murders and rapes.

There is a tattoo that I have heard is specific to the Western Cape: a head with a knife piercing into the skull. This man's body is resplendent with knifed heads. I concentrate on listening to his lungs to prevent myself from imagining his victims. But it is difficult. Between breaths I wonder how many girls he has raped, girls like my two younger sisters or like Leah and Gina. I don't know much about the gangs of the Cape Flats but the little that I do know is too much. I have treated the girlfriends of gangsters who are gang-raped annually to ensure their subjugation to the gang. Animals marking their territory. I have done crime kits on six-year-old boys sodomised by gangs; HIV tests on grandmothers raped by their gangster grandsons. I have lost too many lives to senseless drive-by shootings. Wrong place, wrong time, wrong-colour car. The criteria for killing are altered randomly.

And so I struggle to treat this man. I struggle to see him as human. I write up the correct medications but I avoid eye contact and disregard his attempts at conversation, and when I am eventually forced to speak to him, I am abrupt.

'It's most likely TB that's causing the bleeding in your lungs. We'll try to treat it with medication, but if that doesn't work we'll have to burn the vessel that is bleeding.'

'Burn it? *Brand dit – met wat?*'

I ignore his question. I don't want to talk to him. Ridiculously, I believe that by showing my dislike I will somehow be making his punishment worse. He starts asking me about the bleeding again but I cut off his questioning.

'Justine, please do a full blood count and clotting profile on this man in case he needs an embolisation.' I know that I should be treating him more humanely. I should at least bother to find out his name and answer his questions. My guilt confuses me and I walk sharply from his room. I am angry at myself for my lack of compassion and angry at the patient for presenting me with this dilemma of conscience.

\* \* \*

I'm busy speaking to the pathologist on the telephone in the sisters' office when I hear Justine pass my phlebotomy instructions on to Matthew. The office door is open to the corridor and her voice filters through my concentration. I specifically asked her to draw the bloods on the prisoner because I wanted someone more experienced than a fourth-year student doing it. I tap the desk, willing the pathologist to finish giving me the biopsy results so that I can tell Justine to draw the bloods herself. But his voice drones on through the telephone receiver. As I finish speaking to him my bleeper goes off again. I answer immediately. It is Sister Booyse with a query about the dose of medication that I prescribed for a patient three days ago. By the time I have put the telephone down for the second time, I know that I wanted to do something but I can't remember what it was. I glance around the room for a visual clue to remind me, then give up and get ready to do a lumbar puncture on an eighty-year-old woman who I fear has neurosyphilis. I am busy trying to explain the madness of King George to the demented octogenarian when Justine's voice interrupts me.

'Sue?'

'Yes.'

'I need to talk to you urgently.'

I have already unsheathed the lumbar-puncture needle and I pierce the old woman's leathery skin as I answer.

'Now is probably not the ideal time. Please could you wait until I'm finished here.' The old woman has little fat, and as I advance the needle it grates against her osteoporotic vertebrae. I imagine archaeologists from the future wondering what caused the linear scratches on her lumbar bones.

Justine cannot contain herself long enough for me to finish the lumbar puncture. 'It's Matthew,' she blurts out. 'He pricked himself taking blood from the prisoner. He was struggling to get enough blood and the prisoner knocked the needle out of his arm and into Matthew.'

Oh God. I concentrate on keeping my hands steady. I still have a twelve-centimetre-long needle sticking into a demented woman's back.

'Justine, I asked you to draw the blood. If I'd wanted Matthew to do it, I would have asked him.' To my astonishment, my voice sounds calm, even polite. I push the needle deeper into the woman's back and reach the cerebrospinal fluid. It drips clear through the bore of the needle and into the collecting tube. I watch the meniscus sway up the sides of the clear plastic tube as each drop hits the surface of the fluid.

'Justine, go and draw blood from Matthew for an HIV test straight away, then get consent from the prisoner so that we can also test him. I will organise AZT for Matthew when I have finished here.' I speak slowly, trying to concentrate simultaneously on withdrawing the needle from the old woman's back and on what I am saying. Shit, shit, shit. I should have drawn the prisoner's blood myself. Justine should have drawn it. I should have told the pathologist on the telephone to wait for a few seconds. I am sure that the prisoner is HIV-positive. I don't need a blood test to confirm it. Many prison sentences are effectively death sentences because rape is widespread

47

in the prisons, part of the gangs' intricate hierarchical structure.

Matthew doesn't seem to notice my presence when I get to him. He is sitting in the doctors' office staring at the pulp of his index finger.

'Matthew, are you okay?' I ask. Stupid question. 'Sorry, don't answer. Listen, I've organised antiretroviral therapy for you. You know how it works, don't you?' He nods, but I carry on speaking. At least it makes me feel like I am helping. 'You start with the antiretrovirals now. If the prisoner is positive and you are negative, then you need to carry on taking them for a month and then we'll check again. To be absolutely sure, we check again after three months and then six months.' Six months. A lifetime.

I want to go and tell the prisoner that he can get a new tattoo done, replace the knife with a needle. I want to congratulate him on adding another murder to his tally.

## Role-playing

It is Thursday, philosophy class day. The whole Matthew saga is still bothering me, has been since it happened two days ago. I cannot help feeling responsible to a large degree.

I discuss it with Leah and she tries to convince me that perhaps Matthew will learn some lesson from it and that often we don't know why things happen until afterwards.

Ja, right, I think, what lesson? What it feels like to die of HIV? It's a cop-out answer.

By the time I join the philosophy class, I am keen to hear what the take of the wise is on it. After all, the reason that I signed up for the philosophy workshops was to try to find some answers. I stay behind after the lecture, after everybody has left, and it is just the lecturer and me in the big faded-red room. There is a moth fluttering against one of the velvet curtains, smearing it with a trail of gold-brown dust.

'Mrs De Marigny, do you mind if I ask you a question? It's not really to do with beauty or what we have been discussing. Is that okay?' I suddenly remember someone telling me that the dust is actually made up of tiny scales that line the wings. Remove the scales and the moth cannot fly.

'Fine,' says Mrs De Marigny. 'I can't promise that I'll be able to answer you, though.'

I shake the moth from my mind and start telling her about the prisoner. I try to describe my moral dilemma in treating him. I spill out my guilt, my secret desire that he should be punished even more than his measly thirteen-year sentence. I ask her if she can explain the justice in Matthew's needle-stick injury. She is silent when I eventually finish my tirade. Perhaps I should not have been so honest. I am sure she despises my lack of compassion and my disregard for human rights. I wait for her to advise that I consider a change in profession. Maybe I will have the distinction of being the first person asked to leave philosophy classes, my immorality unredeemable.

'It's a difficult situation and I don't know if I have an answer for you,' Mrs De Marigny says. So far so good; at least she hasn't threatened to report me to the Health Professions Council of South Africa. 'We play different roles in life,' she continues, 'almost like the clothes that we put on and take off. When I am at home, I play the role of mother; when I am at work, that of lawyer; when I visit my mother, I am again the daughter; and when I am here, I play the role of teacher. The roles are all different and I play each one to the best of my ability, but when I move from one role to another, I leave the previous one behind. Almost like dirty clothes. It would not be appropriate if I took on the role of mother in court or if I took on the role of lawyer while tutoring philosophy. I can draw on the experience that the other roles provide, but ultimately my behaviour must be appropriate for the role that I am playing at that moment. I find that it makes it a bit easier to play the role if you act according to the needs of the moment, uninfluenced by thoughts, feelings and emotions from the past. I hope that helps you.'

Our conversation ends there, mostly because I am too scared to say anything more. A lawyer? Thank heaven she was not playing the role of lawyer while I was confessing my sins.

I walk to my car sorting through her advice. What she has said makes some sense. At work I play the role of doctor and I play it as best I am able to. When I am with the prisoner, that is all I am: a doctor. Not a woman, not a judge, not some moral policeman. Just a doctor. Unfortunately, in reality the boundaries between roles are not always so clearly defined.

## An unlikely fling

Hooray for public holidays. Through some lapse in Murphy's foresight, my name is not on the call list for the long weekend and I actually have three-and-a-half completely free days to do with what I will. To the chagrin of my bank manager I decide to splurge on three nights at the Beacon Isle Hotel in Plettenberg Bay. I call in every favour owed to me and am ready to leave by Friday lunchtime. Everything is sunshiny: the weather, me, the fact that I will not see a single patient until Tuesday morning. Even the potholed national road looks great. I have my sunglasses on, the car windows down and Lenny Kravitz blaring.

I arrive at the Beacon Isle Hotel at seven o'clock, just as dusk starts blurring outlines, and decide to celebrate my arrival with sundowners on the deck overlooking the sea. I order a pink and orange cocktail that comes with a paper umbrella stuck into a piece of pineapple and drink it too quickly. I suck the alcohol from a maraschino cherry and ponder the technicalities of having sex on the beach. I order a second drink and buy an unaccustomed box of cigarettes from the vending machine so that I have something to do in my loneliness.

I leave the deck only when the last hint of colour has been bleached from the sky. I smell unfamiliar, too smoky. When I reach my room, I throw away the rest of the cigarettes, then shower and wash my hair to try to get rid of the leftover smoke. Recognisable to myself again, I spreadeagle myself on the double bed and pick up *Northanger Abbey*. I have lost my place but know the book well enough for it not to matter. My hair dampens the pillow; tomorrow it will be musty. I order room service for supper, with a bottle of real champagne all to myself. The blinds are up, the windows are open and I fall asleep with the silhouette of the overhead light burnt red into my eyelids and the rhythmic lull of waves breaking in my ears.

\* \* \*

The harsh light of the morning sun wakes me. Everything in my room is salty-sticky. The view from my window is of Robberg Beach, a long expanse of cappuccino-coloured sand still unblemished in the early morning. I cannot resist the temptation to make my mark on it, as though by leaving my footprints on the water-ruffled shore I can somehow lay claim to it. Or perhaps I just need proof of my existence. I tie my ginger curls into a ponytail, pick up my running shoes and make my way down to the beach.

If I am looking for proof of my existence though, it is fleeting. The soft indentations of my soles on the sand are washed away almost as soon as I lift my feet, symbolic, I think, of the transience and fragility of life. Is it in defiance of this that people build giant monuments, pyramids, great walls? Is the measure of one's existence proportional to that which one leaves behind? Perhaps not; perhaps one exists only for as long as one is held in the memory of those who still live.

A middle-aged couple runs past me, chatting. I can tell, without knowing them, that they have been together for many years. Their body spaces have integrated so that they can predict each other's moves. The arm unexpectedly flung out in emphasis becomes anticipated. I walk faster, digging my heels hard into the sand. I can fool myself into thinking that I enjoy being on holiday alone. I can even fool those around me: I tell them that I work with people all day and that I need some time alone. What am I afraid of, I wonder? Why am I unable to expose myself to love? Is it a fear that I am not worthy of existing beyond my allocated lifespan?

By the time I return to the hotel, the sun is high in the sky. I make my way to the poolside lawn and glance at my watch: half past twelve. Wonderful. I have made a pact with myself that I will refrain from drinking before twelve o'clock, a time I have arbitrarily designated in order to convince myself that I have control over my drinking habits. I order an ice-cold gin and tonic and settle into the last few chapters of *Northanger Abbey*.

'Are you using this umbrella?' A voice interrupts my

reading. I look up at a lanky man with piercing blue eyes and the hypopigmented wrinkles of someone with fair skin who spends a lot of time outdoors.

'No, not at all.' I move my bag from under the sun umbrella, leaving space for the man. He spreads a bleached green kikoi onto the grass and sits down on it. I turn back to my book but the peace of my semi-somnolence has been disrupted. I fiddle with my towel, trying to make myself comfortable. The man has started reading. I squint at his book, trying to make out its title, but my eyes are too weak. He looks up, catching me squinting at him, and I can feel my face redden.

'I'm sorry, I wasn't staring at you. I was just trying to see what you're reading,' I explain.

'Max du Preez.' He turns the book over so that the title faces him, as though to refresh his memory. '*Of Warriors, Lovers and Prophets.*'

'Oh, that's a fantastic book.'

'You've read it?' He looks surprised and immediately I become defensive. I don't know why, because there was nothing accusatory or malicious in his tone.

'Yes, I read it when it first came out,' I say, a little too sharply.

'What are you reading?' he asks, rolling onto his side to face me.

'*Northanger Abbey.*' And suddenly I feel embarrassed, as though Jane Austen is far too frivolous a read. God, what is wrong with me? It hardly matters what he thinks of my choice of books.

'I often think that a person's choice of book gives away a lot about them,' he says, as though confirming my silent insecurities.

'So, what does my book say about me?'

'You're reading a classic: you are obviously well

educated and have a basic literary knowledge. Does it extend to modern authors? I don't know. The fact that you have read this', he points to his own book, 'makes me think that you are politically aware and that, as much as Jane Austen would have me believe otherwise, you are not a closet colonialist and do see value in your South African heritage. I think that you are treating yourself to a holiday read, a book that you are comfortable with and that has become an easy read with repeated reading, but that is well-written enough for the language not to start irritating you.'

'I don't know whether what you've said is a compliment or an insult.'

'Neither, merely an observation.'

I have an unexplained, childish need to prove my intelligence to him. He can't be more than ten years older than I am, but I feel inexperienced and flippant next to him.

'My name is Eric Freemantle, by the way,' he says, extending his hand in greeting. I shake it; the skin is surprisingly soft.

'So, Eric, what brings you to Plett?'

'Work, unfortunately. I'm writing an article on the Garden Route.'

We continue chatting. Eric tells me he is a photojournalist. He writes commercial articles on holiday destinations for a popular magazine so that he can afford to spend his free time writing what he describes as 'travel literature'.

The sun has turned the pale, hospital-adjusted skin of my shoulders pink and I move under the shade of his umbrella. I ask Eric how frequently his job takes him away from home and he tells me that he spends two weeks of every month travelling.

'Doesn't it bother you?' I ask. 'The instability?'

'No,' he replies. 'I get irritable if I spend more than two weeks in one place. One develops a great sense of self-sufficiency by travelling a lot.'

'It can't be conducive to good relationships though.'

'No, it's not.' He is silent for a while and I think that he is going to leave his answer there, but he doesn't. 'I was married for a year but we separated two months ago. It's an institution I wouldn't recommend.'

I want to tell him that perhaps he is unfairly blaming the convention of marriage, that perhaps the problem lies with him, but I don't. We both turn back to our books, but even when the sun's rays have become oblique enough to become harmless I do not move from under the shade of the umbrella. My eyes glance from the page occasionally. His body is lean, with muscles defined more by lack of fat than by exercise. He fidgets continuously, his fingers drumming the side of his whisky glass even when he is lying still. I wonder what it would feel like to lie next to him, whether I would be comfortable against the hardness of his body.

'Are you here alone?' he asks me.

Again I feel slightly violated, as though he can read my thoughts. 'Yes, I am,' I tell him. Unusually, I don't feel the need to explain my solitary state.

'Do you want to do dinner?'

I nod. 'Sure.'

We have dinner at a sleek restaurant full of chrome and cherrywood. Perhaps because of his lean muscularity, I expected him to be a fastidious eater, but he isn't. He orders a well-done steak and eats quickly, hardly chewing the meat. Instead of dessert we order another bottle of red wine. I know, even before we get back to the hotel, that I will sleep with Eric Freemantle. I will sleep with him because I am lonely, and because I am aching for the touch of a man, and because tomorrow morning he will expect nothing of me.

\* \* \*

Eric is already packing his bag when I wake up.

'I have a meeting with the manager of a bird park at ten and then I drive down to Knysna,' he says.

I nod and look down at my watch. It is already nine o'clock.

'I'll make sure I'm out of your room by ten,' I say. He pulls the zip of his tog bag closed.

'Goodbye, then.' The door clicks shut behind his retreating back.

I roll over onto the side of the bed left vacant by his departure. I am sore from the unaccustomed sex. Eric has left a faint trace of his deodorant on the sheets, but, apart from that, my pain is the only proof of his having spent the night with me.

I get out of bed and pull on my dress from the night before, clasp my high heels in one hand and sneak barefoot back to my room. Under the harsh scrutiny of daylight, I feel uncomfortable in my crumpled black cocktail dress and unbrushed hair and I pray that my sojourn has gone unnoticed by the hotel staff. I wonder, briefly, what my patients would think if they saw me as I am now, sneaking back from some stranger's room with inner thighs stained and sticky with sex. But does it matter? Should it matter? Does my private life have any influence on my capabilities as a doctor?

By lunchtime I am packing my bags. I want to get home. I feel like a coward. The worst betrayal to face is of oneself. I have enough insight to know that my behaviour is unhealthy, not only physically (I can't remember when last I used a condom) but emotionally. Too fearful to commit to a relationship, I have prostituted myself to satisfy my craving for intimacy. This self-destructive pattern has to stop. I make a resolution: no more sex with strangers and an HIV test in six weeks' time.

# Chapter Four

## Shouting at the parasuicide

I am mentally checking off my essential call list as I drive to work, making sure that I have packed everything. I have clean underwear for tomorrow, a clean shirt and, most importantly, clean socks. It is not a pleasant experience to peel used socks from your feet after thirty-odd hours. It is even less pleasant for anyone else in the vicinity. I have my toothbrush and toothpaste, invaluable for preventing post-call dog breath. I have my cool bag with three half-litre Cokes and two packets of two-minute noodles and some emergency Jelly Tots. I have money because I cannot stretch two packets of two-minute noodles over four meals. I have my white coat. (When I first started working, just after qualifying, I never wore a white coat. I subscribed to the ideal that we were taught by certain of our professors at medical school of the doctor being more approachable to the patient sans white coat. One day, for a reason I have subsequently forgotten I wore a white coat for a call, and at the end of the night the coat was no longer white but various shades of red, brown and yellow. Ever since that call I have felt that wearing a white coat makes me far more approachable to patients.) And I have my stethoscope. For once, I think that I actually have everything I need.

I get to the hospital and trundle through my ward round. It is strangely hot for March, thirty-three degrees, and everyone has wilted. The students mope around the corridors searching out the cooler patches of cement wall that provide some temporary relief from the stifling heat. If there ever was air-conditioning installed in the hospital, it has long since given up working. The sisters are, if possible, even more recalcitrant than usual and I know that anything I ask for will be out of stock. At one o'clock we eventually get through the ward work and the students and Justine go to the cafeteria for lunch. But I can't afford to take a lunch break as I need to see the ward referrals before I go down to casualty.

The list of ward referrals, or referrals for in-patients that have been admitted by other disciplines but that warrant the opinion of the medical registrar on call, is hung up on the department secretary's door each day at eleven o'clock. She writes the time that the referral was received in red pen on the upper right-hand corner of the page. I need to see all patients referred before eleven o'clock. Today there are six.

The first three referrals are from surgery. Two I see quickly: they are for pre-operative optimisation of treatment of their medical conditions. The third referral is more complicated. It is a woman in her fifties with end-stage emphysema, diabetes, high blood pressure and heart failure. She is fifteen years younger than my mother and too short of breath to lie flat in her bed. Too many cigarettes, fried chips, pies, samoosas and chocolates. She needs an amputation of her right lower leg, which has become septic, but she is too sick for any kind of anaesthetic. The anaesthetists have said they will not dope her until she is medically stable, so the surgeons have referred her to me.

I phone the surgery registrar with a list of the changes that I suggest be made to the patient's management. His immediate response is to ask me if I am going to transfer the patient to a medical ward. I know that this is the real reason for the referral, but I can't take her over because I have too many patients already.

'I haven't got any open beds,' I tell the surgery registrar, which is not a lie, 'but I'll come and see the patient every day in your ward.'

'This is bullshit!' he snarls. 'She can't stay in a surgical ward. Her problems are medical. I'll take her back when you've stabilised her.'

I know that he is angry because he also has too few beds. I know that there are critically ill patients sitting on benches in the surgical admission ward waiting for this woman's bed. I try not to take his anger personally. 'I'm sorry. I can't take her,' I tell him. 'I have written a list of things that she needs done. I will take her over as soon as I have an open bed.' We both know that I will never have an open bed.

The next referral is from orthopaedics, a woman with a history of unstable asthma who has broken her leg. They are managing the latter; I have been called to help manage the former. I examine the patient quickly and then glance over her prescription chart to check her current asthma management. The asthma is being treated correctly, but I notice that she is on a tablet for her high blood pressure that is contraindicated in asthmatics. I scratch out the offending drug and hope that will be enough to control her asthma.

My last two referrals are in the gynaecology ward. The first is a woman with cancer of the cervix. The gynaecologists have done a chest X-ray and have seen a suspicious-looking lesion that may be a metastasis from the cancer. This is an important referral: if the cancer has spread to the lung, there is nothing more that the patient can be offered except palliation, but if the lesion in the lung is benign, the gynaecologists will do surgery and give radiotherapy in an attempt to cure the cancer.

I have not looked at the patient's age on the referral letter and I get a fright when I walk into her room. I was expecting someone older. She looks forty at most. Her hair is braided and she has piled the plaits up onto her head in a loose bun. Little pink clasps hold the bun in place. The femininity of the hair clips looks oddly incongruent with the asexuality of the blue hospital gown.

'Mrs Dlamini?' I ask, checking that it is, in fact, her.

She nods.

'Hello, I'm Doctor Carey. The gynaecologists have called me because they've seen something on your chest X-ray that looks like it may have spread from the cancer on your womb.'

She nods again. They have explained this to her. I pull the curtain shut.

'I need to examine you quickly. Is that all right?'

She starts talking while I am examining her. 'What if it is cancer?' she asks.

I try to avoid answering. 'We need to get some tissue from the lesion first, before we can tell whether it's malignant or not.' I have resorted to jargon to cover my hesitation.

'And if the tissue shows that it is cancer?'

I stop my examination and give her my full attention. 'Mrs Dlamini, if the cancer in the womb has spread to the lungs, then we will not be able to treat it. If it has not spread to the lungs, then there is a chance that we can cure it.'

'So if it has spread to my lungs I am most probably going to die?'

What am I supposed to say? I nod, feeling useless. Nothing that I say can soften the fact. So I tell her what I am going to do, how we are going to take a specimen of the lesion from her lungs. At least it makes me feel like I am doing something.

'I'm going to organise a CT scan for you,' I tell her. 'It's a very detailed type of X-ray that will show us exactly how big the lesion is and where it is in relation to the other structures in your chest. After that, we'll put a tiny camera, which is attached to a thin pipe, down your throat and into your lungs. The camera is smaller than the diameter of my pen.' I show her my pen. 'With the camera we'll be able to see the lesion and take a small sample of it. That sample will tell us if it is cancer or something harmless, like old TB. Do you understand?'

She nods.

'Any questions?'

'Not at the moment.'

I fill in the scan forms and write a response to the gynaecologists on the referral letter.

'That's all for now. I'll see you again as soon as we have a date that we can fit you in for the bronchoscopy. It will probably be in a day or two.'

'Doctor?'

'Yes?'

'I have two children at home. My son is in grade two.'

Everything that I can think of to say sounds condescending or false. I wish that I believed in miracles.

'I'm sorry,' I tell her. 'I really hope that it is just old TB.' And that is a true statement.

* * *

My last referral is a young mother who had a Caesarean section five days ago. She is spiking temperatures and the obstetricians can't find the source of the infection. They want to send her home but they can't until the fever has settled. They have checked her operation wound and it is not infected, so they have referred her to me to help locate the source of the fever. She is breastfeeding when I get to her bed.

'Hello, Sisi.'

'Hello.' She smiles at me. She doesn't look very sick.

'Boy or girl?' I ask, nodding towards the baby.

'Boy.' She removes him from her breast and shows him to me. His fat face crinkles up in irritation at being torn from his food source, and for a moment he looks as though he is going to cry. I put my finger next to his palm and he wraps his hand around it. I know this is just a reflex, but I manage to pretend to myself that the infant actually wants to hold my finger.

'Sisi, tell me, how are you feeling?'

She beams at me. 'Good. Very good. Just my ear. There is water coming out of it.'

'Does it smell bad? The water, I mean.'

She nods. I check her ear. She has a middle-ear infection. That is the source of her fever.

'You have an infection in your ear,' I tell her. 'I'm going to write up some antibiotics for you to take home.'

'Home?' Her face lights up. I nod and she breaks into Xhosa. The other five women in the ward start laughing and clapping. For a few moments I am transformed into a hero. Nothing like a little bit of easily earned appreciation to improve one's mood.

\* \* \*

I have half an hour left before I have to be in casualty so I go down to the cafeteria to get some coffee. The cafeteria is on the lower ground floor of the hospital. It is made artificially cheerful with vases of dusty plastic daisies on the tables and posters advertising meal specials stuck up on the walls. The woman behind the counter wears a mustard-yellow apron and matching cap.

'Filter coffee, please.' My stomach grumbles and I realise that I haven't had anything to eat all day. 'And a slice of cheesecake. The one with the berries on top.' I resolve to start my diet tomorrow.

I make my way to a seat at an empty table, pick up a forgotten newspaper and glance through it. There is nothing particularly interesting. The lead article is about the government's reassurance that the Zimbabwean elections will be free and fair.

'Sue, is that you? I don't believe it. How are you?' A familiar-sounding voice interrupts my reading, but I only place it after looking up.

'Donald.' I force a smile. Donald was in my class at medical school but I haven't seen him since graduation. I preferred it that way.

'It's so good to see you.' He leans over the table and gives me a damp kiss, then pulls up a chair and sits down.

'What are you doing here?' I ask him. I hope that he will say that he is on an isolated visit, that he is working somewhere very far away, like Canada, and that he has just popped in to Bellville Hospital to remind himself how glad he is that he is not working in South Africa.

'I have a post here, specialising in surgery,' he says. 'I started at the beginning of the month.'

Surgery, of course. He fits the profile. Not that all surgeons are arrogant pricks. I note with satisfaction that Donald has put on weight. But then, he is no doubt thinking the same thing about me. He digs at my cheesecake with his coffee teaspoon.

'And you? What are you doing here?' he asks.

'Internal medicine. I started at the beginning of the year.' I watch my cheesecake disappear as I talk.

In my second year of medical school, for about a month I thought that I was in love with Donald. The problem was that Donald, and Donald's parents, were as much in love with him as I was. In fact, there were altogether far too many people in love with Donald. I discovered this only after sleeping with him. A day after, to be precise, when I burst into his residence room with a carefully iced cake that I had baked for him and found him in bed with an occupational therapy student. Donald and I were never particularly good friends for the remaining four years of medical school.

'So, are you married yet? I heard you were engaged to some guy in IT.'

How like Donald to go straight for my weakest spot.

'No, things didn't work out between us,' I say as casually as I can. Such a nice, neat little parcel wrapping up so many months of pain. I check my watch. 'Oh dear, it's five to six. I'd better run. I have to be in casualty at six. It was good to see you.' I've never been so glad to have to get to casualty.

'Yes, you too. I'll page you sometime and we can meet up for a coffee.'

Maybe not, I think. I smile vaguely and make a dash for the cafeteria door, the remaining cheesecake a small sacrifice for my escape.

My previously good mood has dissipated completely by the time I reach casualty and my temper on arrival is worsened by Justine's obsessive, ineffectual wanderings around the unit.

'Justine,' I snarl, 'you can also see patients, you know. The unit will not fall apart if you stop checking up on everything twenty times.'

She rushes off. I know that she has gone to the bathroom to cry and I feel terrible about snapping at her, but I don't have the energy to go and apologise. I dispatch the students to see the stable patients and start with the more seriously ill ones myself.

The sister calls me just as I am about to examine a woman with chest pain. 'Doctor, the ambulance is here with a resus.'

I run to the resuscitation bed. The paramedics are wheeling in an unconscious man, ventilating him manually with a bag. He is young, with greasy ginger hair tied into a ponytail. One of the paramedics starts talking to me as I pull on gloves.

'Thirty-year-old man. Collapsed at home and his mother called us. When we got there he was in PEA. We started CPR and gave adrenaline, got a rhythm back after about six mg but he was still pulseless. He went into VF and we shocked him twice but then he reverted back to PEA. We intubated him at the scene and have been ventilating him the whole way. There is an adrenaline infusion running. According to the mother he has an alcohol history but no drugs. I gave Naloxone anyway and he did have some response but relapsed again.'

'Thanks.' I turn my attention to the patient, trying to sort out in my mind what the paramedic has told me. No organised heartbeat initially. No spontaneous breathing. I don't know how long he was like that before the paramedics got to him. A poor prognostic factor. Alcohol and a probable drug history, most likely heroin if he responded to the Naloxone. My hands have already started examining the patient while my mind is running through the possibilities. I can't feel pulses. The pupils are fixed and dilated and don't respond to light. I attach the ECG electrodes and an irregular green line appears on the monitor.

'Sister, please give an adrenaline bolus, two mg.' I start chest compressions. He is a big man, fat, and I tire too soon.

'Jono!' I shout for one of my fourth-year students, a prop for the Stellenbosch rugby team. 'Can you do compressions?' He nods. 'Good, please take over here.'

I can hear the pop of ribs cracking as Jono starts pressing down on the patient's thorax. I attach the patient to the ventilator and then listen to his chest to check that the endotracheal tube is positioned correctly and that it hasn't been pulled out of his lungs or slipped too deeply down the right main bronchus during the journey to the hospital.

'Sister, one mg of atropine, please,' I order. 'And get the Naloxone. It's worth a try.'

But there is no response to either of the drugs. The patient is still, in effect, dead. Jono continues chest compressions and sweat runs down his face onto the man's wobbly white stomach. I am checking for clues, trying to figure out what caused the patient to collapse. His lungs are clear. It is unlikely that he has had a heart attack at thirty, although he is overweight. How bad an alcoholic is he? Can that be the cause of his collapse?

I call another of the students. 'Zahira, please come and draw bloods. I want a blood gas for pH, full blood count, urea and electrolytes, toxicology screen, alcohol level, liver functions.' Everything, anything that might give me a clue. I scan the soft skin of the patient's cubital fossae for signs of intravenous drug abuse. There is nothing visible. I check between the toes because sometimes people hide their addictions in unlikely places, but there are no clues there either.

'Sister, did you get the time that he came in?' I ask.

'Ten to nine.'

It is now ten past nine. Twenty minutes. I decide to give him the benefit of the doubt; I won't include the time that the paramedics were resuscitating.

'I am going to give it ten more minutes. Please give him another bolus of adrenaline and atropine and let's give sodabic and some magnesium as well. Jono, are you okay?'

He nods, too breathless to talk.

The sister gives the drugs but there is no response. At twenty past nine I check everything again: there is still no pulse, no discernible heart rhythm, no pupillary reaction to light, no spontaneous breathing.

'We have been resuscitating for half an hour with no response. I'm terminating the resus.' I say the legally necessary words. 'Jono, you can stop the chest compressions.' I am the doctor in charge of the resus; it is my decision to stop the procedure. I try to remember that I am not really making the call on life or death; he was already dead when he came in. There are dark blue sweat circles under the armpits of Jono's light blue shirt.

'Thanks, Jono, you did well. Go and get a Coke or something. I'm sure you're exhausted.'

He thanks me, then disappears onto the trauma deck for a cigarette. I wish that I could join him. I turn to the sister who helped me.

'Thanks, sister. There was nothing more that we could do. I think that he was dead for a while before he got to us. There was nothing on the ECG from the time that he arrived here.'

She nods in agreement, to reassure me that we have done our best. It's especially difficult with young patients.

This is the extent of our debriefing. There are other patients still to be seen.

The dead man's mother and a younger woman are waiting in the corridor outside the unit. The mother has watery blue eyes and bleached strawberry-blond hair with dark grey roots. Her resemblance to the man that I have just spent the last half-hour trying to resuscitate is disconcerting. I falter momentarily before speaking to her.

'Hello, I'm Dr Carey,' I eventually manage to say. The mother drove in behind the paramedics and I hope that, because she saw the first part of the resuscitation at home, she has some idea of how serious her son's condition was. 'Are you the mother of . . .' Oh God, I don't know his name. Luckily she interrupts me.

'Yes, and this is Lucille, his fiancée.' She points to the younger woman with her.

'Do you mind coming with me?' I grab the dead patient's folder, quickly check his name and then lead the mother and fiancée to a small waiting room next to the sisters' office. It is a dingy, windowless room, the floor lined with the standard-issue grey hospital linoleum. There are dried blood splatters on one wall and a faded oil painting of a church and cemetery on the other. I don't know which is worse, the blood or the cemetery.

'I am very sorry to have to give you this news, but Elmo is dead.' I feel awkward, as though I am somehow responsible for his death. There is silence for a fraction of a second, so that my words seem to have been absorbed by the plastic walls, and then the fiancée starts screaming and collapses to the floor. I am glad that we are not still in the passage.

'But the paramedics said that they got a heartbeat back.' The mother is angry, her mouth twisted in accusation.

'I'm very sorry. They may have got a heartbeat back initially, but from the time that he arrived at the hospital he didn't have any heartbeat. We tried to resuscitate him for thirty minutes and gave him all the drugs that could possibly have helped, but unfortunately he didn't respond to anything. There was nothing more that we could do. I'm sorry.'

The girlfriend is writhing around on the floor, her eyes rolled back, as though she is possessed. Although she is not really having a seizure, I know that it will be useless to try to calm her down. This is her way of dealing with her grief. I move a chair to ensure that she doesn't hit her head on it.

'Would you like to see him?' I ask the mother.

She nods.

'I'm just going to speak to the nursing sister and then she'll come and fetch you to see his body,' I tell her. 'Oh, one more thing, before I forget. We don't know how he died. Because of this we will need to do an autopsy, to ascertain the cause of death. Do you understand?'

'Do you think I killed my son?' the mother screams at me. 'She thinks I killed my son!' This she yells to a hospital cleaner walking past the room.

'No, that's not what I meant.' But she is not listening. The girlfriend's wailing and rolling continues. 'I'll speak to you later about the autopsy,' I say and rush from the scene, glad to escape. I don't know how to comfort the mother and fiancée. I have no answers for them because I have absolutely no idea how Elmo died. It's impossible for me to deal with their grief while I am still asking myself whether there was anything else I could have done to save the young man's life.

I find the sister who helped me with the resus. She is busy writing her notes about the resuscitation. 'Sister, the family are in the waiting room,' I tell her. 'Please would you call them to see the body when you've finished. You can give the fiancée an Ativan tablet to calm her down. Oh, and remember that you mustn't remove any of the lines or tubes from the body, even if the family requests you to, because he'll need a post-mortem.'

I want an Ativan tablet. I want to leave casualty for a minute, get away from bleeping monitors, students' questions, wailing girlfriends. I want to sit on the trauma deck and watch the smoke from the cigarette that I am desperately craving fade into the cool night air. But there are patients waiting for me. I walk back into the casualty unit.

\* \* \*

The first chance that I get to sit down is at half past two in the morning. I collapse into the threadbare bottle-green armchair that someone has decided is old enough to be relegated to the casualty doctors' office. The springs are broken and the base of the chair sags so that my bottom nearly sinks to the floor. I am starving and curse Donald for guzzling my cheesecake lunch. I open both packets of noodles. The microwave is broken so I cook the noodles in a cup of boiling water from the kettle. Two packets of half-cooked two-minute noodles at two thirty in the morning, washed down by five hundred millilitres of Coke. My healthy lifestyle: exemplary. The sister opens the door of the doctors' office just as I start eating.

'New patient, Doctor. An OD.'

'Is she stable?'

'Yes, she walked in. Overdosed on flu tablets or something. She's seventeen. Her mother brought her in.'

'What time did she take the tablets?'

'About an hour ago.'

'Give her some activated charcoal in the meantime. I'll

see her as soon as I have finished eating.'

It is a constant source of wonder to me that the overdose patients always pick between two and four o'clock in the morning to come in, the time when I am most tired, most hungry and most irritable. I finish off my rubbery noodles and get up from the chair, still hungry.

When I get to her bedside, the girl's teeth and lips are black from the activated charcoal that the nursing sister has given her to drink. The girl's mother is standing next to her bed.

'What did you take?' I ask the girl. She starts sobbing and the mother hands me an empty box. Paracetamol.

'How many tablets were in the box?'

'I don't know,' the mother answers. 'I think there were about six left.'

I turn to the girl. 'How many tablets did you take?' She bursts into tears again and I struggle to keep my voice level. 'I need to know how many tablets you took so that I know how serious this is. Please can you try to remember.'

She snivels and looks away. I take deep breaths to stop myself from screaming at her. The cup of activated charcoal at the patient's bedside is almost untouched.

'You must please drink that up, the whole cup,' I say, pointing to the charcoal. 'I know it tastes awful but it binds the paracetamol that you took so that it doesn't get into your bloodstream.' I simplify the explanation of the drug's mechanism of action so that it will make sense to her.

'But it tastes horrible,' she says between tears.

'She doesn't like the taste,' her mother clarifies, as though I am deaf or an imbecile.

'Well, neither does paracetamol taste nice and you managed to swallow that. Drink it up. I am going to get the stuff to draw your blood; I need to do paracetamol levels.' I get up to fetch a needle and some blood tubes and the girl lets out a wail and clings to her mother.

She is still crying when I return. I tie a glove around her upper arm as a tourniquet.

'Hold your arm out straight for me, please.' As I approach the girl's arm with the needle she screams and bends her elbow.

'I haven't even touched your arm yet! How old are you?'

'Twenty.'

'You're not a baby. Hold your arm still and it'll just be a small prick.' I try a second time and again she withdraws her arm before I get anywhere near the vein. She grabs on to her mother.

'You're acting like a baby,' I say, crosser than ever. 'Stop this now! If you carry on crying I'm going to tell your mother to wait outside.'

'Please don't,' she sniffles.

'Straighten your arm. Let's try again.'

As I reach her arm she pushes the needle out of my hand. It scratches the skin of my forefinger, leaving a thin, red stripe. Thank God the needle is still clean. I rip the glove that is acting as a tourniquet from the girl's arm.

'If you do something stupid like drink tablets, you must face the consequences.' I realise that I am shouting and lower my voice. The other patients are staring at me. 'Quite frankly, I don't want you here. I have sick patients waiting for me, patients that are dying, and you are wasting my time and theirs. If you are not going to let me treat you properly, then you leave, now! I do not have time to waste on silly girls who decide that they want to drink five Panados at two o'clock in the morning because they want a bit of attention. Do you understand me?' Heil, Hitler. At least my shouting has frightened away her tears. 'Now, are you going to hold your arm still for me?' She nods, white-faced. I manage to draw blood this time. And start feeling guilty.

'We're going to keep you overnight. I'll check the blood results in the morning and if they are normal then I'll discharge you, but you must see the psychiatrist before you go. I'll arrange it. Okay?'

She nods again, sniffling.

I feel bad. I wish that I had the patience or time or compassion that, as a doctor, I should have. I wish that I wanted to sit down next to her and ask her what made her so sad and why she even thought about taking her life. That is what a good doctor would do. But right now I am too tired even to try to be a good doctor.

*　*　*

We have a ward round with the consultant at seven o'clock in the morning to see the patients that I have admitted overnight. I have managed to get forty-five minutes of sleep, and in that measly forty-five minutes I have been attacked by a mosquito. It has bitten me on my right eyelid, which is swollen shut, leaving me even blinder than usual. The ward round is a teaching round and the consultant, who has probably had eight hours of sleep, is more than usually eager to pass on his superior knowledge to the students. He questions them on each patient, asks them about chemistry and haematology results, checks that they have remembered to test urine specimens, quizzes them on chest X-rays that, through my swollen eye, are no more than a black and white blur. By eleven o'clock I would sell my body for a cup of coffee. Unfortunately nobody makes the offer, probably because of my puffed-up eye. At last, at half past twelve, the round finishes.

Before tackling the ward work that the consultant has left in his wake, I decide to go to the cafeteria to get some coffee and a muffin. Appeasing my hunger pangs is worth the risk of seeing Donald. I turn to Justine and the students. 'You guys are welcome to come to the caf with me or you can start the ward work so long. Whichever you want,' I tell them. They elect to come with me.

I down two cups of coffee, a stale muffin and two pieces of fudge. Hope the sugar and caffeine will get me through the afternoon. Over my third cup of coffee, Justine and I divide the list of ward work that still needs to be done. I notice that she chooses all of the easy stuff to do herself but I am too tired to argue. I figure it will take more energy to fight with Justine than just to do the work myself.

At four o'clock on Thursday afternoon, more than thirty-two hours since I arrived at the hospital, I am finally done. I am walking to my car with my backpack of sweaty clothes and my empty cool bag when I remember the surgery referral patient whom I promised to see. Shit. I want to forget my promise, but I know that if I do I will spend the whole night worrying. I squeeze my bags into the remaining bit of open space in the boot of my car, then turn around and walk back to the hospital. I can't remember the patient's name when I arrive at the ward.

'Sister, Dr Carey from internal medicine. Where is that woman with the septic leg lying? The one who was referred to me yesterday.'

'Mrs Mentz?' the sister asks.

'Yes, that's her.'

'Room seven.'

'Thanks.'

The patient looks much worse today than when I saw her yesterday. And the surgeons have done nothing that

I asked them to, not even put her on oxygen. I wonder if they bothered to look at my response on their referral note. The sister has followed me to the room and is standing at the door.

'Sister, I need oxygen for this woman and a CVP set. Please be quick because if we don't do something soon she's going to collapse and I don't feel like a resuscitation now. And you can page the surgery intern to come and help me. They should be doing this, not me.'

The sister rushes off and I sit down on the chair next to the patient's bed. I close my eyes and rub my fists into the sockets to stop the tears. Hard, so that I see little flashing lights. I don't want to do this now. I want to go home to a bath and some decent food and bed. I have two minutes to feel sorry for myself and then the sister is back. She puts an oxygen mask on the patient and I quickly draw blood for an arterial gas analysis. Organise a mobile chest X-ray. Start an adrenaline infusion. All stuff that should have been done yesterday, and the surgery intern still has not arrived.

I scrub my hands at the basin in the patient's room and put on sterile greens. I feel over the patient's neck for the landmarks to insert the central venous catheter. I run my fingers along the inner border of her sternocleidomastoid muscle, from the medial end of the collar bone to the angle of her jaw, then measure out two-thirds the length of the muscle. I feel for the pulsation of the carotid artery and go in laterally with the needle to avoid it. The needle goes in deep under the muscle until I see the flashback of dark purple venous blood. I thread the guide wire through the needle. It is difficult with clumsy hands that have had too little sleep and I am worried that I am going to prick myself. I run the plastic dilator over the guide wire and then follow it with the catheter. I put in two stitches to secure the line, then cover it with a plaster.

The patient needs to go to intensive care. I doubt that they will take her because her baseline function is too poor, but I am too tired to be the one to make that decision. I page the ICU registrar.

'Hi, it's Sue Carey here. I have a patient that I would like to refer to ICU. She's a fifty-three-year-old woman with multiple underlying illnesses, including heart failure and diabetes, who has now collapsed in septic shock secondary to a gangrenous leg. The surgeons will not remove the leg until she is more stable. I have put up a CVP and started adrenaline but she needs ICU care.'

'What's her baseline?' the intensive-care registrar asks.

'I actually don't know,' I answer carefully. This is the deciding factor. 'She was already quite sick when she was referred to me. Surgery admitted the patient and I saw her for the first time yesterday. I think it's Dr Van Zyl looking after her. Speak to him. I can't make a call on it.'

'We don't have any open beds at the moment, anyway. I'll come and see her later, and if her baseline function is okay I'll put her on the waiting list.'

'How many on the waiting list?'

'Three in front of her.'

'Thanks. She's in ward D2.'

I put the phone down. She won't make it into ICU. Even if she does get onto the waiting list, she'll be dead by the time there is room for her. There is nothing more that I can do, but I wonder whether I managed everything properly. Perhaps if I had taken her over yesterday, or if the surgeons had actually done what I asked when I asked, she would not be so sick today. I know that the surgeons' lack of response was not because they were lazy. They were probably just too busy. But I'm too tired to think of possibilities. It's six o'clock. I have been at the hospital for thirty-four hours.

'Sister, you should probably call her family,' I tell the nurse looking after her. 'She's not doing well and the ICU is full. I don't think she's going to make it.'

My pager goes off as I am walking out of the hospital for the second time. I hesitate before answering it. Curse my conscience as I walk back into the ward to find a telephone. It is the pathologist, with the biopsy result of the patient with the cervical cancer and the lung lesion. It is malignant. The child in grade two will have to finish school without the help of his mother. I will tell the patient and the gynaecologists tomorrow. One more night will not make a difference and I am too tired now. Too tired to think. Too tired even to cry.

# Chapter Five

## Why not to date guys from the gym

There is a guy at the gym with whom I have built up a tentative relationship over super-circuit intervals. He drives a metallic green car with leather seats, and he does not wear a wedding ring. I first noticed him a few weeks ago, when he complimented me on my fitness after watching me struggle through ten minutes of the super-circuit. If I were fit, his overture would probably have been effective in impressing or at least charming me. But I am not fit, and at the time that the compliment was given I felt as though I was about to succumb to a myocardial infarct. Being preoccupied with my imminent heart attack, I had little energy to respond to his flattery. It must have influenced me on a subconscious level, though, because the next time that we did super-circuit together, I greeted him. Super-circuit chirps progressed to discussions of training habits (I lied), which in turn progressed to name-swapping. So now I know that his name is Deon.

Today Deon is already doing super-circuit when I arrive at the gym. I greet him as I sit down on the first weight machine. He looks up, smiles and carries on running up and down the metal stairs that facilitate cardio intervals between the weight machines. He does it with such ease that, were I a newcomer to the gym, I could be fooled into thinking that super-circuit training is not strenuous. I am halfway through the circuit when he finishes. The green light signalling the change from weight machine to stairs flashes and I start jogging up and down. In my peripheral vision, I see Deon approach me. He looks relaxed, as though he has just done a gentle warm-up.

'Sue, how are you keeping?'

I turn my head to answer him and my foot slips so that my shin slams into the edge of the metal super-circuit stair. 'Oh shit! Eina, eina, shit, eina!' The fatal error was taking my eyes from the steps. My coordination, bad at the best of times, has always had the tendency to deteriorate in the presence of a good-looking man.

'Oh shit, this is sore.' I sit down and grasp my degloved shin, aware that everyone in the gym is staring at me. Already several aspiring paramedics have run to the circuit.

'Are you okay?' Deon kneels down next to me.

I really have only one option now: to die. But somehow my body doesn't feel that a skinned shin and bruised ego warrant giving up altogether. God, I am so clumsy. At least the damage looks serious. A rectangle of my skin is hanging from the edge of the stair. Blood pours down my leg. I press my sweat towel over my shin to try to control the bleeding. It burns like the fires of hell.

'I'm okay, thanks for the concern,' I say in the general direction of the crowd staring at me. I get up on slightly wobbly legs. Deon reaches to take my arm.

'Let me help you,' he offers.

'No, I'm fine, really. It's just a graze.'

'Well, at least let me help you to the changing room.' Deon grabs my sweaty arm and helps me to the door of the changing room.

In the safety of the women's bathroom I search frantically for a fire escape. There must be a fire escape in the changing room. What about those poor women caught in the shower when a fire breaks out? But nothing. I put my jeans on and try to stuff my towel up the leg to contain the bleeding. It doesn't work and I leave an embarrassing trail of bloody droplets behind me. I am doomed to be known forever in the gym as the girl who slipped on the super-circuit.

Deon is waiting for me when I eventually muster up the courage to leave the changing room.

'Feeling a bit better?' he asks.

'Marginally.'

'How about dinner tonight to cheer you up?'

I am cheered up already, and respond with good-humoured self-deprecation. 'Are you sure that you want to risk taking me out? I mean, I might just slip on the restaurant floor and spill red wine on you or something.'

'Shall we meet at Prima Pasta at eight?'

'Great. I love Italian food. See you there; just keep a look-out for the woman with a limp.'

At home, it takes me an hour to curb the bleeding from my shin and another hour to decide what to wear. Obviously, anything shorter than ankle length is out of the question. I am counting on Deon having selective retrograde amnesia for traumatic events and I would hate the sight of an ungainly red scab to recall any suppressed memories. Eventually I choose black pants and a maroon shirt. I leave the top two buttons of the shirt undone, hoping that my ample cleavage will distract him from remembering anything to do with the super-circuit.

\* \* \*

Deon is late and I curse the one time in my life that I have actually arrived on time. I inspect the menu, then re-inspect it, then try to memorise it so that I look as though I am doing something other than sitting drinking on my own. I have finished my second gin and tonic by the time he arrives.

'Hello, beautiful. Sorry I'm late.' Deon kisses me on the cheek and whips a bunch of red roses from behind his back.

'Waiter, please bring us an ice bucket for the roses,' he shouts to a waiter five metres away. I cringe as the entire restaurant turns to stare at me and my red-rose date. The huge bunch of roses takes the place of honour in the centre of the table, making eye contact between us dependent on skilled gymnastics.

'Do you mind if we move the roses?' I ask. 'I'm struggling to see you past them.'

He hesitates for a moment before placing them on the table next to us. 'I have to confess to being a bit of a romantic,' he says.

In the process of moving the roses I have not noticed the waitress's arrival. She asks me if she can get me another drink.

'Please, that would be wonderful. I'll have a glass of dry white.' She scribbles down my order, then turns to Deon. I can't help staring at her notepad. It has 'Thick Dik' written on the cover in bright red letters. I turn my head to one side and try to figure out if I am misreading it or if this is some kind of sign. The proverbial writing on the wall, in red miniature. It takes me a while to remember that *dik* is Afrikaans for 'thick'.

'Just a sparkling mineral water for me,' Deon says. 'I don't drink alcohol. I think it's an awful habit, very unhealthy. Might as well drink a glass of oil.' Perhaps, I think, but who in his or her right mind would want to? 'Do you know how many calories a single unit of alcohol contains?'

'No, but please don't tell me,' I say. I'm tempted to add that I do drink, that I'm not planning to stop and that occasionally I think it is a life-enhancing, if not life-saving, habit. But Deon ignores my request and ploughs on with his tirade against alcohol. By the time that my glass of wine arrives, lovely, ice-cold, gooseberry and guava sauvignon blanc, I actually feel guilty for taking a sip.

'So, tell me about yourself,' he says.

Without the roses between us, there is altogether too much eye contact. 'Well, what do you want to know? I'm nearing thirty, work at Bellville Hosp—'

'No, I don't mean the superficial stuff. I don't want to know about Sue the nurse or Sue the dietician or whatever job it is that you do. I want to know the real Sue, the Sue behind the job.' For once I am not being defined by my job and I don't really know how to handle it.

Oh God, an impromptu psychology session. Not my forte.

'You aren't a psychologist, are you?' I ask jokingly.

'No, not yet. But I am studying psychology via correspondence. I've done eight months so far. I have to confess that I think I have a bit of an aptitude for it. I have a knack for listening to people, as I'm sure you've noticed. I'm actually an estate agent slash property developer and I love my job, but I feel that if I can combine it with psychology, I'll become so much more successful. It's all a matter of visualisation, of focusing your inner self. Close your eyes for me for a moment.'

I look at him with raised eyebrows, not sure he is being serious.

'Come on, just close your eyes,' he says. 'That's right. Now, imagine a happy space for yourself. A pond with white swans gliding on the surface and a rainbow lighting up the sky. Have you got that?'

I wonder whether he's going to ask me to imagine 'My Little Ponies' prancing at the side of the pond, whether he's pulling my leg.

'Now imagine me,' he continues, 'a successful property developer cum psychologist selling million-dollar properties on a luxury golf estate . . .'

'That was once a nature reserve?' I blurt out.

'Shh, focus! Go back to the pond. Remember, happy place.' I wonder what the pond has to do with a golf estate. Deon continues to guide my visualisation. 'Imagine my power, my charisma combined with what I have learnt from my psychology degree. Imagine my confidence drawing people to me. Now leave the pond. The sun is setting and the first star is twinkling in the sky. Imagine me driving away into the distance in my brand-new silver C-class Mercedes with the sunset behind me, DEON on the number plate.'

I have decided that I am cancelling my gym membership. I can't believe that I am being asked to visualise someone else's fantasy. I consider leaving immediately but the temptation of seeing how his bizarre egotism will evolve keeps me at the table.

Deon prattles on for a while longer. I am glad that I inspected the menu before he arrived, as I have only just been allowed to open my eyes by the time the waitress appears to take our order.

'I'll have the pasta primavera,' Deon says. 'Please bring it asap because I need to eat before nine.'

The waitress turns to me. 'I'll have the same, please,' I tell her. I decide against ordering another glass of wine, although I could use one.

'I'm so glad that you didn't order a dish with flesh in it,' Deon says. 'Meat is so bad for you. It's full of hormones and antibiotics and other artificial poisons. I stopped eating it four months ago, haven't touched it since, and I feel so much better. Like a new person. Like I have been cleansed from within.'

'I do eat meat, actually,' I admit. Italian names are not easy to memorise: pasta primavera was about all I could manage.

'You must stop. It will help you lose some of that extra weight as well. I can't begin to tell you the benefits of being a vegetarian. I have to admit that I'm a bit of a health freak.'

I want to suggest that he leave out the 'health'. Fortunately his monologue is cut short when our food arrives, and he begins to eat immediately.

'I have to eat before nine,' he says between mouthfuls of spinach. 'It affects my metabolism if I eat later than that. I'm convinced that it's because of my healthy habits that I look so young for my age. Lots of water, eight hours of sleep a night, no alcohol, no meat, no eating after nine o'clock.' No life, I think. 'How old do you think I am? Guess.' He doesn't wait for my estimate. 'Only thirty-four! Can you believe it? If you just follow my advice, you could also look about five years younger than you do. I could help you, if you want.'

'No, thanks. Being a doctor precludes eight hours' sleep a night. Speaking of which, I'd better go and catch some shut-eye.'

'Sue, it's been wonderful meeting you. I've had a splendid dinner and you are a very, very special person. I feel that we have a real connection. I'd love to see you again.'

'Thanks, but unfortunately I'm so busy at the moment that it's really difficult for me to find time to do social things. Tonight was really a bit of an exception.'

'Well, if you do have some time off, give me a call.'

He hands me a business card. 'And do yourself a favour, go and buy a copy of the book *Seven Steps to Learning to Love Yourself*. It will transform your life. In fact, I wouldn't even consider dating anyone who hasn't read it. It's essential for self-development. Sorry, I'm keeping you. Good night, and good luck with your nursing.'

That's one reading tip I won't be taking. Perhaps to my detriment, I'm not a big fan of self-help books. I glance at Deon's business card on the way back to my car before throwing it away. The card is almost entirely taken up by a photograph of himself: a calling card for the image-conscious.

## Dispensing the government's disability grants

'Mrs Beukes!' I yell. Blank faces lined up along both sides of the out-patient department corridor stare back at me. I try again. 'Mrs Beukes!'

'Coming, Doctor.' From far along the row of seats a woman extricates herself from the mass of people. I wait for her while she gobbles down the last bite of her pie. Wait as she gathers together her numerous parcels. Wait as she goes back to her seat for the can of Coke that she left behind. Wait as she heaves her obese frame to my examination room.

'Hello, Mrs Beukes, how are you today?' I ask. She sits down and her bottom rolls over the edges of the seat, diminishing it to a child-size play-chair.

'Fine, thank you, Doctor,' she says rather breathlessly.

'That's good. Shall we check your blood pressure? You'll need to take your shirt off for me.'

She takes a good five minutes to struggle out of her sweaty polyester blouse. I try to stretch the cuff of the sphygmomanometer over the wobbling mass of her upper arm without success.

I leave Mrs Beukes waiting in the cubicle and go off to find the clinic nursing sister. I ask her whether there is a blood-pressure cuff for obese patients.

'I don't think so. Doctor can check in the A clinic.'

No obese cuff there. I check the C clinic. Again I am unsuccessful. Eventually I manage to locate an obese blood-pressure cuff in the gastro clinic a floor below our clinic. I return to the examination cubicle to find Mrs Beukes fully dressed.

'Sorry, Mrs Beukes. Let's try again.'

I wait another five minutes for her to take off her blouse for the second time. This time the cuff fits and I take her blood pressure: 180/110. Far too high.

'Mrs Beukes, your blood pressure is very high.' She shakes her head, dismayed at her blood pressure's apparent waywardness. 'Are you taking all of your medication?'

'Yes, Doctor.' But this is a standard response, as is 'no' when I enquire whether a patient drinks alcohol. There are only about three people who drink in the Western Cape. I am one of them.

'Which tablets are you taking?' I ask her.

'The water tablet. I take half every morning.'

I nod; she is taking her diuretic correctly. 'What else?' I ask.

'Then the other one, I take one in the morning.'

'Which one is that?'

'I don't know the name. The white one. It's a round one.'

Aha, that explains everything. Mentally, I run through the extensive list of round white tablets that I can remember. 'Does it come in a bottle?' I ask, trying to limit the selection.

She nods. I have now reduced the number of possibilities to about two hundred different kinds of tablets. 'What else do you take?'

'The pinkish-brown one. I take one in the morning.'

Pinkish-brown? 'Is it in a white box with black writing on?'

'Yes.'

'That one you need to take one in the morning and one at night. Anything else?'

'They gave me another one but I stopped taking it because it wasn't working. It's also a pinkish kind of colour. I think it's called XL.'

I know which tablet she means. It's a good anti-hypertensive. 'How did you know it wasn't working?'

'It made me feel very weak. It made my legs weak.'

A new side-effect, perhaps? I wonder how many boxes she has collected at home. 'You can bring the unused tablets back so that we can give them to other patients. Those ones are quite expensive.'

'No, I give them to my neighbour. They work for her. She uses them whenever she has headaches.'

Oh God. I press on. 'Are you taking any other tablets?'

'Just the sugar one.'

For her diabetes, I presume. 'The big white one?'

'Yes, Doctor.'

'And how often do you take that one?'

'When my sugar is high.'

I am momentarily impressed. 'Do you have a machine at home to measure your blood sugar?'

'No, I can feel when it's high. It makes me feel very weak and tired. It makes my legs weak.'

'So is your sugar high at the moment?'

'No, it is quite fine now.'

Not after that Coke and pie, it isn't. 'Please go back to the sister. She's going to check your sugar quickly, just to make sure it's fine.'

She comes back with a small slip of paper. I take it from her and read the blood-glucose measurement.

'Nineteen! Mrs Beukes, your sugar is much too high, it should be less than eight.'

'Aai, Doctor, I don't know how it got so high. Maybe it's all the stress. Or the piece of cake that I ate yesterday for my granddaughter's birthday.'

Or the pie and Coke, perhaps?

'You need to take the sugar tablet every day, three times a day, even if you feel fine. I am going to make an appointment for you with the dietician. You weigh one hundred and twenty-five kilograms. You need to lose some weight, at least sixty kilograms, otherwise you are going to have a heart attack or a stroke. Okay? Are you going to try for me? And remember to take all your medication?'

'Yes, Doctor. I'll try.'

'And no more Coke and pies, okay?'

'Yes.' She smiles.

'I know it's difficult but you must try, for your own good. I can do my bit for you but you must also do your bit.'

'Yes, Doctor. I'll try.'

I wonder whether I have made any difference, whether the next time I see her it will be in casualty with one side of her body paralysed.

* * *

My next patient is a young woman in her early thirties. She comes in with an older woman.

'Hello, I'm Doctor Carey. How can I help you?'

The older woman speaks. 'She is having pains in her head.'

'What kind of pains?'

A discussion in Xhosa between the two women

follows, and then the older one speaks again. 'Bad pains. Pains that start in her head and move all the way down her back and into her stomach and then into her legs. Sometimes she becomes weak and loses all of her power.'

'How long has she had the headaches?'

'For many years. And she also has arthritis in her knees. It causes her too much pain.'

'Please tell her that I need to examine her. She must undress and get onto the bed.'

I examine the young woman thoroughly but can find nothing wrong with her. Her blood pressure is fine. She has no evidence of a meningitis or an encephalitis. Her neurological exam is normal, and when I do fundoscopy, her retinas and optic discs are normal.

'I think the headaches are from stress.' I give a common but reasonable diagnosis. 'I am going to give her some headache tablets. Is she very stressed?'

'She has four children and she must also look after her sister's child because her sister is dead. The oldest girl is eight. Her husband is a bad man. Too bad.' The older woman shakes her head and clicks her tongue in emphasis. 'Sometimes he works, but he drinks and spends all the money. When he has been drinking he hits her.'

Slightly stressful circumstances to be sure. More than enough to cause headaches. But I suspect painkillers will not have much effect.

The older woman digs in her bag and the ubiquitous green disability grant form makes its appearance in her hands. 'Please, Doctor, can you fill this in for her?'

I take the form. It is not a social grant and the young woman has no medical disability. 'Is she getting grants for the children?' I ask the older woman.

She nods. 'But it's not enough and the husband is sometimes taking it to buy beer,' she says.

'I'll fill in the form but she doesn't qualify for a grant,' I explain. 'There's nothing wrong with her. I can't give her a grant.'

'But what about the headaches? She has five children to look after. Some days she is too weak.'

'I know, I'm sorry, but this is a grant for people who are too sick to work. She is not that sick.'

I tick the box next to 'Does not qualify' and hand the form back to the woman. The couple shuffle from the room heavily and I feel that I have betrayed them. I want to shout to them that it is not me who has let them down, that I am a doctor, not a social worker or a politician. I wonder if I should have lied for them. But then where would I draw the line? How can I decide who deserves a grant and who doesn't?

\* \* \*

'Mrs Geduld!' I call my next patient. She is an elderly woman who bustles down the corridor to my cubicle. 'How are you today?' I ask.

'Fine, thank you, Doctor.' She has dressed up to come to hospital. She's wearing a red and white polka-dot dress with a bow that ties underneath her neck, stockings and brown court shoes, polished to hide the scuffs on the heels and toes.

'Are you taking your medication?'

'Yes, Doctor, every morning.'

While measuring her blood pressure, I notice a safety pin holding the dress closed where she has lost a button, and for some reason it makes my heart ache. How can a safety pin so easily pierce through all my defences? All at once Mrs Geduld is a human being and I want to buy her a new button, a new dress, a new wardrobe.

'Your blood pressure is perfect,' I tell her, forcing myself to concentrate on what I am doing. 'Well done! Any other problems? Are you still managing to do some work around the house?'

'Of course. I live on my own. I must do the housework. My daughter is in Port Elizabeth and my husband died ten years ago.'

'Shame, you must get lonely.'

'No, I go to church every morning and evening.'

'You go to church twice every day?'

She smiles. 'Every day, seven days a week. Without the Lord Jesus Christ I would not be where I am now. He gave me the strength to get through the time when my husband passed away and He gives me strength every single day. Without Him, I would not be alive. With Him, I am happy and strong enough to care for those people in the church who are old or sick.'

'I think that you are incredible, Mrs Geduld.' I fervently wish that I had some of her faith. 'I'm going to give you an appointment in two months' time. Keep well until then and don't work too hard.'

'Thanks, Doctor. Hard work keeps me young. God bless.'

No, God bless you, Mrs Geduld. Sometimes there are patients who doctor me.

\* \* \*

'Mr October!'

He is young, forty at most. Dirty, yellow nails. Smells of mandrax. He hands me the disability grant form as soon as he enters my cubicle and requests that I renew it.

'Why can't you work?' I ask.

'Fits.'

I open his file. He has epilepsy, poorly controlled. 'How many fits are you getting a week?'

'About three or four.'

That is a lot. I check his prescription chart; he is on almost maximal therapy. 'Have you had seizures since childhood?'

'What?'

'Fits since you were a baby?'

'No, only after the time I was stabbed in the head.'

Multiple scars criss-cross his hairline. Ugly purple worms. I do not bother to ask which one caused the epilepsy. 'When was that?'

'In 1988. I was still in prison then.'

If telling me this is a ploy to get my sympathy, it has failed. Somehow I doubt that he was a political prisoner. 'When did you get out of prison?'

'2002.'

'And you have been on a disability grant since then?'

He nods.

'When did you go to prison?'

'When I was twenty.'

'Have you ever worked in your life?' I am angry. He can hear it and he doesn't answer. Doesn't have to. I start filling in the form so that I don't say anything else. He qualifies for a grant. This man, this drug addict, who spent fifteen years in prison being supported by taxpayers' money, who has never worked a day in his life, qualifies for a grant because of a fight that he got into while incarcerated. I can't help feeling that there is something wrong with a system that allows this man a grant and withholds one from a woman who is struggling to bring up five children on her own.

Or perhaps there is something wrong with me. Perhaps I should have lied, should have given the young mother debilitating arthritis and cured this man's epilepsy. Perhaps then I would not be so bitter or so angry. Perhaps then I wouldn't need three glasses of wine before bedtime to help me sleep. I wish that there was an instruction book on how to play the role of doctor. That I didn't have only my dodgy moral conscience to guide me.

# Chapter Six

## More on the nature of beauty

Philosophy class meets again, and I'm not getting any answers. We're still discussing beauty, and the more we delve into the nature of beauty, the more my dismal outlook on life seems to be a function of me and not the world.

Gilbert the builder raises his arm and Mrs De Marigny nods at him to speak. 'Maybe Shakespeare was right when he said beauty is in the eye of the beholder. Isn't that what he said?'

The group is divided in their opinion of the origin of this quote. I notice the dream-catcher woman, the one named Carol who asked me about lymphomas, shaking her head.

'But does it really matter?' she says. 'I mean, does it matter whether the beauty is in the eye of the beholder or the beholden? Perhaps what we should be concentrating on is our perception of beauty.' Her voice is deep and smooth, like cocoa made with cream instead of milk. She could be a radio presenter. 'Everyone likes beautiful things. Perhaps what we should be discussing is our receptiveness to the beauty or our connection with the beauty. I'm sure there's so much beauty out there that we all miss just because we're not open to it, or because we have preconceived ideas about what is and what is not beautiful.'

Perhaps I'm looking for beauty in the wrong places. Or not looking for it at all.

I go over to speak to Carol during the tea break. She had noticed that I missed the lecture last week and asks me if everything is okay. I explain that I was too tired to make it and then ask her if she has found out anything more about the lymphoma. I have remembered to update my knowledge of lymphomas, albeit rather superficially.

'My friend spoke to the oncologist,' she says. 'He called it a Hodgkin's lymphoma, stage three. I don't know if that means anything to you? He seemed to think it was good news.'

'Well, if one had to choose a cancer, probably Hodgkin's lymphoma would be the one; it has a very high five-year survival rate. Much higher than most other cancers.' My mind feels boggy, too thick to make a proper sentence. Who on earth would want to choose a cancer?

'Sorry to sound stupid, but what do you mean by a five-year survival rate?'

'Basically, in cancer terms if you're still alive and haven't had a relapse five years after being treated, then the chances are very high that you've been cured from the cancer. So a high five-year survival rate implies a large number of people who've been cured from the cancer. As far as I know, Hodgkin's lymphoma has about an eighty per cent five-year survival rate.'

'But that's still twenty per cent who don't make it to five years.'

'Yes, I know. But I think that most of those twenty per cent are stage-four disease.'

Mrs De Marigny signals to us that the lecture is about to resume.

'Have you got a cellphone on you?' I ask Carol.

'Yes, why?'

'Let me give you my number quickly. If you've got any questions you can give me a call, any time. Okay?'

'Thanks, that would be great. I'm sure my friend will appreciate that.' She types my number into her cellphone as we walk back to the lecture room.

I have noticed that the Camel-man yacht owner is not at the lecture. I wonder if he has given up on philosophy or if he is gallivanting around the world. I hope that Carol calls me. It would be nice to feel like I'm doing some good for a change, even if it is just answering someone's questions.

## Successfully reinventing myself

I have decided that the answer to relieving my semi-permanent state of depression lies in dyeing my hair. Reinventing myself, as in the movies. I am going from faded ginger to feisty red. From fat and drab to slender and well-groomed. And of course, this will all be accomplished in an afternoon. After all, in movies it only takes about ten minutes.

The hairdresser has given me a selection of fake-hair swabs of different hues of red to choose from. They range from strawberry sunset to scarlet surprise (either for the very daring or for prostitutes, I presume). I choose a colour closer to the scarlet than to the strawberries.

'Are you sure you want that one? It's very red.' The hairdresser looks worried.

'Yes, I'm sure. I'm trying to make a statement.'

'You do know that it's permanent? It doesn't wash out in eight washes.'

'Yes.' Yes, I do understand the meaning of permanent. The hairdresser sighs as she starts mixing the colour.

I spend thirty minutes reading a crumpled fashion

magazine from two years ago and then the hairdresser starts rinsing off the dye. It has seeped onto the skin of my forehead, staining the light, downy hair of my hairline, so that I look as though I am wearing a red skullcap.

'Do you want a blow-dry?'

'Please. I'd like to see the colour properly.'

The red emerges as she blows the hot air through my hair. Delicious, sexy, bold. I leave the salon a redhead and the whole world has changed. Men stare. Maybe the movies are right. I stop for coffee at the Latino Café and steal glances of myself in the wall-mounted mirror. Flirt with the teenage waiter. Get a manicure. Splurge on a black lace bra. It doesn't matter if nobody sees it, the magazine at the hairdresser assured me a few hours before. It's all about how you feel.

My new life lasts until I reach home and realise that I have three hours left before I have to be at Paarl Hospital for a trauma shift. The sophisticated redhead disappears into the worn jeans and scuffed tackies that are specially reserved for Paarl Hospital trauma shifts.

* * *

There are five doctors on call in the hospital, excluding the anaesthetist. As the locum, I get the choice job of casualty officer. The other doctors are on for gynaecology, medicine, paediatrics and surgery and are supposed to help me out in trauma between whatever needs to be done in the wards or theatre. I have noticed that when certain doctors are on, the ward work increases exponentially after midnight.

I pick up the first folder on the pile waiting for me and call the patient, a drunk thirty-four-year-old male with a laceration over his left eyebrow. He has been stabbed with a broken bottle. I fetch a suture pack, inject some local anaesthetic and start suturing. I am about halfway through stitching the wound when one of the other doctors approaches me.

'Hi,' he says. 'I don't think we've met before. I'm Julian.'

I finish tying the stitch before looking up to greet him. The stab victim notices my distraction and takes the opportunity to try to make his escape.

'Sit down. I haven't finished yet. If you don't keep still I'm going to end up hurting you,' I say to the patient, then look up again. 'Sorry about that. I promise I'm not always so rude. I'm Sue. I would shake your hand but I fear we'll have another attempted escape if I do.'

Julian is wearing theatre greens, which means he is most likely on for surgery. Or he has decided that it is safer not to bring his own clothes into the trauma unit. He is tall, with floppy blond hair, blue eyes and thick, unruly eyebrows. He reminds me of a large puppy dog.

'You on for surgery?' I ask.

'Good guess.'

'Do you work here permanently or are you just doing a locum?'

'Permanent.'

The edges of the wound are jagged and I have difficulty opposing them: the difference between a broken bottle-top stab and a knife stab. At least knife wounds are clean.

'I haven't seen you here before, so I presume you're just doing a locum,' he says.

'Yes, I'm actually a registrar in internal medicine at Bellville. Shit!' The edge of the skin breaks as I pull the knot through. 'Sorry. I do a few extra calls a month to keep the bank manager off my back.'

My patient is becoming restless again. 'Sit still!' I say to him. 'I can't stitch this up properly if you keep moving your head.'

'Listen, I'll come and chat to you later,' Julian says. 'I don't think your patient likes divided attention.'

During the course of the evening we get to know each other over suture packs. I stitch up a laceration on a man's arm while convincing Julian of the downfalls of having Greek–Irish ancestry. He tells me about his father, who owns a wine farm near Bonnievale (which immediately heightens my interest in Julian), and his mother, who is an artist living in Simon's Town, while he sutures an eyelid. I probe more deeply into the wine-farm connection while he holds down a man into whose chest I am trying to insert a drain. We decide we are hungry and fantasise about pizza while stitching up the face of a drunk man stabbed by his best friend. We discover that our pizza desires are infinitely distant. How can anyone actually choose to have banana on a pizza? A father and son come in. They have had a fight over a girl (both are married, neither to the girl in question) that ended in a mutual stabbing. The son's wounds are worse, extending from his upper lip through the right nostril, so that the lip flaps open with every breath. This will be a difficult wound to suture, not only technically but also because stitching it up will require close contact with the patient and the second-hand alcohol that he is exhaling. We flip a coin for the father and Julian wins. I suture the son's face and he orders pizzas that get cold in the doctors' tearoom.

Julian is called to theatre for a laparotomy just after midnight and time slows down in casualty. I notice my stomach rumbling for the first time. At three o'clock I decide that I am drunk on exhaled alcohol fumes.

'Sister,' I say to the nurse who is working with me in casualty, 'I'm taking a quick break. Call me if there's an emergency.' It is thirteen minutes before I get called. Enough time to have downed a Coke and gagged on half a cold pizza.

The emergency is a stabbed chest and the wound is bubbling as the patient breathes, which means that the stab is communicating with the lung: with each breath the patient takes, air from outside rushes into his chest cavity, compressing his lungs. Usually one needs an X-ray to diagnose a pneumothorax, but I am certain enough clinically that this is one to decide to put a drain in without confirmatory X-rays. Besides, X-rays can take up to an hour, and this man cannot wait that long. The sister gets the instrument tray ready while I try to get the patient to lie on his back at a forty-five degree angle with his left hand behind his head. He is drunk and restless and refuses to lie still and I shout at him because I am afraid of cutting myself.

I inject local anaesthetic, then make a laceration on the chest wall between the fourth and fifth ribs. I dissect down to the pleura quickly and then lean on the forceps to enter the pleural space. As I enter the chest cavity, a wave of blood, at least a litre, sprays over my jeans and shoes. I quickly grab the chest drain and force it into place. Blood runs down the tube into the collecting bottle, filling it so quickly that it needs to be replaced almost immediately. I stitch the drain to the skin so that it doesn't pull out, put a bandage over the wound and then survey the damage to my clothes. I am glad that I decided on jeans and tackies and not a skirt and open sandals, even though anyone who sees me – including Julian – would have to assume that I have absolutely no dress sense.

\* \* \*

Just before eight o'clock in the morning, Julian reappears in casualty.

'I ended up having to do some impromptu plastic surgery,' he says, 'so I took a bit longer than I thought I would. Did you survive here?'

'Just. Everything was sort of déjà vu: drunk man with stab wound to $x$, variation provided by the instrument used to inflict the wound. The broken bottle is popular but the knife seems to be the instrument of choice. I did have one panga and, interestingly, one garden fork. Oh, and let's not forget the six-year-old boy who stabbed his three-year-old sister in the ear with a pen. The damage to my clothes is from a haemopneumothorax; the guy was stabbed, surprisingly, in the chest with, even more surprisingly, a knife.'

'Welcome to Paarl Hospital on a Saturday night!' Julian laughs. 'Listen, if you're serious about wine tasting, give me your number and I'll give you a call next time I visit my dad. I'd like to see you again, under different circumstances.'

I look down at my bloodstained jeans and shoes and wonder if I'm hallucinating. I'm too scared to answer. Perhaps my tired imagination is working overtime, influenced by the high alcohol content in the air.

'Sorry, I don't even know you.' Julian, blushing, breaks the pause. 'I suppose you have a boyfriend. It was a bit presumptuous of me just to ask you like that.'

'No, no. That would be great. I'd really like that. I've never been known to say no to good wine. And I don't have a boyfriend.' *But you thought that I did!* says a gleeful voice in my head. Must be the hair.

I float back to my car. Turn on the radio and sing my way out of Paarl. Halfway home I realise that I am singing the words of 'Everybody Hurts' to 'Night Swimming', and drifting across lanes. I pull off the road to stop at a twenty-four-hour convenience shop, where I pay too much for an energy drink and a glucose bar for the drive home.

* * *

The clattering of pots wakes me. It's Leah, attacking the kitchen.

'What are you doing?' I shout through my closed bedroom door.

'Making us a Sunday roast. Gina's coming.'

'Leah, I haven't slept for the last twenty-four hours.'

'I know. I thought you would like some decent food. I'm making a good ol' roast chicken with roast potatoes and gravy and cauliflower with cheese sauce. It will only be ready in two hours so you can sleep until then.'

Oh God, two hours of clanging pots. I wrap my head in my pillow to try to block out the evidence of Leah's kitchen experimentation. It only transforms the clang of pots to the muffled clang of pots. Eventually I give up. I put on my dressing gown and make my way to the kitchen.

'Pour me a glass, please,' I say, holding out an empty glass to the bottle of red wine that is standing open on the kitchen counter. The wooden surface is stained with multiple crimson rings from the bottoms of too many bottles of wine. Leah does not move from the stove.

'Pour one yourself, I'm busy. I thought you were sleeping.'

'No, for some reason I'm struggling to sleep. Can't think why.'

The first few sips of wine go straight to my head. No sleep makes me a cheap date. And grumpy.

'When is Gina coming?' I ask.

'About half an hour ago. You look exhausted. Was your call busy?'

'That would be a gross understatement. I think I sutured about fifty lacerations, erring on the conservative side. I don't understand why every argument they have seems to end up in a stabbing. Actually, usually in two stabbings. And it's not a friendly jab either. They stab in places meant to kill, or at least severely maim: chest, head, eyes. Some of the men are so drunk when they come in that they pass out with huge open gashes; often I don't even have to use local anaesthetic. It's ridiculous. I don't know if it's a cultural thing or a class thing, the stabbing, I mean. Is it the poverty or some cultural psyche? And before you crap on me for being racist, I'm just trying to understand why people do this. I can't imagine anywhere else in the world where one would see so many stabbings in one night. The worst thing is that most of the time it's friends or relatives stabbing each other and the next day they're best buddies again. How can you go back to being best friends with someone who came half a centimetre away from blinding you? I feel like I'm dealing with a completely dysfunctional society.'

'How can you make such generalisations? You keep on saying "they". Who is "they"?'

I can see that my outburst has shocked Leah, but she has no idea of what my night was like. She doesn't know what it feels like to spend twelve solid hours stitching up rude, intoxicated men. She doesn't understand the wasted money, time and energy. She doesn't realise how many people I could be helping if I weren't spending all my time on stab wounds. She can't relate to my helplessness, the awful, inevitable momentum of the situation. I'm jealous of her protected office job: a job that allows her naivety, that allows her to believe in good and not to generalise.

'Leah, I don't blame these people for the situation they're in and I'm not cross with them. I'm cross because nobody seems to be making any effort to change what's going on. Everybody is very quick to blame the past but that's where it ends. Nobody seems to want to do anything about the future.'

'What crap!' Leah flicks her hair over her shoulder and strides angrily to the stove. 'I'm doing something about it,' she says, vigorously stirring the gravy.

'What do you mean you're doing something about it?'

'My art classes.'

Every Sunday morning, from nine o'clock to twelve o'clock, Leah gives art lessons to underprivileged children in the Kayamandi township. Our fridge is an ever-changing mosaic of potato prints and brightly coloured stick people.

'Don't take me the wrong way, but do you really think that by teaching some kids to draw for three hours once a week you're going to change the situation? I think you have no idea how bad it really is.'

Leah slams the pot lid down. 'Well, at least I'm doing something,' she says, black eyes drilling holes into me.

'And I'm not?'

'I don't know. It's about your attitude, not about how many stab wounds you stitch up. If one child in my class learns something from me, if I can change one child's life in some way so that he grows up to have a better future than he might have had, then every single Sunday that I have spent in that stinky, dusty, makeshift classroom is worth it. Don't you understand, Sue? It only takes one person's life.'

No, I don't understand. Her eye drilling has turned me into a sieve. Everything has drained out of me and all that's left is a punched-out skeleton. Just then Gina arrives, and her presence saves the rest of the lunch from being incinerated by Leah's fury.

'Hello, you two. Why so serious?' Gina's voice is exaggerated, fills the room. She puts a parcel down on the wooden counter and lights a cigarette. 'I brought some treats: Chipnix and a blue-cheese dip for starters and real Swiss chocolate for dessert,' she says, unpacking the articles from the parcel one by one.

I open the packet of chips and balance one in my mouth. The polyester yellowness crackles and pinches my tongue. Tiny pinpricks. More holes.

'I have to tell you guys what happened last night,' Gina says excitedly. 'It was so embarrassing!' She's wearing tight jeans and a bright red strappy top. An orange push-up bra slides up over her artificial cleavage. She is too manic for a Sunday afternoon. She has forgotten about the cigarette that she lit; it burns down in the ashtray to leave a smoking grey ash-tube.

'I went out with some friends to this place in town...' She shovels chips into her mouth as she speaks, hardly chewing them. I notice a lovebite on her neck, a brown-purple tattoo marring her smooth olive skin.

Leah glances at me, eyebrows raised. Her look says, You're the doctor, sort it out.

'Gina, have you been drinking?' I ask her.

'No, just one or two glasses of champagne before I got here. I went to breakfast with some friends. Nothing wrong with that, is there?'

What am I supposed to say? It's long after twelve o'clock.

'What was I saying? Oh yes, I went to this place in town with some friends. You should see this place, it's stunning. It has this fish tank in the centre of the room, massive, right up to the ceiling. I love fish. It's so relaxing watching them. I thought I might get some but then I realised that my cats would probably eat them. Shame, my one cat, the tortoiseshell one, was in a fight and got half his ear bitten off. I got this antibiotic from the vet that I'm supposed to give him . . .'

'Well, I have some good news from my call, if either of you is interested.' I interrupt Gina's monologue. She's talking too fast and her thoughts are all disorganised. She started telling us about her night and ended with her cat's ear injury. I wonder if she's just drunk or if she's been taking drugs. I consider confronting her but then realise that it would be pointless while she's in this state. 'I met a guy,' I continue, 'quite a decent-looking chap, and he actually took my number.'

'Who is he?' Leah asks.

'A doctor who works at Paarl Hospital. His name is Julian Beresford. His father owns a wine farm and his mother is an artist.'

'Wow, is he single?'

'I'm assuming so, since he asked for my number. I know this will come as a shock to you both, given my usual anti-male bias, but he actually seems like a really nice guy. I could be wrong but I don't think he's an arsehole.'

'So, when are we going wine-tasting?' Gina wants to know.

\* \* \*

I fall asleep at the table, in the middle of lunch, sitting up. Leah puts me to bed, takes off my shoes, closes my bedroom curtains. I wake up again sometime during the early evening, dreaming of a doctor with floppy blond hair trying to stab me. I get up to brush my teeth and then fall back to sleep.

## Revealing identities

I go over to talk to Carol during the philosophy lecture

tea break. She is not wearing any make-up and the nudity of her face seems to highlight its beauty rather than reveal any flaws. I ask her how she manages to keep her skin so perfect and she laughs and tells me that she has to keep it unblemished because she is a beauty therapist. 'People will hardly want to come to me if I look awful,' she says.

She tells me that she owns a health spa in Constantia that specialises in food wraps. I am immediately interested: a spa that promotes eating! I realise my error as soon as she starts talking about the Azuki bean-and-papaya wrap, which is exceptionally good for cleansing and nourishing the skin, and the chilli-and-rooibos wrap, which quite literally melts cellulite away. If all goes well, she's planning to open another spa in Camps Bay next year and would like to incorporate fresh sea-water scrubs into the cleansing regimen. She grew up in Camps Bay, she tells me, so she wouldn't mind moving back there. Her parents still live there, in a lovely old house that is ten minutes away from the beach and that backs out onto the mountain.

We walk to the tea table and I ask for a cup of coffee with lots of milk and two sugars. Carol has black rooibos tea with a squirt of lemon. Perhaps that is what keeps her skin so clear.

'About my friend with the lymphoma,' Carol brings it up suddenly, out of nowhere. I nod my head and gulp down a sip of coffee. It burns the lining of my oesophagus.

'Yes?'

'I . . . it's actually me. I'm sorry I misled you but it was easier than, you know, telling you straight away.'

'Don't worry. I figured that's how it probably was.'

She promises to show me around her Constantia spa, if I ever happen to be in the area. Throws in a complimentary massage.

# Chapter Seven

## The day of reckoning

I admit a new patient to the ward, a woman with full-blown AIDS. She is thirty-one years old and was referred to Bellville Hospital with respiratory distress. I see immediately that she is seriously ill: her thorax caves in and her nostrils flare with the effort of each breath, tiny beads of sweat glisten on her nose and cheeks, her heart flutters beneath her thin chest wall as though even it is trying to escape the disease ravaging her body. I put a thermometer under her arm and the mercury rises to forty degrees Celsius. Across her one thigh and spreading to her buttocks are the painful blisters of shingles. They have become septic and are crusted with pus, too painful even to wipe clean. She lies twisted on her side to avoid putting pressure on them. Her body is covered with raised papular lesions that she scratches continuously, until they break open and leave chunks of skin beneath her nails. A virus, *molluscum contagiosum*, has attacked her right eyelid. It is swollen shut with dimpled carbuncles.

I speak to her while I am examining her. Her mind is still unaffected by the AIDS. She is from Cape Town, grew up on the mountainside in Hout Bay. Beautiful place, I comment, and she nods. But she can't swim, she tells me, because she was always too scared of the sea. Until she got sick she was working as a waitress in a restaurant at the Waterfront. She found out at the beginning of the year that she was on the shortlist for a scholarship to study as a chef, but she had been too ill to go to the interview. She pronounces it 'tchef' and it takes me a while to understand what she is saying. I ask her to sit forward so that I can auscultate her lungs posteriorly, but she is too weak to get up on her own. Eventually we manage together, she pushing with her left arm and me pulling her up by her right arm. Then suddenly it is too much for me. I lower her down, drop my stethoscope on the side of her bed and run to the doctors' office. Slam the door shut against my frantic breathing. That could be me. I feel my neck, searching for tell-tale lymph nodes. I need to get an HIV test. Today, after work.

*　*　*

I go straight from Bellville to a nearby private hospital. I park my car, then ask the way to the pathology department, sure that everyone I pass can tell that I am going to have an HIV test. I force myself to turn the handle of the pathologist's waiting-room door, push it open and walk to the reception desk. The receptionist glares at me accusingly as she fills in the form.

'Name?'

'Susan Carey.' I am glad she doesn't ask me how to spell my name.

'Age?'

'Twenty-eight.' I hide my hands behind my back so that she doesn't see them shaking.

'Are you having the test for insurance purposes?'

I hesitate for a moment. 'No, I'm a doctor. I've been sprayed with blood a few times. I just want to make sure.' Right. It's only a partial lie but she can sniff it out like a police dog on the trail of cocaine.

'Sit down. The sister will be with you in a moment.'

I have already died and embark on an out-of-body experience. I watch a pale red-haired woman sitting in the plastic-covered waiting-room chair. Watch her as she gets up to follow the cheerful sister to another room. Watch her as she rolls up the sleeve of her jersey and straightens her arm. Guilty white skin exposed.

'I'm just going to put on the tourniquet,' the sister says. 'It might feel a bit tight.'

Actions so familiar. The needle pierces the skin and I watch the deep purple blood pulse into the collecting tube. My blood. The sister snaps open the tourniquet and it is over.

'When will the result be available?' I croak.

'I'll send it up as an urgent specimen, if you like. You can phone the lab just before six. It should be ready by then.'

I wonder how she can sound so bright when I am dying.

Six o'clock is only two hours away but my fear has warped time, slowing it down like a stretched tape. What will I do if I'm positive? Will I disclose my status to my friends and family? To my colleagues and patients? Will I somehow try to get hold of Eric Freemantle? I know that I won't have the courage to tell the truth; I will lie and tell everyone that I got splashed with blood or pricked by a needle. And the illness itself? Will I be able to afford antiretrovirals? Probably for no longer than a year, and after that I will be back to where I started. I know what AIDS does: the rotting, pain, wasting, dementia and indignity that are, in most cases, inevitable. Would I have the strength to continue living knowing what the future holds? I think not.

\* \* \*

'Path lab, hello?'

'It's Doctor Carey here. I'm phoning for the result of an HIV test that I had earlier today.'

The woman on the line spells out my name to me.

'That's right.'

She checks my date of birth and identity number.

'The test came back negative,' she says.

'Are you sure?'

'Yes, the result was negative.'

'Thank you.' *Thank you, thank you, thank you!* I'm not going to die just yet. I kneel down and thank God or whatever good there is that deep down inside myself I believe in. Swear that I will never have sex with a stranger again.

I think about my new patient later on in the evening. I wonder how she became positive. Did she have multiple sexual encounters or did she have one steady partner who cheated on her? Perhaps she was like me but just unlucky. I feel uncomfortable, almost guilty. Why did I get away with my behaviour? There are many women who have slept around far less than me and who are HIV-positive. Is it my social class protecting me? My skin colour? My genes? Or is it simply random, the luck of the draw?

## An exclusion to intimacy

Julian has still not contacted me. I have resisted calling the Paarl Hospital switchboard to get his number. I decide that today is his last chance to call before I admit that I was mistaken and label him an arsehole. The day comes and goes and my phone is silent. I run myself a bath when I get home from the hospital and try to convince myself that I didn't really like him anyway.

From the bathroom, I hear Leah arriving home with John in tow.

'Leah, I'm in the bath with the door open,' I shout in warning as they come through the front door. 'Please come and shut it.'

She leans into the bathroom before closing the door.

'What's wrong?' she asks.

'Nothing. What makes you think something's wrong? I'm fine.'

'I know you. You only have candle-lit baths and listen to this morbid music when you're depressed about something.'

'I'm fine and it's not morbid music. It's soulful and intelligent. Julian still hasn't called.'

'Maybe he's busy. It's only been a few days.'

'Well, it doesn't matter anyway. I've decided that I'm better off without any men in my life. What's so wrong with being single? In fact, I think that single women have far more fun anyway.'

Leah closes the door and switches off my music. My blue mood is broken without the strains of a forlorn saxophone floating through my red wine. I get out of the bath and join Leah and John watching a rerun of *City of Angels* on satellite TV. They are snuggling together on the couch, Leah's tiny body curled up next to John's. She picks at a bowl of chocolate-coated peanuts and feeds odd ones to him. On the television screen Meg Ryan and Nicholas Cage clutch each other in a French kiss. Oh God, I'm surrounded by romantic couples.

'I'm going to bed,' I announce. They ignore me, hardly notice my disappearance. I am peripheral to their intimacy. I turn my cellphone off before I fall asleep. I'm not going to spend another half-wakeful night hoping for the bleep of an incoming text message.

# Exposing the unbeliever

I'm meeting my mother for coffee after work. I give her a missed call as I leave the hospital, our pre-arranged signal. She is already waiting for me when I get to the bookshop, where we meet in the coffee bar because we share a dislike for shopping malls. Aside from our noses and large breasts, it's probably the only thing that we have in common. She gives me a hug and a kiss and we sit down at one of the tables. I order a cup of coffee and a cappuccino from the waitress and then ask my mother how she is.

'All right, I suppose,' she says.

I know how to interpret that response: terrible. My mother is Greek. Her world is full of passion: everything is either wonderful or awful. Today, I fear, it is the latter.

'What's wrong?' I ask.

'It's your grandmother. She's driving me insane.' Since my grandmother moved in with my mother, my family home has become the battleground for the war of the control freaks. 'She's now decided that she will do nothing in the house before asking me, but I know that she's doing it just to irritate me. I'm waiting for her to start asking me for permission to go to the bathroom. It's because I got cross with her for making supper the other day.'

'Tell her she can come and live with me. I wouldn't mind someone other than Leah making supper.'

'No, you don't understand. I had already planned what I was going to make. I had already made the supper in my mind. I don't want to come home and find some other supper made.'

It sounds wonderful to me. My mother's voice drones on in the background while I sprinkle sugar on the cappuccino froth and eat it off. I've heard all this before.

'And your father just works and works. You know, I

never get to see him. He spends all his time in that study of his. And then your grandmother goes and takes him tea! It's my job to take him tea.'

'At least he works at home. At least he isn't at the office with the secretary. At least it's not the secretary bringing him tea.'

She ignores me. 'We go out for dinner and he doesn't talk the whole evening. If I don't talk, then there's just silence the whole evening. I watch other couples, they talk. So what's wrong with us? Why can't we talk like an ordinary couple? I'll tell you why, it's because your father has a problem communicating. And this new gardener that he got pulled up all of the seedlings that I planted two months ago. I could have strangled him.'

'Who? Dad or the gardener?'

'Both!'

'Why have you got a new gardener? What happened to George?'

'This is another one of your father's charity cases. He comes on Thursdays, when George is off. He worked for us before, about two years ago, and then just disappeared.'

'What, after borrowing a whole lot of money from Dad?'

'No, it turns out that the poor man went to prison and he was just released recently.'

I look at her in disbelief, wondering if I have heard correctly. 'What? You have an ex-prisoner working for you? Are you crazy? What was he in prison for?'

'I don't know. I think he has a gambling problem. He looks like a gambler.'

'How the hell can you tell what a gambler looks like? He could have been in prison for anything. He could have raped someone. He's probably a gangster. I can't believe that you're letting a prisoner into the house. He's probably scouting it out to see what he can steal.'

'Susan, stop it. You should see him. He's skinny. He couldn't hurt a fly. I'm probably stronger than he is.'

'Mom, stop being naive. He can just bring the rest of his gang along with him and then it doesn't matter how small he is. I've seen the victims of gang attacks. I've tried to save their lives. You don't know what the gangs are capable of. Even the police have no power over them.'

'Susan, calm down. You're overreacting.'

The couple at the table next to us have stopped talking. I glare at them and the woman looks down at her cup.

'Mom, I'm not overreacting. I've worked with these gangsters. They place no value on life. Don't come running to me when Nikki or you get raped. You can't have him working for you. I'm going to phone Dad right now.'

'Sue, what's wrong with you?' My outburst seems to have shocked my mother from her depression. 'What about rehabilitation? People are not all bad, you know. None of us would get anywhere without second chances. Maybe the work we are giving him is the only thing keeping him from going back to his criminal habits. What's happened to the girl that used to want to save the world?'

'The world isn't worth saving any more.' But even as I say it I know that I have overreacted. I wonder when I stopped believing in good. How many murdered or raped patients ago was it? I apologise to my mother and flash a smile at the couple next to us.

'I'm so tired of it all. The poor guy is probably just trying to survive and here I am slating him.' I lean my elbows on the table and put my head in my hands. What is wrong with me? Why have I stopped being able to see good? Is it because I have been disappointed too many times? Or am I drowning in self-pity like a selfish child?

\* \* \*

116

There are two messages on my phone when I get home. One is from Carol asking me to call her when I have a moment. The other is a text message, from Julian: *Hello comrade-in-arms. Am thinking of hiking up Table Mountain on Sat and would love some company if you're free. Let me know.* Perhaps I was too hasty in judging him. I SMS him back asking what time and where he wants to meet.

## The case of the difficult daughter

The sister at an old-age home near Bellville has sent in one of the residents: a woman who has been getting progressively more confused over the past three days. As the patient comes in, I take a quick look at her to make sure that she is stable and then ask one of the students to see her. Jono starts examining the woman and I tell him to call me once he is ready to present her to me. Even without having examined her properly, I suspect that she has a urinary tract infection. It is a common cause of delirium in elderly patients.

I am busy putting up a drip in a critically ill twenty-year-old man with a diabetic ketoacidosis when a shrill voice shouts my name. I turn around. The woman calling me is in her early forties. She is wearing fuchsia pink lipstick and her thin blond hair is puckered into a perm. I don't recognise her.

'I will be with you in a second, ma'am. I just need to finish here.' I connect the drip and complete the man's prescription chart, then turn my attention to the woman.

'My mother has been waiting to see you for over forty minutes now,' she says.

'Sorry, who is your mother?' I am confused.

'Mrs Van der Walt.'

117

The name is unfamiliar. I stare at the woman trying
to figure out who on earth her mother could be and then
suddenly make the connection. I think it is something in
the sharpness of her nose that enlightens me.

'Was she referred from the old-age home?' I ask.

The woman nods. She has the dry, almost leathery skin
of a heavy smoker. I check her index finger; it is stained
deep nicotine-yellow.

'My mother is very ill, you know. I want to know why a
student is seeing her and not the doctor. This is absolutely
ludicrous.' She draws out the first syllable of ludicrous to
*loo*dicrous. Too much lunchtime American television.

'The way that it works in a tertiary government
hospital', I explain to her, 'is that the less-sick patients in
casualty are often seen by the students before the doctor
sees them. That is the way the students learn and I do
always check everything. In any case, forty minutes is not
a long time to wait at all. Most of the patients here, some
far sicker than your mother, wait for hours. You're actually
lucky that she's only been waiting for forty minutes.'

'Well, I refuse to let a student see my mother.'

Well, then pay for her to go to a private hospital, I'm
tempted to snap. I walk over to Mrs Van der Walt. The
daughter follows me.

Jono is busy listening to the old woman's chest. 'Jono,
this is Mrs Van der Walt's daughter,' I tell him. Jono
stands up and greets the daughter. I ask Jono what Mrs
Van der Walt's vital signs are. Apart from the temperature,
they are within the normal ranges. I ask the patient a few
questions and, although she is confused, she is not acutely
ill or distressed.

'Mrs Van der Walt is obviously fairly stable,' I say,
making sure that the daughter can hear me. 'Jono, you
can carry on seeing her. I'll come and discuss her with you

when I have sorted out the unstable patients.'

'This is unacceptable!' the daughter shouts. 'I refuse to let a student see my mother. How old are you anyway?' she says, turning to me. 'You don't even look like a proper doctor. When did you graduate?'

'Ma'am, I assure you that I am a proper doctor. If you have any doubts about that, or my age, you are welcome to go and check with the medical superintendent.' I walk off calmly and start swearing under my breath as soon as I am out of sight.

An hour later, I return to Mrs Van der Walt's bedside. The daughter is sitting on a chair next to her mother's bed. Folds of white flesh, visible where her blouse has pulled up, hang over the waistband of her too-tight jeans. She plays with a set of gold bracelets on her right wrist. As I arrive, she stands up and I smile sweetly at her. I know it will piss her off.

Jono presents the patient to me and I check his examination and confirm that she has a urinary tract infection. I write up a prescription chart for her, ask Jono to draw some bloods and then explain to the daughter what is wrong with her mother.

'Will she have to stay here?'

'Yes. She needs intravenous antibiotics and some rehydration fluid. She'll have to stay in hospital because she needs a drip.'

'I hope she'll have her own room.'

'I think that's highly unlikely, ma'am. We'll put her in whichever bed we have available.'

'What? You mean she has to lie with these people?'

'What do you mean, ma'am?' I put on a baffled smile, appear concerned, but I know exactly what she means.

'I don't want her picking up AIDS or something here. I'm not joking, I'll sue the hospital. And look at this place; I've got a good mind to write to the newspapers.' Go ahead, I think. 'They brought her the most disgusting meal for lunch. It looked like tinned dog food.' I want to tell her that many of my patients really appreciate the meals but she doesn't give me a chance to talk. 'The floors are filthy. Earlier I saw one of the students wipe up some blood off the floor with tissue paper – just tissue paper, no disinfectant or nothing. You can't tell me that is good hygiene. My poor mother doesn't even have a pillow.'

'We don't have any pillows here but you are welcome to bring one for her from home.' In fact, I think, you are welcome to take a little of the money that you spend on jewellery and cigarettes and pay for her to go to a private hospital. Or perhaps spend a little more on your premiums each month and put her on your medical aid.

But I also know that, in a way, what she says is right. Just because this is a government hospital does not mean that the quality should be substandard. Patients should have pillows. There shouldn't be old bloodstains on the floor. People shouldn't have to wait for hours before being seen. Unfortunately, those things require more staff. And more staff costs money.

## A walk up Table Mountain

I drag myself out of bed extra early on Saturday and open my curtains. The weather is conspiring with me; it is still and sunny and the mountain, which I can see if I stand on a chair and peer through the kitchen window over the neighbour's roof, is clear.

Julian is already waiting for me when I arrive at the Kirstenbosch parking lot. It's still early, so the usual tourists and picnickers have not yet arrived, just a few eager hikers and runners. I walk over to him and say hello.

He's standing in front of an old Land Rover that is too covered in mud for me to be able to discern whether its original colour is white, cream or brown.

'Is that your car?' I ask. Obviously it is, but I can't think of anything else to say.

'Yeah. She's gone quite a distance with me: all over southern Africa. Nothing luxurious but she runs well. Since I got her she's made this weird noise whenever I go downhill, so I've christened her "Crackling Rosie".' He waits for a response from me but I don't know what he's talking about. 'From the Neil Diamond song?' he prompts.

'You're not a Neil Diamond fan, are you?'

'Of course I am. What, aren't you?'

'No! But my father is. When exactly were you born?'

'That's irrelevant. Good taste is ageless.'

'Good taste is obviously also subjective.'

'Just wait, I'll soon have you listening to decent music.' He dips his head to one side and looks at me. 'You look different out of your hospital gear.' He leaves it up to me to decide whether it is a good or a bad change. 'Shall we go?'

Julian lets me walk in front of him as we follow the route up Skeleton Gorge. The name has always held a grim fascination for me. When I was young I was convinced that somewhere along Skeleton Gorge was a hidden cannibals' cave or some other horror waiting to be discovered. It was a genuine disappointment when my mother told me that the gorge was named after a horse's skeleton found along the route. Despite this disillusionment, it remains my favourite trail up Table Mountain. The path runs under a canopy of bowing trees and vines so that most of the walk is shaded. During winter a river gushes down the gorge, but even in the dryness of midsummer the air carries the scent of water.

It takes thirty minutes of walking up an almost vertical path, albeit shaded, without a single break for me to realise that Julian takes his hiking more seriously than I do mine. To me, a hike implies a brisk yet pleasant walk with frequent breaks to view the scenery. I wonder what Julian would call that? I feel like I am walking through dough and my chest is burning. I haven't had an asthma attack for years but I fear that one is imminent. I decide that I can take it no longer and ask Julian if we can stop for a water break.

'Of course,' he says, taking a bottle from his backpack and handing it to me.

'Thank you.' I try to drink but am so out of breath that half of the water spills down the front of my shirt.

'Are you okay?' he asks.

'Fine,' I answer monosyllabically, trying to control my gasping. The thought crosses my mind that at least he has medical training.

'I'll slow down a bit.'

'No, really, it's okay.' I try to ignore my heavy breathing, the sweaty wet patch below my breasts, the sunscreen film covering my eyes. I drink slowly, trying to prolong the break. This is ridiculous, I tell myself. Why can't I tell him that he's going too fast for me? Can I not show any form of weakness to anyone?

'Well, should we carry on, then? We're almost at the top.' He starts walking again and I follow. Even though he has slowed down slightly, he's still moving quite quickly. I force myself to keep up with his pace, and by the time we reach the summit I am exhausted. The end of the path spills out onto the top of Table Mountain and suddenly all of Cape Town lies at my feet. I lean against a rock and try to submerge myself in the flood of endorphins pulsing through my blood.

Julian looks at his watch. 'Not too bad,' he says. 'Just over an hour.'

'How long do you usually take?' I ask.

'A little bit shorter.' He's blushing.

'How long is a little bit shorter?'

'Oh, usually about half an hour.'

Great, I think, and I was under the illusion that we had actually been walking quickly.

'Should we find somewhere to sit?' Julian asks me. 'I brought some snacks.'

Sitting sounds wonderful to me, but I am still slightly too nauseous to consider the snacks.

We walk along the prehistoric seabed that forms the top of the mountain until we find a huge rock, tumbled into its current resting place by an ancient tidal wave. It has a flat surface on which I can not only sit but, joy of joys, lie down. The sky is bluer on top of the mountain. Far above us, an unidentified black streak circles and dips and dives. I wonder if we look like prey from that high up. My nausea subsides and we eat bacon croissants and then a slab of chocolate. Julian lies down next to me and I wriggle closer to him so that my head leans against his shoulder. I want him to kiss me. I want to taste his sweat. I want him to make love to me on top of the rock on top of the mountain on top of the world. But he doesn't. I must be satisfied with the comforting warmth of his T-shirt on my cheek.

The walk down is easy and quick by comparison, and too soon we are back in the parking lot. I don't want to part yet.

'Do you want to go for lunch somewhere?' I ask. 'I would kill for a cold beer right about now.'

He glances at his watch.

'Unfortunately, I'm working at three so I'd better go.

Thanks for the hike; I enjoyed it. We should do it again sometime, sooner rather than later.'

I don't move my mouth throughout the drive home. I want to preserve the feeling of pressure that his lips have briefly left on mine.

## Rooibos tea and tears

Leah has gone away for the weekend, to a music festival up the West Coast, and so the house is a mess. Without her around, dishes seem to stack up in the kitchen and items of clothing that are usually contained in my room reproduce and start taking over the rest of the house. This is a problem because I have invited Carol for Sunday-afternoon tea. I am busy trying to repack my wardrobe, which I turned out prior to dressing for my hiking expedition, when she rings the doorbell. I throw the last few items into the bottom of the cupboard and close the door.

Carol is wearing jeans and a tight T-shirt and has pulled her fine hair back into a ponytail. She looks little older than a teenager. I wish briefly that I could look that young and then remember that she has a lymphoma, which makes me feel guilty for wishing for anything instead of just being thankful that I am healthy. By the time that I invite her in, my cheeks are warm and I know that I am blushing. She must think that I'm an idiot.

'Can I make you some tea or coffee?' I ask as I direct her down the entrance hall and into the lounge.

'Have you got rooibos tea?'

I nod. We always have a stock of it because Leah drinks rooibos tea with honey and lemon whenever she has a hangover.

'I'll have black rooibos without any sugar,' Carol says. She sits down on the couch in the lounge. I go to the kitchen and make myself a cup of coffee, rooibos tea for Carol.

'I've been trying to watch what I eat and drink,' she says as I hand her the mug of tea. 'You know, trying to be healthy. Since they diagnosed me with the lymphoma I think I've bought every health book I can find that contains the words "cure" and "cancer". Silly, isn't it?'

'No, not at all. I'd probably do the same.'

'I keep on wondering what caused it, if it was because I was eating too unhealthily. You read all these articles in magazines condemning preservatives. I used to be permanently on a diet so I always drank sweetener in my tea and coffee. Perhaps it was that. Otherwise I was always so healthy. I never smoked, I exercised every day, I hardly drank any alcohol. It would be easier if I just knew why it happened to me.'

Unfortunately medical school often leaves out the 'Why me?' part.

'It's most likely that it was a mix of things,' I tell her. 'Perhaps something in your genetic make-up. Cancer is usually caused by a combination of different factors.' I listen to the impersonal words coming out of my mouth, because in truth I don't know the answer. I am almost her age. She has a much healthier lifestyle than I do. Why her? I hesitate before I speak again because what I want to tell her is instinct, not soundly based medical knowledge.

'Carol, I'm going to be honest with you, but I'm speaking as a friend, not as a doctor. Please don't quote me on this and remember that it may all be nonsense. I think that there's more to some cancers than just genetics and environment. I'm quite sure that there is something deep in one's psyche that contributes as well, some hidden hurt or anger or pain. Perhaps on a level that even the individual cannot recognise.' I regret having opened my mouth. What I am saying has no scientific basis. I don't even know why I think it. But she latches onto the idea.

'That makes some sense to me,' she says. 'At least that would explain why it happened to me and not someone else. Do you think that if I could resolve those issues, the cancer could be cured?'

Oh God, I've made a huge mistake.

'Carol, the only sure chance of recovery that you have is with chemotherapy and radiotherapy. I'm certain of that. What I meant was that you should also try anything else that may help, like meditation or acupuncture. Anything that opens you up to some form of self-exploration. Healing needs to take place on all levels, emotional and physical.' Amazing how I can carry on, even though I am way out of my depth.

'I understand that. It's one of the reasons that I started going to the philosophy workshops. I thought that maybe I'd be able to learn a bit more about my true self.' She fiddles with the slender silver watch around her left wrist as she talks. 'To be honest, I'm a bit scared of the chemo. I've heard all these stories about how awful it is and how it does more damage than good.'

I have finished my coffee but her cup of tea is standing on the coffee table virtually untouched. I can't imagine anything worse right now than black rooibos tea without sugar. I lurch back to delivering medical information. 'Previously chemo had awful side-effects, but there have been so many advances recently that modern chemotherapy has far fewer adverse effects. When do you start?' I don't know that much about chemotherapy, but the little I do know is more than I know about alternative healing.

'I go for my first chemo next Tuesday, so I'm quite nervous. I'll have eight sessions of chemotherapy, then a short break and then a course of radiotherapy.'

We sit in silence. I don't know what to say to her. I keep imagining how I would react if someone told me I had a lymphoma. I wonder if I would stop drinking coffee and change to black rooibos tea.

'My fiancé has been great,' she says. This is the first time she has mentioned she has a partner and I look down at her left hand. She has picked up the cup of tea and her fingers are wrapped around the handle. There is a thin silver band set with tiny sapphires on her ring finger. 'He's so supportive. He's come to all of the doctor's appointments with me and he came with me when I had the CT scan and the bone-marrow biopsy. That was sore. I don't want another one of those; I felt like I'd been run over by a truck.' She sips her tea. 'We were supposed to be getting married this June but obviously the lymphoma has put a spanner in the works. We're postponing the wedding until . . . until I'm better. I'm almost thirty-four, Sue. I can't wait much longer to start a family.' An urgency has crept into her voice. 'I was planning to be pregnant by the end of the year. I stopped the pill and everything. This wasn't supposed to happen. I don't even know if I'll be able to have children after the chemo and radiation. In just six weeks, all my dreams for the rest of my life have been shattered. I don't understand why it had to happen to me.' She starts crying. 'I'm sorry I'm so tearful.'

'Don't apologise. You need to cry sometimes. Let me get you a tissue.'

I don't have any, so I run to the kitchen and grab some paper serviettes.

'Here.' I hand her a lavender-sprigged napkin.

'Thanks, I'm so sorry.'

'Don't worry. Everything will be fine. Remember, you can have children until you are at least forty.' I feel uncomfortable, but I lean over and hug her.

'I'm sorry, Sue, I really am. I didn't mean to collapse in tears like this. It's just so nice to have someone to talk to. My fiancé has been supportive but he's really taking strain and I've been trying to be the strong one. The same with my parents. I haven't really been able to voice my fears to anyone and I think they all just came pouring out now.'

'It's okay. You also need some support; you can't always be the strong one. You need to allow yourself to feel these emotions.' I hear the clichés pouring out of my mouth, but occasionally they have a place. I suppose they haven't become clichés because of underuse.

Carol smiles at me and I try to think of more comforting things to say. But I can think of nothing, even further clichés elude me, so I blab on about my mother and the gambling gardener. I know that I must be boring her but I can't seem to shut up. The silence is too awkward. Eventually she gets up to go and I tell her that she can phone me any time and that my cellphone is always on. She gives me a hug before she leaves and I suddenly wish that I was not her friend but her doctor because then at least I could do something for her other than bore her with family anecdotes. It is the first time in a very long time that I have genuinely wanted to take on the role of doctor.

She has raised the fundamental question, the one that my medical training cannot answer: Why me? I pick up the half-empty cup of tea and take it to the kitchen, watch the liquid swirl down the drain. It was the six weeks that got me: dreams built up over so many years, over a lifetime, annihilated in just six weeks. That's not even two months.

# Chapter Eight

## The attack of the fleas

I am busy putting up a drip on Mr Moloti, who is somehow still clinging to life, when I first notice my itch. He is a difficult patient to drip; AIDS has shrunk his veins in the same way that it has shrunk him, so that they are barely palpable tracings on his dark skin. I have already pricked him five times without success. This is the sixth time and the last remaining vein; I cannot afford to lose it just because I have an itchy leg. I ease the needle into his flesh slowly, waiting for the tiny drip of blood at the end of the catheter that marks my entry into a vein. At last the dark purple appears. I withdraw the needle, throw it on the floor and smoothly slip the plastic catheter into the vein. I connect the line and check that the fluid runs in freely, then pick up the six needles from the floor and throw them into the 'sharps' container before I focus on the itch, which has now moved from my calf up to my thigh. I roll up the leg of my trousers. Flea bites.

Usually I avoid the hospital bathrooms, which seldom have toilet paper and as infrequently have toilet seats, but this is an emergency. I run to the ladies' room, hold my breath to avoid smelling the stale urine fumes and slam the door shut. The door bangs against the frame and swings back to attack me. A broken door, what a surprise. I push against the filthy door with one hand to keep it closed and remove my trousers with the other. I can't see the flea. I shake out the pants. Still no flea. I twist my head around to try to see the back of my legs, then bend down to inspect the floor. I concentrate on picking out a jumping black dot from all of the other black spots on the dirty floor. I want to shower and change but I can't go home in the middle of the day. I put my trousers back on and try to ignore the creature attacking me.

By the time I finally get home to the luxury of a clean bathroom and mirrors, the flea has travelled up my leg to my waist, eating on the move. From the evidence, it appears that it got stuck at my waistband and decided to take a ninety-degree turn. I get into the shower with a belt of red spots. Altogether I count eighteen bites. I can't imagine that the flea hasn't popped from all the blood it has sucked from me. Or perhaps it wasn't a single flea; perhaps it was a whole flea colony that relocated from a patient to me.

\* \* \*

My phone rings as I get out of the shower and I run to answer it, slipping on the bathroom floor in the process. I'm hoping that it's Julian. I still haven't heard from him since the hike.

'Hi, you'll never guess what.'

No Julian. Instead I get manic Gina.

'No, I won't, but I am sure you'll tell me.'

'I got that shoot I told you about. Can you believe it? I actually got the shoot!'

I move the phone away from my ear to protect my sensitive tympanic membrane. 'What shoot?'

'The German one. Remember, I told you about it?'

I have a vague recollection of some foreign advertisement

that was supposed to be her big break. 'The beer advert?' I think people call it an educated guess.

'Yes, that one. This is big, Sue. It's international and I'm going to make over a hundred thousand rands.'

'Wow, that's amazing.' I try to sound excited for her but it is difficult. One hundred thousand rands! I have to work almost impossibly hard to make so much money. One hundred calls. One hundred nights not slept. One hundred nights risking my life taking blood from HIV-positive patients. One hundred nights trying to make sense of hopeless situations. Gina just has to look good. I can't help being jealous, can't help feeling that there is something wrong with a society that puts a higher price on looking good than on saving lives.

'Aren't you excited for me?' she mopes in my ear.

'I am happy for you, Gina. I'm just tired. Well done. I'm sure you're going to look stunning. I hope that you won't forget us when you're rich and famous.'

'I'm going out to celebrate on Saturday night.' She is happy again. 'Are you working?'

'No, I'll come and celebrate with you. Let me know the details on Friday. I need to go now, I just got out of the shower and I'm dripping water everywhere. Congrats again, hey.'

She says goodbye and I put down the telephone. I walk to my bedroom and stand in front of the full-length mirror that is leaning against the wall. I keep meaning to hang it but haven't yet found the time and, because of the angle at which the mirror is propped against the wall, my calves look disproportionately large. The hot water from my shower has agitated the flea bites so that they stand out on my pale skin in angry red welts. I am valueless, discarded by the world because of my too-heavy breasts, the convex curve of my stomach, fleshy thighs that rub together when I walk, a face that reflects too much of the pain that I have seen. The world does not want to be reminded of suffering; it wants a giddy face, a face that disregards reality.

I am not going to be pictured on billboards, displayed on the covers of magazines, flown around the world for interviews in exotic places. That is the price of a vocation, I am told.

Sainthood is not a prerequisite for acceptance to medical school. Perhaps it should be.

# The doctor strikes back

I cover myself in insect repellent before going back to the hospital. I'm hoping that it will deter the fleas, but these are seasoned veterans. I catch two on me: big, swollen things that pop in a splatter of blood when I squeeze them between my thumbnails. I wonder whose blood it is that is left on my nails.

Mr Mohammed's malaria is at last under control and he is ready to be discharged. He makes a thumbs-up sign with his right hand and smiles at me, a big white smile in a blue-black face, when I tell him that he can go home. I wonder if home is a universal word. Wonder if he will survive the deception of the South African Dream. Wonder if I will see him selling contraband cigarettes on the side of Voortrekker Road.

When I reach Mr Moloti's bed, it is empty. This time he is not in the bathroom. He has slipped away overnight. He hasn't died. Died implies a suddenness. He has simply faded until our weak human eyes can no longer distinguish his dark skin from the shadows that envelop him. I fill in his death certificate and wonder what I should write under 'Cause of death'. I am not allowed to write HIV because it contravenes patient confidentiality. Eventually I settle on pneumonia and sepsis.

I admit a new patient: a twenty-three-year-old woman who has been trying to eat her eight-month-old baby. She has wild eyes and an angry mouth, and she explodes into incoherent torrents whenever anyone goes near her. There are no single rooms available so I have to put her in the general ward with five other women, a move that will surely alleviate the boredom of their hospital stays. I write 'Please restrain patient' on the top of the prescription chart, and the nursing sisters tie the patient's hands to the bedsides with pieces of linen so that she doesn't pull out her intravenous line. I question the woman who has brought her in, an aunt.

'Has she been sick like this before?'

'No, this is the first time that she is like this.'

'Does she have any pain?'

Not that the aunt knows. Her niece was fine, perfectly healthy, until one day she started eating anything she could get her hands on: plates, glasses, plants, even shit. They had to lock everything away. When she tried to eat her baby, they decided to bring her in to hospital.

'Has she lost weight?'

The aunt does not understand.

'Has she got thin?'

The aunt nods her head rigorously. 'Too thin.' She indicates with her hands how much weight her niece has lost.

'Where is she from?'

'Kraaifontein.'

'Before Kraaifontein?'

'Ciskei.'

'Did she come to Cape Town to have the baby?'

The aunt nods.

'How is the baby?'

'The baby is too sick.' She sighs and shakes her head. 'He is coughing all the time. And the stomach is running. Every day and every night it is running. He has been in hospital too many times.'

'Has she got a boyfriend?' I am trying to piece together the puzzle.

'No, no boyfriend.'

'But the baby? Eight months ago?'

The aunt shrugs her shoulders, shakes her head.

'Thank you, Mama. We'll try to find out what the problem is. She will have to stay here for a few days.'

I fetch Justine and Jono from the next bay and ask them to help me by holding the crazy woman still while I draw blood. 'I'm sure that she is RVD-positive,' I explain to them, 'so please don't let her move. I'd prefer to leave the hospital today without a needle-stick injury.' RVD is doctors' code for retroviral disease; using the code keeps the rest of the ward from knowing the patient's HIV status. Jono and Justine lean on the patient while I draw the blood.

'Justine, she may have a dementia secondary to the RVD, but we need to make sure that she doesn't have cryptococcal or TB meningitis, neurocysticercosis, syphilis or anything else that is potentially treatable. We will need to do an LP and a brain CT.' Panic appears in Justine's eyes. 'Don't worry, I'll do the lumbar puncture. You can organise the CT scan. But I will need you two to hold her still while I do the LP.' Delirious patients are seldom as cooperative as one wishes.

Once I have finished taking the blood, I dispatch Jono and Justine to send off the specimens and to arrange a CT brain respectively while I try to find a lumbar-puncture pack and a needle of the correct size. By the time I get back to the patient's bed, she has soiled herself and, even without the use of her hands, is making every effort to eat the faeces. I decide that the urgency of the lumbar puncture is negligible. It can wait until after the sisters have cleaned the patient (I can't help feeling glad for a moment that I studied medicine and not nursing). I leave the lumbar-puncture pack next to the patient's bed and go off for lunch.

When I return, the patient is clean and the linen has been changed. It is difficult to comprehend that this woman, five years younger than me, is probably dying. That she has an eight-month-old baby who is also probably dying. That she might never recognise her baby again. Except perhaps as her next meal.

Justine and Jono arrive and we roll the patient onto her side, then force her into the foetal position, knees drawn up to her chest, to open up the spaces between her vertebrae. I kneel on the ground so that I am level with her back and palpate along the lumbar spine until I locate the correct space. I edge the needle in but every time I get near to the bone she arches her back, closing the intervertebral spaces. I try four times, unsuccessfully. My knees are sore from pressing on the hard floor and my back is cramping from bending over. I can feel sweat trickling down my cleavage and the back of my neck. I stand up and peel the sterile gloves from my hands. Stretch my legs, my waist, massage my lower back.

'This isn't working. The position is wrong,' I say to Justine and Jono. 'She will have to sit up. You guys will just have to use all your strength to hold her still.' We try to coerce her into sitting hunched forward over the edge of the bed, but after a few seconds she tries to bite us.

'Justine, please go call Matthew and Zahira. I'm going to need you all to help me restrain her. I'm not risking her thrashing around while I have an unsheathed needle in my hand.' I take over the arm that Justine has been immobilising and start speaking to the patient.

'Try to calm down,' I say quietly. I hope that a soothing tone of voice will convey my English message to the patient. Wish, not for the first time, that I spoke Xhosa. 'This is not going to be sore if you just keep still. We need to find out what's wrong with you so that we can treat you.' Obviously my tone of voice suggests something else. She breaks free from my grip and scratches me, leaving a long red stripe down my arm. I will have to sedate her in order to have any chance of doing the lumbar puncture.

I tell the students that I think continuing in this way is pointless and we let go. The woman calms down. I decide to find out whether I can get someone to translate; perhaps she will cooperate more if she understands what we are trying to do. I would probably also bite and scratch if someone came near me with a lumbar-puncture needle without telling me why. I turn around to go wash the scratch on my arm and she vomits up her lunch, which I have just seen her finish. Fish, carrots and coleslaw land all over the back of my jeans, my shoes, the bag that I have left at her bedside. I try to rinse off my bag and shoes in the basin in the women's toilet. The drain is partially blocked and the water collects in a murky yellow pool of diluted vomit. The jeans are beyond saving and I throw them away in one of the hospital bins to be incinerated. I spend the rest of the day in theatre greens, but the smell of puke follows me around, fills my nostrils so that I feel nauseous.

When I get home I wash my bag and shoes properly, twice, in the washing machine with half a bottle of fabric softener. But the stink of vomit remains. Sour, like spilt milk that has been left in the sun. Eventually I throw them away but I can still smell regurgitated, partially digested fish and carrots when I get into bed.

## Shopping for customised jewellery

The number of flea bites on my body has increased to thirty-five. Two different kinds of insect repellent have proved ineffective. I have tried eating mounds of raw garlic, which has repelled everything except the fleas. I have smeared myself with citronella cream and burned citronella incense, both to no avail. As a last resort, I am making a visit to the pet shop. Smelling like flea powder is a small price to pay for my sanity. I am busy reading the blurbs on the backs of different flea powders, in the hope that one of them mentions something about use for humans, when my phone rings. It's Carol. She asks if I am free to talk and laughs when I tell her that I am in the process of choosing myself a flea powder.

'I just wanted to let you know how my chemotherapy went.'

Shit! I forgot that yesterday was her first chemo session. I should have at least remembered to send her a text message.

'And how did it go?' I ask. At least she can't see me blushing over the phone. I feel like an absolute failure as a friend.

'Well, fine, actually. I'm a little bit nauseous but otherwise I feel quite normal.'

'That's great, Carol. When's your next session?'

'In a week's time.'

I decide not to tell her that the worst effects of chemotherapy usually occur later, well into the course.

She says goodbye, and before I put my phone away I set a reminder to call her in a week's time.

A shop assistant has been hovering around me since I started talking on my phone. I wonder if she is going to tell me to turn my phone off, that cellphones are not allowed in the pet shop. But she just wants to know what type of animal I am choosing the flea powder for. I hesitate for a moment before answering.

'A cat,' I say. Yes, I could picture myself with a sleek Siamese cat. Not a converted stray like Gina's, but a decent thoroughbred feline of pure Thai descent.

'Then you should get this one.' She hands me a small bottle. 'There are different strengths for different-size animals.'

Oh God, I am hardly the size of a cat. 'And a dog,' I blurt out. 'A very big dog, like a kind of Labrador. Actually, probably bigger than a Labrador. More like a Great Dane.'

She crumples the bridge of her nose in bewilderment. 'A mixture of Labrador and Great Dane?' she asks.

I nod.

She hesitates for a moment, then hands me another bottle. 'That should do the trick. You can pay at the counter when you're finished.'

I'm walking to the till with the chosen flea powder when I notice the flea collars. Baby-blue with pretty silver buckles, and just the right size to fit around my ankles and wrists. I put the flea powder back on the shelf and pay for four flea collars.

'What about your dog? Those are too small for a dog,' the shop assistant says as I walk away from the counter. I make a dash for the door.

* * *

Leah is busy treating her hair with a ceramic hair straightener when I get home. As her hair is naturally straight, I think the treatment is more ritualistic than cosmetic.

'What's the big event?' I ask.

'John's taking me out tonight and he won't tell me where. He says it's a surprise. I think he's going to ask me.'

'Ask you what?'

'*The* question, silly. I know he's bought the ring. I was looking for a piece of paper on his desk while he was in the shower the other day and I saw the receipt.'

'Wow, and what will you say?'

'Yes, of course.'

I give her a hug. 'Congratulations. I'm so excited for you. You guys make a perfect couple and I know that you'll be happy together.'

'Thank you.'

'I can't believe my best friend is getting married. It sounds so scary.'

'I know. I'm actually quite nervous but I know it'll be fine. John and I are right for each other.'

'You're so lucky.'

'It's not just luck, Sue. It's also hard work.'

'You sound like you're already married, like one of those wise old women who've been married for years. Have you told Gina yet?'

'No, she's been acting all strange lately. I'm a bit pissed off with her. Since she got this big modelling thing she seems to think she's in a different league, way too cool for us mere mortals. She's hanging out with this rich druggy crowd. She can phone me if she wants to speak to me. If she's sober enough to.'

The last time I saw Gina was when she came for Sunday lunch, drunk. The last time I spoke to her she was also drunk.

'Do you think she's okay?' I ask Leah.

'I don't know. I tried to talk to her about it but she said I was being all neurotic "as usual". Her words, so I left it. Am I neurotic?'

'No, not really. Why didn't you say something to me?'

'You're always so busy. You're always either at work or too tired. What do you mean, "not really"?'

'No, forget it. You're not neurotic. Gina is confusing neurotic with responsible.'

I feel terrible. Too busy to notice that one of my closest friends is becoming an alcoholic. I spend my time helping strangers but I'm too tired to know what is going on in my friends' lives. I try to call Gina but her phone just rings. I leave a message and decide that I will try to speak to her on Saturday night at her celebratory dinner. If she's not already too drunk by the time I get there.

I receive a text message from Julian just as I am about to get into bed: *Hey, busy past few days. Are you up for sundowners at Clifton beach tomorrow evening?*

Though I'm supposed to go to philosophy class, Julian presents the more tempting offer. I should be excited but I'm too worried about Gina. Despite my exhaustion it takes me a long while to fall asleep.

# Chapter Nine

## A green glass-bead sunset

I get one compliment and more than a few strange looks, but the flea collars work. The bite count stays at thirty-five. I toy with the idea of developing my own range of designer flea collars for doctors working at Bellville Hospital.

Matthew is off sick and I am worried about him. I ask Jono if he knows what is wrong with him.

'He phoned me this morning to say that he spent the night throwing up. He thinks that it might be food poisoning. He ate some bad-tasting chicken take-away yesterday.'

Good, I think, sounds harmless enough. Unlikely to be related to the needle-stick injury.

I get back the blood results of the crazy woman, whose name I have subsequently discovered is Lindiwe, and they help me to put some more of the puzzle pieces together. Slowly a picture is emerging. As I suspected, she is HIV-positive. Despite her indiscriminating appetite, she is also severely malnourished and in early renal failure secondary to dehydration. I must wait for the lumbar-puncture results and the CT scan before I can solve the puzzle completely. The brain scan could take up to a week to be done, as there is only one scanner working at the moment and a large backlog of emergency CT scans that get priority.

Lindiwe's aunt is waiting in the ward when I get there. She has brought her niece a tub of pink yoghurt and a packet of bright orange chips to eat. Far more dangerous than fish and carrots. I stand far from the bedside, as I don't particularly fancy having to throw away another pair of jeans.

'Good morning, Doctor. Did you find out what is making her head crazy?'

Technically not, but I have found out what is contributing to the cause of her madness. 'We're still waiting for some more results and for the special scan of her head. We won't know what is causing her behaviour until we have those results.'

'And did you get back the blood results?'

Now I'm put on the spot. We drew the blood for the HIV test without consent and before counselling. 'Yes, they show that she has an infection in the blood. She is very sick.' I am not lying.

'Can you treat the infection?'

Oh shit. 'No, we cannot cure it completely. But we can make it get less. We can make it a bit better, but not completely better.' The aunt looks justifiably confused by my tentative, poorly worded explanation.

The ward sister calls me aside to tell me that Lindiwe kept everyone awake during the night. According to the night staff, she stripped and tried to run away. They had to call security to bring her back. They want her transferred to a psychiatric ward. I try to explain to the ward sister that the psychiatrists will not take her unless the CT scan and LP results are normal and that we are still waiting for these. She grunts, raises one eyebrow and says something to the nurse next to her in rapid-fire Afrikaans that I cannot understand. I interpret it as her unhappiness with my explanation. Eventually we reach a compromise. I will discharge another of my patients, who is in a single room, so that we can move Lindiwe into that room, and I will write up some strong sedation for her.

\* \* \*

I manage to leave the hospital at four thirty. When I get to my car I try to phone Gina, but her phone just rings until a deep male voice starts talking about Hannibal Lector. I quickly end the call, sure that I dialled the wrong number, and try Gina again. I did not make a mistake. Her voicemail is a corny recorded message of an Anthony Hopkins impersonator inviting the listener for dinner. Sometimes the two-year gap between Gina and me feels like ten years.

I rush home and get changed into clothes for sundowners on the beach. I opt for a light cotton long-sleeved shirt and a pair of trousers so that I will not have to expose Julian to my bite-riddled limbs. I stop at a bottlestore on my way to pick up some champagne and reach the beach by five thirty.

Julian's Land Rover chugs and shudders into the parking lot as I am getting out of my car. I walk over to where he has parked. He is wearing the same black board shorts and blue T-shirt that he wore on our hike up the mountain.

'I picked up some champagne on the way,' I say, handing him the bottle.

'Well, I have to commend you on your taste.' He retrieves a picnic basket from between the surfboards in the back of his Land Rover and opens it to reveal an identical bottle of champagne.

We walk single file down the narrow flight of cracked cement steps that leads to the beach. The loose sand deposited by countless feet that have traversed the stairs feels slippery underneath my bare soles and I need to concentrate not to fall. Deep green hedges and dark, private gateways line our descent. At one point there is an opening between the houses and I catch a brief glimpse of turquoise unblemished by white: a promise of what awaits us below. Julian takes off his slip-slops when we reach the sand. We walk together across the small crescent-shaped beach to the cluster of grey granite rocks on the far side. The air is chilly but the rocks are still warm with retained daytime heat. I stretch myself out against the stone so that its hard prickliness pokes the back of my shoulder blades. We have caught the sun in its setting and it hovers on the horizon, a great disc shrouded in thick orange ether. Julian pours two glasses of champagne. I notice that the glasses he pulls from the picnic basket are proper crystal champagne flutes.

'That's brave of you. I wouldn't risk bringing my glassware to the beach.'

'It seems sacrilegious to drink good wine from plastic glasses,' he says, pouring me a glass of champagne. 'I think I must have inherited the trait from my mom. We used to hike a lot as a family when I was young, before my parents got divorced, and my mom always took a china cup with her in her backpack because she refused to drink her tea from those enamel hiking mugs. I know it's rather ridiculous but I'm like her: I'd rather risk breaking the glass. Cheers! It's nice to see you again. How has your week been?'

'I've been attacked by hospital fleas and have resorted to wearing flea collars around my wrists and ankles.'

He laughs. I decide to let him wonder whether I'm joking or not. 'A friend of mine has just recently been diagnosed with cancer,' I continue, 'and she went for her first chemotherapy session, which luckily went well.'

'Oh, speaking of which, I wanted to tell you that I know,' Julian says, somewhat hesitantly.

'Know what?' I ask.

'Don't worry. I'll tell you later. Carry on telling me about your week.'

'Well, apart from that, nothing else interesting has really happened. How was your week?'

'Quite stressful. I did a right hemi-colectomy and primary anastomosis on a patient with colon cancer, but he became really sick post-op and we had to take him back for a re-look. For some reason the area around the anastomosis had become necrotic, and so we had to resect even more bowel and then take out a stoma. Not ideal.' He opens a bottle of olives and offers them to me. 'Help yourself to some olives. My dad cured them; it's one of his hobbies. Oh, I almost forgot.' He digs in the picnic basket and pulls out a small brown paper packet that is stapled closed. 'I bought something for you. I thought it would look nice on you.' He hands the parcel to me and I try to identify the gift through the packet, but my fingers do not recognise its shape.

'Thanks. What have I done to deserve this?' I ask and he blushes deep crimson.

'Open it. It's nothing big.'

Inside the packet is a craft-market bracelet of green glass beads strung onto a brown leather thong. It's beautiful.

'Thank you. It's lovely. I . . . don't know what to say. You should be proud of yourself. It's not often that I'm speechless.' I put the bracelet on. It's far more attractive than the flea collar to which my wrist has become accustomed.

'See, the green is the same colour as your eyes,' Julian says.

I can't remember what shade of blue his eyes are; I certainly wouldn't be able to match beads to them.

I move closer to him, hoping that he will put his arm around me. But he doesn't. We talk until nine o'clock and then walk back up to the parking lot. My head is buzzing with champagne and his closeness. He gives me a hug goodbye and I pull his head towards me and kiss him. He yields to my kiss and I can taste the salty bitterness of olives. I know that he will come home with me if I ask him to. I know that we will have sex and I know that in the morning I will panic and push him away. I know, because this has been my pattern for the last few years. I am not going to do it again. I pull my lips away from his.

'Julian, do you mind if we take things slowly?' I ask.

'No, not at all. You call the shots. I'll wait for you.'

'Thanks. I appreciate it.'

'Well, you're worth waiting for.'

Somebody laughs on the beach and the sound floats up to the parking lot on the still air, oddly disembodied. I hope that I will prove Julian right. I hope that I am worth waiting for.

\* \* \*

I check my eyes against the beads in the mirror when I get home. He was right about the colour, and I realise it means more to me than the bracelet itself.

# Cultural healing

Friday rolls around, and the whole world is ready for the weekend. I am wallowing in my depression alone. I turn on my car radio and the pleasure of Friday is being discussed on every station that I tune into except for one, which appears to be hosting a phone-in panel discussion for UFO enthusiasts. After learning that Velcro was developed using alien technology, I decide on silence. Once I have finished my day at Bellville, I can look forward to going directly to Goodwood Hospital for a Friday-night paediatrics call. Hardly something to be excited about.

I get to the ward at twenty past eight and Justine is already panicking that I am not coming in. I ask her what she will do if I am actually sick one day. She doesn't answer but my question disconcerts her: she drops her precious green folder. It splays open and blank X-ray request forms, discharge pages, prescription charts and referral notes scatter across the floor, underneath patients' beds and out of the ward into the corridor.

'Justine, why on earth have you collected all of these forms?' I ask as I bend down to help her collect the strewn pieces of paper.

'Because the ward often runs out. I like to keep them on me, then I don't have to run around looking for forms.' She sniffs. A tear rolls down her cheek and makes a crinkly wet splotch on one of the pages. I wonder if my questioning has upset her or if it is something else. Sometimes dropped pieces of paper also make me cry.

'That's so clever,' I say. 'I should have thought of doing it myself ages ago.' I *have* thought of it, actually, but I'm too lazy to lug a thick folder around with me. But I hope that my comment makes her feel a bit better.

\* \* \*

Carol calls me sometime in the middle of the morning.

'Hi Sue, I missed you at philosophy last night. I just wanted to check that you're okay.'

'Yes, I'm okay, thanks. I had a date, so I decided to skip philosophy.'

'Lucky you. Was it someone special?'

I hesitate a moment before answering. 'Yes, it was. It is.' I don't really want to talk about Julian yet. I'm too scared that things won't work out. 'I've been thinking about you a lot,' I say, to change the subject. 'Everything still okay after the chemo?'

'Fine, thanks. I still feel almost a hundred per cent. I can't believe how smoothly it went. Thanks for all your advice about the chemotherapy. I'm very lucky to have someone that I trust, whose opinion I can ask. I told my fiancé all about you and about the discussion we had when I visited you. He wants to meet you sometime.'

'I'd love that.'

I don't know what she is thanking me for: I've hardly given her much advice at all. She says goodbye and I hope, as I put my phone away, that at least I gave her the right advice. She has placed so much weight on what I told her that it frightens me, which is strange because I give advice to patients all day long and never feel any hesitation in my decisions. What if the chemotherapy makes her sick? But I cannot think like that. I would have advised any patient in a similar position to have chemo and I would have had no doubt in my decision. Why is it so different when the patient is a friend?

\* \* \*

Matthew arrives very late, just as we are finishing the ward work. I don't scold him because he looks awful, too off-colour for a simple fast-food gastro. I pull down his lower eyelid and ask him to look up. The white of his eye is discoloured, a deep lemon-yellow.

'Matthew, are you on a medical aid?' I ask.

He nods. 'I'm still on my dad's medical aid.'

'I'm going to speak to one of the private physicians. You're jaundiced. It had to be really bad chicken to damage your liver that much. In fact, if it was the chicken you can probably stop studying medicine today because you can sue whoever you bought it from for enough to never have to work in your life. You need to be seen properly.' Ten minutes later I dispatch Jono to drive Matthew to a private physician who has agreed to see him as an emergency.

I am worried about Matthew, worried that he has developed hepatitis or pancreatitis as a side-effect of the antiretroviral medication he is taking for his needle-stick injury. I still can't shake the feeling of responsibility. And the guilt.

\* \* \*

I finish at five minutes to four in the afternoon and rush directly to Goodwood Hospital. I have to change my mindset from adult to paediatric medicine. Everything is different for children: the normal values for blood pressure, pulse and respiratory rate vary with age; the doses of drugs, which must all be worked out according to weight and then converted to millilitres (most paediatric drugs are, of course, syrups); the flow rates of the drips; the size numbers of the resuscitation equipment. There is one child waiting in casualty when I get there. The doctor who worked during the day hands over to me. 'I'm sorry, I haven't had time to see this little kiddie yet,' he says. 'I think she has a bit of a runny tummy.'

'No problem.' I turn to the mother and sick child. 'How old is baby?' I ask. The mother smiles and nods at me. I try again. 'One year? Two years?'

Her face lights up as comprehension dawns. 'One year three month,' she says.

I transfer my attention from mother to child. The baby is significantly dehydrated and extremely apathetic.

'Is baby vomiting?' The mother nods. 'Diarrhoea?' I can see the confusion on her face and I attempt gestures to symbolise a stomach working. My translational signing is unsuccessful and the mother smiles at me uncomprehendingly. I need to know so much more: if worms or blood are present in the diarrhoea, how long the child has been sick, if the mother has given the child any medication, if the child is allergic to anything, if the child's vaccinations are up to date, if the mother has access to running water at home. But this will take too long with hand signals and there is no translator available outside working hours.

I call the sister to help me put up a drip. The child is so dehydrated that its blood vessels have collapsed and I struggle to find a vein. I start on the hands and arms and, when I have transformed both upper limbs into pincushions, I move on to the feet. Initially the child screams but she soon becomes too tired to cry. The mother stares at me and I wonder what she thinks I am doing. I wish I could explain to her that I am trying to help her baby and not performing some barbaric bleeding ritual. We shave parts of the baby's head to try to find a scalp vein but they are all flat. The baby has lost too much fluid. And she now has a lopsided Mohawk.

I am going to have to put up an intraosseous line and pump fluid into the baby via its bone marrow. I try to explain to the mother the procedure that I am about to do, but I think I only succeed in confusing her further. I hesitate for a moment and then decide that it will be better for her to wait outside. She probably thinks, from my inept hand signals, that I am preparing to amputate her child's leg.

The mother goes outside and I sit down in front of the child. I take a thick needle and feel one thumb's width below the knee for the hardness of the tibial bone beneath the skin of the shin. I drill the needle into the bone applying constant pressure with the palm of my hand. The child is too sick and exhausted even to cry. I feel the needle give and know that I am through the hard bony cortex and into the spongy marrow. I aspirate some blood just to be sure and then attach the drip line and check that the fluid runs in easily. The child will live a little longer. I bandage the leg and call the mother back in.

But the child does not respond as well as I expect it to. I push in fluid boluses, waiting for her at least to start crying again. They have no effect; the child remains obtunded. I draw blood for a blood-gas analysis and then run with the specimen to the neat box-like machine at the back of casualty unit. I turn the machine on and a thin metal proboscis rises and sucks up the blood specimen that I present to it. After two minutes of mechanical churning counted down by a digital timer, the machine shoots out a piece of paper with the results of the blood-gas analysis. Every time I use the blood-gas machine I imagine little goblins inside the box quickly analysing and assessing the blood sample, then typing a result for me. After checking the values printed on the piece of paper, I understand why my fluid resuscitation is not having the effect that I expected. The electrolytes are completely abnormal. The sodium and the potassium are sky-high and the child is severely alkalotic. This imbalance is incongruent with the history that the mother has given me, unlikely to be caused by the acute diarrhoea alone, and I try to think what else could be wrong with the child. I look at her prune-like face, willing her back to life. I call the sister to get the resuscitation trolley.

A flash of red catches my eye as I lean over the child to intubate her. I lift her T-shirt and notice a twisted red and yellow rope tied around her stomach, almost hidden by the nappy. And suddenly everything makes sense and I curse myself for having taken so long to realise it. After intubating the child I call the mother back into the room. 'Mama, did you take baby to a sangoma?' I ask her.

She does not reply.

'Sangoma?' I repeat. I know that she has heard me and that she understands. 'Did the sangoma give the baby medicine?' The mother nods. I wonder what concoction of drain cleaner and soap and other chemicals this child has received. One of my patients once told me that Handy Andy cleans the stomach as well as it cleans a dirty rim from a bath. The all-purpose cleaner.

I struggle to resuscitate the child, struggle to correct the electrolyte imbalance. She has stopped breathing and I have to connect her to a ventilator. At this late stage, the fact that I know the cause of the illness makes no difference to my ability to treat it. The child's body is floppy, as though it has already been disinhabited. The mother stares at me with pleading eyes, eyes that I avoid because I don't know how to meet them. I think she realises that her child is dying.

\* \* \*

I wish that the mother had brought her child here before going to the sangoma. I am angry with the mother, angry with the sangoma, angry with myself because I cannot speak Xhosa. The whole system is wrong. I have no right to be pissed off with the mother for going to a sangoma, someone who speaks her language and who provides answers to her questions. She comes to me after the sangoma's medication has not worked and I prick the child more than ten times, on all four limbs. I shave her hair into a weird pattern and prick her head. Eventually I stick a thick needle into her leg and put a tube down her throat. And when the child dies, all I can say to the mother is that I am sorry. She probably thinks that I have killed her child. Perhaps she will go back to Khayelitsha and tell all the other mothers that the white woman doctor at Goodwood Hospital killed her baby. And more of them will take their children to sangomas before coming to the hospital. That is what *I* would do.

The mother has picked up the body of her dead child and is rocking it backwards and forwards, close to her chest.

'I'm so sorry, I'm so sorry.' I repeat myself because I don't know what else to say. I don't even know if she understands me. I am frustrated by this unnecessary death, frustrated by the socio-economic factors that caused it and over which I have no control, I am angry at the faceless monster that poisoned the child, and I am cross with myself because I have been too lazy to learn to speak Xhosa. There is nobody that I can shout at. It would be better if I could yell at someone, or even pick up the telephone and leave a rude message on an answering machine. At least that way the anger would be outside of me, not inside me, slowly eating away at my sanity. But there is only me and the mother and her dead child in the room. So I go outside to the parking lot and fetch a cigarette from the ashtray of my car. I slam the door shut and sit on the steps at the entrance to the hospital and smoke to keep my tears at bay. Doctors don't cry.

# Chapter Ten

## Celebrations to forget

I struggle to sleep after my call, kept awake by thoughts of the child who died. Would it have made any difference if I could speak Xhosa? The mother would still have gone to the sangoma first. And even though I would have been able to explain to her what happened to her child, I would not have been able to tell her why her baby got sick in the first place. That question the sangoma would have been able to answer for her. Nevertheless, I resolve that I must try to learn to speak Xhosa as soon as I have some time.

As I finally start drifting off to sleep, my phone bleeps. I should have turned it off. The more I try to ignore the incoming message alert, the more awake I become. Shit. I pick up my phone, contemplate throwing it across the room for about two seconds, and then check the message. For once I am glad that curiosity got the better of me: the message is from Julian, inviting me for a walk up Lion's Head. I consider declining. That would be the sensible option, given his definition of 'walk' and the fact that I haven't had any sleep. But I want to see him again, so I agree to meet him at the bottom of Lion's Head in an hour.

We walk up the trail slowly. I am glad that I was on call the night before because my lack of sleep gives me an excuse for setting a sloth-like pace, one that doesn't leave

154

me breathless and gasping. We walk mostly in silence; I'm too tired to think up conversation. I explain this to Julian because I don't want him to think that I'm a boring person or that, after two dates, we have run out of things to talk about.

'No problem,' he says. 'I understand completely.'

Unlike Kevin, I think. Then I wonder why I'm comparing him to Kevin.

The evening is still and the air barely moves as we push through it. It's easy to imagine that it never rains in Cape Town: the fynbos is dry and weary, desiccated in the long heat of the end of summer. Blue-headed lizards dart into the bushes on either side of us, their evening sun-tanning interrupted by my heavy footfall. When we reach the top of Lion's Head, we look down over the coast that stretches from Bloubergstrand to Llandudno. Cars buzz along the coastal road like ants. Although they may not know it, it is the scent of Cape Town that they follow, a scent heady with beauty, with the smell of spices brought down Africa in the palms of refugees, with whiffs of Durban poison and the cigar smoke of home-grown jazz.

'What are you thinking about?' Julian's voice breaks the silence.

'Sorry, my mind is wondering. Just how beautiful Cape Town is. Speaking of which, I'd better hurry up. I'm supposed to be at Gina's party in half an hour. Are you sure you don't want to come with me?'

'Yes, I'm sure. Thanks for the invite but I need an early night.'

I'm glad he says no, as I'm not ready to share Julian yet. He takes my hand to help me down a section of steep rock and keeps holding it until the path narrows so that we are forced to walk in single file. Tonight, holding hands is enough.

* * *

Gina has given me directions to the restaurant at which she is holding her celebration, but still I spend half an hour driving up and down the one-way streets of Cape Town trying to find it. The restaurant is expensive and exclusive, so exclusive that it is known only to those eligible to hear about it. There is a small sign, deceptively insignificant, painted onto the wall of an office block that denotes the restaurant's existence. I walk around the office block, my heels clipping the littered tar, trying to find the entrance. Eventually I notice a narrow alley and venture down it, mace spray in my hand because it is dark and deserted, and at the end of the alleyway I come upon the doorway, lit up with swinging lanterns. The decor inside is ultra-trendy, the lighting subdued, the waiters all high on coke.

Gina is already drunk when I arrive. She has lost weight since the last time I saw her. Her spray-tanned skin clings to her bones, making her look older than she is. She is frantic, hyperactive, fluttering everywhere between chairs and tables.

'Oh Sue, it's so wonderful to see you,' she oozes as she catches sight of me. 'I'm so glad you could come. You have to meet everybody.' She introduces me to a group of people whose names I forget the moment she says them. I feel drab and old-fashioned in this group of beautiful socialites. There is only one seat left open, far away in the corner at the end of the table, and I make my way to it, tripping over legs and handbags. The chair is hard and uncomfortable and cuts into my bottom. It is as though even the furniture in the restaurant knows that I do not belong. I drink a cocktail quickly. The alcohol goes straight to my head but I feel no more welcome than before. I want to catch Gina alone to speak to her but she is surrounded by people, the centre of attention, flirting with everyone, male and female. I try to strike up conversation with the emaciated woman sitting next to me but she keeps on drifting off to sleep. I don't fit in with this crowd and I long for Julian's quiet company.

I find myself reduced to staring at someone's cigarette as it glows to ashes in the ashtray. Enough. I make my way over to Gina and pull her away from the group that surrounds her. 'Gina, I have to go,' I tell her. 'I'm really tired and I still need to drive home.'

'No, you can't go yet. The party's only starting and this is my special night.' She's like a sulky child about to throw a tantrum.

'I'm sorry. Call me tomorrow. I want to go for coffee with you and catch up a bit. We haven't spoken for ages.'

'Well, that's your fault, not mine. You're the one who's always working.'

'Gina, please.'

'I'll call you tomorrow.'

I get a peck on the cheek before she drops into some stranger's lap.

Gina's behaviour scares me. Her angry self-destructiveness is both threatening and confusing. Does she hate herself so much, or is she genuinely oblivious to the consequences of her actions?

## Playing psychologist

Gina calls me on Monday morning and we arrange to meet that evening at a café in Long Street. We meet early, at six thirty, before the café becomes a pub. Everything is quiet, holding its breath for the rush of people that darkness will bring. We order coffee. Gina drinks hers black, without sugar.

'Are you on a diet?' I ask. She usually drinks her coffee with milk and two sugars, like me.

'I'm trying to lose weight,' she says. I wonder where she wants to lose weight from. She has no fat left on her. 'You have to, you know, otherwise you don't get jobs,' she continues. 'All of the other girls are so bloody thin. They snort coke all day so they don't need to eat.'

I'm glad that the subject is out in the open and that she has brought it up herself. 'Thank God you said that,' I tell her. 'Leah and I have been so worried about you. We were concerned that you were getting caught up in the whole drug scene.'

'I don't know what the big fuss is anyway. What's the big deal about drugs? I never do them when I'm alone, only when I go out. It's not like I'm addicted or anything. They make things more fun. Life is so bloody miserable; at least some chemical influence makes it a little more interesting.'

'Jeez, Gina! Drugs are psychoactive, they aren't there just to make life a little more interesting. They mess with your brain and deplete your neurotransmitters. And it's not like they have no long-term effects, even if you just do them socially. Look, I've got no problem with smoking a joint every now and then, but the hard stuff, shit, it's not worth it. I should know. I've seen too many substance-abuse psychoses. Do you know how many people are in Valkenberg Hospital because of drugs? It's scary. And believe me, it's not a place you want to end up in.'

'Whoa, stop lecturing. I've got this under control. It's not me you need to talk to, it's the other girls. I don't know why you and Leah always try to be my parents, forever interfering with my life. I know exactly what I'm doing, okay?'

Well, at least she isn't accusing me of being too busy to speak to her.

'What do you mean when you say that life is so miserable?' I ask, picking up on what she said earlier. I wonder whether I should prescribe some antidepressants to make her feel better. At least then I would be doing something for her.

'Just forget it, okay? You're supposed to be my friend, not my bloody shrink. You're treating me like I'm some delinquent kid who's been brought into your rooms.'

I want to tell her that she's behaving like a delinquent kid, that by twenty-six she should have outgrown these kinds of issues. I want to tell her to pull herself together and go see someone qualified in the mental health field to help her sort out her problems. But I know that this will alienate her even more and will probably lead to a screaming match in the café.

'I'm not acting like your doctor,' I tell her instead. 'I'm speaking to you like this because you are one of my best friends and I care about you.'

'Well, I'm fine, thank you.'

I don't know what to say without risking her never talking to me again, so I change the topic. 'How are things with your parents?' I ask.

'Not great. I think they're heading for divorce. I don't know when last I spoke to you. Did I tell you that my dad has been having an affair?'

'No. With who?' I'm not shocked by her news. I suspect that he has had more than just a single affair.

'Some fitness instructor at the gym. Twenty years old. Younger than me. Guys are all such bastards.'

'How is your mom coping?'

'One day she's pissed, the next day she spends in bed crying and won't even get up to brush her teeth. I could have handled it if their marriage had just not worked, but what kills me is that he had to go and sleep with some slut half his age. What's wrong with him? I mean, couldn't he at least have waited? Got divorced first?' She is clenching her fists, her skeletal knuckles white.

I don't know what to say. My parents are still married, relatively happily as marriages go. I tell her that I think the whole thing is crap. I wonder if she's in the state she is now because her parents have never grown up themselves. Is the inability to reach emotional maturity hereditary or learned?

I'm genuinely worried that Gina is losing it but I don't know what to do. I speak to Leah when I get home and she says that she will try to chat to Gina, but I know that it won't help. Gina needs more help than we can give her as friends. I wish that her parents were not so fucked up because at least then I could speak to them. I wonder if they have even noticed what is happening to Gina.

## Unusual weekend plans

Uncharacteristically, I remember to call Carol on Tuesday evening, after her session of chemotherapy, to find out how she is doing. I can hear that she has been crying when she answers the phone.

'I'm so scared, Sue. My fiancé is making all these plans for next year and I don't even know if I'm still going to be here. I just listen to him and I can't bear to remind him that I'm dying. It's making everything ten times worse than if I just had to deal with this on my own. Sometimes I think that it would be better if he just left me and spent his energy finding someone who will be around next year.'

'Carol, stop it! You're not dying. Don't be ridiculous. The chemotherapy will work. Your cancer is treatable. You have to be positive.' Yes, right, it's easy for me to say. Be positive. Smile while your hair falls out, smile while you retch your guts out, smile while you plan your funeral. 'I know it must be difficult to be positive, but speaking from a purely medical point of view, your chances of surviving are far greater than of dying.'

'Twenty per cent don't make it, Sue. You told me that.'

'I also told you that eighty per cent do.'

'But what if I'm in that twenty per cent?'

'The chances are greater that you'll be in the eighty per cent. But listen, what are you doing this weekend? I'm off on Saturday, let's do something. Maybe you need a little break from your fiancé.'

'That would be nice. What do you want to do?'

'I don't know. Something different. Something that you've wanted to do for ages but haven't got around to. I think you deserve to treat yourself.' I also need to do something, to get my mind off Gina.

'I know, let's go ice-skating! I've been dying to go ice-skating for ages but my fiancé refuses to go with me.'

I wasn't thinking of anything quite that energetic or adventurous. More like an evening out to a nice, civilised art film or perhaps a visit to a health spa. The last time I ice-skated was when I was seven and I ended up in the trauma unit with a broken arm. But after all, I made the offer.

'Well, okay, if that's what you really want to do,' I reluctantly agree. I hope I sound reasonably willing, if not enthusiastic. We make plans to meet at the Goodwood ice-skating rink on Saturday morning. I can hardly believe I'm almost thirty and off to ice-skate; I must be going crazy.


## An unexpected coffee date

Matthew is going to be okay. The physician has called to tell me that he will be discharged in two days. He has changed Matthew's antiretroviral prophylaxis to something that is slightly less toxic. His liver should be fine but they are still worried about his pancreas.

I am sitting in outpatients trying to fit thirty patients into as many minutes when my pager goes off. I don't recognise the number that comes up on the screen of my bleeper and go to the telephone outside my examination cubicle to answer it.

'Sue Carey here. Someone paged me.'

'Sue, hi, it's Donald.'

Great, the last person I need to hear from. I'd hoped he had forgotten about me.

'Yes, what do you want?'

'I thought we could go for coffee after work sometime, catch up on old times. When are you free?' he asks.

Oh God, what old times?

'Um . . . I'm really quite busy most days.'

'Well, what are you doing after work today?'

In a near panic I try to think of an excuse. Today happens to be the one day that I have nothing planned.

'So how about after work?' he persists. 'Page me when you're done.'

How like Donald. He has put the telephone down before I've even said yes.

I prolong my ward work for as long as possible. I tell Justine that she can go home early, I write extra-diligent notes for all of my patients, I help a man with half of his body paralysed limp to the bathroom. Even so, I am somehow finished by four thirty. I page Donald to tell him that I am exhausted and am going home to bed and end up making an arrangement to meet him at a small coffee shop in Durban Road, close to the hospital. At least they sell delicious pastries: I need something to look forward to.

* * *

Donald is waiting for me when I arrive, chatting up the waitress. It never ceases to amaze and irritate me that women are so easily impressed by male doctors. I have yet to find a man impressed by *my* being a doctor. It doesn't have quite the same effect; men don't suddenly want to jump into bed with me, or share a future with me, when I tell them what I do for a living.

'Sorry I'm late.' I give Donald my usual greeting as I sit in the seat opposite him. 'Have you ordered yet?'

'No, I was just about to.' He turns to the waitress, flirtation over. 'I'll have a filter coffee, please.'

'Make that two, and you can bring me one of those chocolate-mousse-cup things. With extra cream, please.'

'Sue, listen, I need to talk to you because I can feel that there's some awkwardness between us and I want to clear the air.'

So my abruptness over the phone has not gone unnoticed.

'I know that things between us were not always great at medical school,' he continues, 'and that we had our little hiccups.'

Whatever you want to call it, Donald dear. This is becoming interesting. I nod to show him that I am still listening and he carries on talking.

'I've always liked you and I'd really like it if we could start over again, with a clean slate.'

I don't know whether I can trust my hearing. I wonder if they have suddenly started putting hallucinogenic drugs in the chocolate mousse.

'First, you need to apologise.' I say. I'm not letting him get away so easily with all the months of agony that he caused me in my naive youth.

'Apologise for what?'

'For leading me to believe that I was the one for you,

just so you could sleep with me, while simultaneously deceiving at least three other girls.'

Donald's face flushes dark red. I don't know if his colour change is caused by anger or embarrassment, and I don't really care. I notice that, unlike Julian, who looks even more endearing when he blushes, Donald just looks guilty.

'I'm sorry, Sue. I was young and had raging hormones that were completely out of control and I really didn't think about what I was doing. Is that okay?'

'Mmm. Do you really mean it?'

'I do, I do, I promise. Really.'

'Methinks the man doth protest too much. But your apology is accepted.'

'So, when can I ask you out on a date?'

'Aren't you going a little bit too fast? We've only just got through the truth and reconciliation bit.'

'Ah, but we haven't got to the best part of the reconciliation bit yet. Let me show you, since you suffered so badly, just how much a good reconciliation can make up for it.'

'It seems as though little has changed since medical school days, then.'

'Okay, I retract what I said.'

'God, I'm stuffed. This chocolate-mousse thing is so filling.'

'Thank heaven. At last I can ask you for a taste without trembling in fear.'

'Sorry, didn't I offer? How rude of me. Finish it.' Payback for the cheesecake.

'So, are you going to give me an answer?' he asks.

'To what?'

'The date? When are you free?'

'You're really persistent, aren't you?'

'How do you think I got into medical school?'

'Obviously not as a result of your intelligence or tact.'

'So?'

'Okay, okay. How about next Saturday night?'

I'm dumbfounded by myself. How can I have been manipulated into agreeing to a date with Donald? Bastards don't suddenly become nice guys.


## Childhood revisited

I get lost finding my way to the Goodwood ice-skating rink. The face of Cape Town has changed since I last went ice-skating twenty-one years ago and a casino posing as an over-the-top French chateau now stands in the place of the somewhat dilapidated ice rink of yore. Eventually I approach a security guard and he directs me to the rink.

Carol is already waiting in the queue to get in. We are the only adults in line without children running between our feet or pulling on our arms and I can't help worrying about how this makes Carol feel. I talk about anything other than offspring in an attempt to distract her from thinking about children. It occurs to me that I may be dwelling more insistently than she is on the possibility that she may never have the opportunity to bring her children ice-skating, that she may never even have children.

We hand in our shoes and the woman working behind the counter pulls out ice-skating boots for us to try on. I try not to think of how many different feet have sweated in the boots. My one foot is slightly bigger than my other and I imagine I can already feel a blister forming through my thick socks.

'So, you ready?' Carol asks me.

I can't wait, I think sarcastically, sure that I am going to leave here with plantar warts, athlete's foot and blisters.

'Remember,' I warn her, 'I haven't done this since I was seven and my memories of that time are still rather traumatic. I spent the whole of summer with a plaster cast on my arm. Do you have any idea how itchy casts are? Oh, and not to mention the fact that I missed out on an entire season of "Marco Polo" in the pool because I wasn't allowed to swim with the plaster on.'

Far more confident than I am, Carol immediately glides out onto the ice in front of me. While she skates effortlessly in figure-of-eights and backward circles, I shuffle along the side of the rink, gripping the rail and trying not to trip over the toddlers sharing the safety bar with me. Carol is so graceful and perfect as she skates that it is difficult for me to imagine there is something growing inside her, taking over her cells and distorting their normal function. That is what cancer is, really: a collection of aberrant cells that multiply far more rapidly than they should, that have lost the ability to obey the usual signals to stop growing when they reach the body's natural borders, that cannot function in the place of the cells of the organs they take over because they are largely undifferentiated. In a rather macabre way cancer is like a community in revolution, a *coup d'état* in which anarchic rebels take over and kill all the professionals but then do not have the expertise and experience to replace them properly. Perhaps chemotherapy is like a UN peacekeeping force.

Carol whips past me and grabs my hand, pulling me away from the security of the safety rail.

'Carol, stop, I'm going to fall.' I tense my muscles, trying to slow her down, and brace myself for the inevitable.

'Just loosen up. Don't fight, otherwise we'll both fall. Follow me.'

I relax and suddenly I am flying, around and around. People pass me in a blur. I cling to Carol's hand and let her pull me along. She will survive the cancer, I think. Somebody so powerful and so graceful cannot just be extinguished. Dizzy, I spin faster and faster until my blade gets caught in Carol's and we are both on the ground with our faces in freezing cold slush. People skate to either side of us, splitting and then rejoining so that their blades etch a little seed pod around us. Carol gets up, laughing. Her nose is red from the cold and her blond hair is plastered to her face in thick wet strips. I don't want her to move away. I want her to be like a child forever, inside the safety of the seed pod.

I get up, my wet jeans sticking to my legs like a dirty nappy, and try to make my way back to the rail. Children whiz past me. Teenage couples pull each other along, first one leading and then the other, an excuse to hold hands. I feel like I am trying to cross an Italian highway. Carol has got lost among the skaters. As much as I would like to, I cannot remain forever standing still in the centre of the circle of movement. I take a few steps towards the edge and get hit by a flying pre-adolescent. He immediately gets up and resumes his adrenaline rush. I, however, have the added challenge of old age and imminent osteoporosis to deal with. I look at my wrist, which feels as though it has just gone through an old-fashioned iron press. It resembles a purple tennis ball. I realise I should have succumbed to propaganda and drunk my daily glass of milk. Somehow I manage to dodge bodies and make my way back to the railing. I imagine that this must be how the characters in PlayStation games feel.

I cannot move my wrist. Carol panics and tells the ice-rink manager to call an ambulance. I explain to her that it is okay because, unless the paramedics carry a portable X-ray machine around with them, they will probably be about as much help as I am at the moment. Besides, an injured wrist definitely does not warrant flashing lights. Instead, Carol drives me to the casualty unit of a private hospital and I have X-rays taken of my wrist. This time there is nothing broken and the sister bandages my wrist and tells me to ice it every hour with a packet of frozen peas.

'RICE,' she over-enunciates, as though I have injured more than just my wrist, 'rest, ice, compression and elevation.' I nod, too embarrassed to tell her that I am a doctor. 'And stay away from the ice-rink, dearie. No use trying to pretend you're still a youngster.' The cruellest yet probably the soundest advice that she gives me.

Carol takes me home and goes with Leah to pick up my car. Meanwhile I collapse on the couch in front of the television with a cup of coffee and a packet of frozen peas on my wrist and swear that I will never, ever be coerced into going ice-skating again. This is the lesson that I should have learnt when I was seven. I have an awful thought that perhaps I will spend the rest of my life having to learn the same lessons over and over again. Perhaps I am one of those people that have to have things drummed into them, literally. I hope not; it could make for a painful existence.

Leah and Carol come back with my car and we spend the rest of the afternoon watching soppy romantic comedies and eating popcorn. Between movies, Leah cooks some pancakes and Carol and I pour syrup onto them while they are still warm. Carol rolls mine into a sausage for me because it is too complicated for me to do with one hand. We squeeze lemon juice over the pancakes and then eat them with our fingers, so that our hands become sticky with syrup and lemon juice. I am worried that my clumsiness has ruined Carol's special ice-skating morning and I apologise to her.

'Don't be ridiculous!' she scolds. 'This is just as much fun. Since I got sick, everybody has been treating me with kid gloves. Even my fiancé has been panicking about absolutely everything I do. It's such a relief just to be able to act normally. So don't apologise. This has been fantastic, exactly what I needed.'

## Dinner with Donald

My injured wrist means that Donald has to pick me up for our Saturday-night date. He arrives at seven o'clock, while I am still in my dressing gown and trying to straighten my hair with my one functional hand. I hear him making polite conversation with Leah while I squeeze myself into a push-up bra and a possibly too-small black dress. After a further ten minutes of acrobatics, I admit that my ceramic hair straightener was not designed for those with disabilities. I manage to pile my hair onto the top of my head in what I hope looks like a purposefully messy bun.

By the time that I am ready, Donald and Leah are remarking on the weather for the third time.

'Wow, you look stunning!' Donald says to me as I walk into the lounge. 'I'm glad you don't dress like that at the hospital; you'd give all of the old men heart attacks.'

I catch Leah's eye and she raises one eyebrow before slipping from the room. I know exactly how to interpret her look: cheesy. I turn my attention back to Donald. 'You are quite the Mr Charming tonight.'

He nods. 'As always,' he says. I wonder how many James Bond movies he has studied to perfect his nod.

'Let me see this ice-skating injury of yours,' he says, and I show him my bandaged wrist. He starts unravelling the bandage and my wrist is revealed: ugly, purple and swollen.

'It looks sore,' he says. 'Let me see if I can make it better for you. There are some tricks I know that they didn't teach us at medical school.' He starts kissing my palm and moves his way up my arm. I wonder if he thinks that just because he slept with me a hundred years ago he retains rights to my body whenever he feels like it.

'Hey, don't think that you're getting away with a cheap date tonight,' I tell him. 'I need at least a three-course dinner and a few glasses of very good wine before I'll condone this type of behaviour.' My tone is probably too aggressive. I'm irritated with myself because, as much as I want my body to be impervious to his teasing, my arm has come up in goose-flesh where he has been kissing and I can feel my nipples hardening.

We walk outside to his expensive black car. It has tinted windows and a significantly large chrome exhaust. Donald is a fast driver, and soon we arrive at a restaurant in the Malay Quarter in the centre of town. It is a sushi bar with minimalist decor and a giant fish tank as a centrepiece. I wonder if it was the same fish tank that Gina told me about.

We sit down and Donald leans over the table to offer me a cigarette. I hesitate before taking one. 'I've actually stopped smoking,' I tell him. 'It was worsening my asthma.'

'Yes, it looks like it.'

'I haven't bought a box since I can remember.' He leans over the table and lights my cigarette and I inhale deeply. What am I doing?

\* \* \*

Donald and I share one sushi platter and then another, and I can see that he thinks he is getting laid tonight. I toy with the idea briefly but almost as soon as the thought enters my mind I am flooded with self-disgust. What is wrong with me? I like Julian; what am I doing out with Donald? Is my self-esteem so low that I have actually fallen for his superficial flattery? Or was it the coward in me who made the date with him in order to ruin my chances with the man I really like? After the frozen litchi dessert, I tell Donald that my wrist is hurting and that I think it's time for me to follow the RICE advice.

'Are you sure that I can't tempt you with coffee at my place?' he asks, before dropping me off.

'No, neither coffee nor sex. I don't think I'm up for either.'

'It's a pity. You're missing out.'

'I'm sure you'll easily find someone else willing to replace me,' I say, closing the car door behind me.

I'm glad that I get into bed alone, that I decided not to go home with Donald. Perhaps I am growing up at last.

# Chapter Eleven

## The definition of madness

When I get to the hospital on Monday, my voice is still hoarse from smoking half a box of Donald's cigarettes on Saturday night. I meet Justine in casualty and she asks me if I am getting sick.

'No, it's from smoking,' I tell her.

'I didn't know you smoked.' Her tone of voice clearly conveys her disapproval.

'I don't. I used to but now I only smoke occasionally. I was on a date with a guy who smokes.'

'Was it that doctor from Paarl Hospital?'

'No. It was a guy that I was with for a short time at medical school. He's a surgery registrar here now.'

'*The* surgery reg?' Justine asks.

'What do you mean?'

'The gorgeous one. Dr Levine?'

'Yes, that one,' I say. 'He is good-looking, but I think it would be pushing it to call him gorgeous. I think that the Paarl doctor is actually far more attractive.'

'All the female interns are in love with Dr Levine. I know of one girl who swapped from paediatrics to surgery just so that she could work with him.'

'I hope that you're not being serious,' I say. Please tell me that the poor girl had another, really good reason for swapping to surgery. I find it hard to justify swapping rotations for a guy, no matter how good-looking.

'I am being serious, it's the truth. He's divine.'

Divine Dr Levine. 'Well, please don't let him in on it. He already has a God complex.'

It irritates me that Donald has a female-intern fan club. None of my interns are falling in love with me or swapping rotations to be close to me. The only fan I've ever had was a hospital janitor who used to send me slabs of nutty chocolate and little keyring teddy bears until he was admitted to a psychiatric hospital.

Casualty is quiet and I leave Justine in charge while I go up to the ward. Sister B has called me because Lindiwe has pulled out her drip and the sisters cannot sedate her. When I get to her room, the patient is sitting at the head of her bed with her arms wrapped around her knees. Her wrists are still bound where they were tied to the bedsides, but she has managed to undo the knots that kept her restrained. She looks vulnerable, like a frightened animal. I wonder what she is thinking, *if* she is thinking. I wonder if it is fear that has made her crazy. She has gone from eating everything to refusing to eat anything. Her skin is dehydrated: thick and sluggish when she moves, slow to follow the underlying muscles. I sit down on the edge of the bed and reach out to touch her hand. She shrinks away from me, habituated into associating hospital staff with pain. I try again, opening my fingers and exposing my palm to show her that there are no needles in my hand. This time she does not pull away.

'Sisi, you need to take these tablets. They'll make you feel better,' I tell her, although I know she cannot understand what I've said. I stroke the top of her hand, a maternal gesture remembered from my childhood. What would madness be for me? Being tied to my bed in a grey-linoleum room surrounded by people who speak a language that I cannot understand? Being pierced continually in my arms and my back without explanation? Having tubes of blood taken from me daily? Being given drugs that make me drowsy, make me lose track of time, make me forget who I am? Yes, perhaps that would be madness for me.

I hand her the sedative tablet and she puts it into her mouth. I know that she has not understood me and that I will never know what made her accept and swallow the tablet I held out to her, but I cannot help hoping, as much as my cynical side scorns the thought, that it had something to do with my holding her hand. She falls asleep and I put the drip up again and re-tie her hands to the bedsides. I feel like I am betraying her, even though I know that without the intravenous fluids she will dehydrate and end up in kidney failure.

\* \* \*

When I get back to casualty, Justine rushes to meet me outside the unit.

'I did it!' she shouts, with uncharacteristic exuberance.

'What?'

'I put a chest drain in on my own. Remember that man that you sent for X-rays? Well, the X-ray showed a pleural effusion and I stuck a needle into his chest and the fluid that came out was pus and so I put in a chest drain.' Her words tumble over each other in their excitement to escape, in her desire for approval.

'Well done. I knew that you'd be fine. I hope you realise that from now on I'm leaving all the drains for you to put in.'

Justine laughs and hangs the man's chest X-ray up on the white X-ray box. She turns on the light so that it transilluminates the film. The opaque fluid in the chest blocks out the dark translucency of normal lung tissue. I trace the faint white outline of the plastic drain tube entering the chest wall and passing into the pleural space. It is positioned perfectly. I tell Justine that she is going to be fine next year. And I think that she will be. She has only two more weeks left with me before she moves on to her next rotation. I realise that I am actually going to miss her.

## The nature of man

Man, we are assured by Mrs De Marigny, includes woman. We have moved on in our philosophy classes from the nature of beauty to the nature of mankind. This interests me because it is something that I have thought about a lot. Mrs De Marigny asks us what we think the true nature of mankind is.

'I think that it is essentially good.' Carol answers first, in her soft, creamy voice. 'I think that everyone is born good and that things happen in life that cover up that goodness.'

'Yes,' Gilbert the builder responds. 'Some people have bad childhoods – they grow up to be abusive. Or maybe they are poor, then they grow up to be thieves. I firmly believe that circumstances make you what you are.'

'Which means', Carol says, nodding in agreement, 'that people can be rehabilitated. If you can undo what the world has done to them and re-educate them, then perhaps you can find that essential goodness again.'

I wonder whether Carol and Gilbert actually believe what they are saying. I wish I could be so sure that mankind is essentially good. I don't speak out to raise my objections to their blind faith because I don't think that they will understand me. I doubt that they have ever seen, much less had to examine, a two-year-old child who has been raped. I find it hard to accept that the person who raped that child should be forgiven or can be re-educated. I am envious of Carol and Gilbert because they are not constantly reminded of the worst side of human nature, of the violence, strife, addictions and anger. I wish that I had their lack of cynicism. If Carol is right, if everybody is born essentially good, what is wrong with our society that it so often allows the goodness to go into hiding? It is easier, I suppose, just to believe that some people are born inherently evil. That way I am not responsible and that way I cannot do anything about it. Perhaps my cynicism is my escape.

## An interesting lecture

In a display of unusual foresight, the hospital administrative staff has decided to implement a policy of preventive medicine. The result is the establishment of various health education clubs, including an asthma club, a diabetic club, an epilepsy club and a hypertension club, for patients with the relevant illnesses. The principle is that the patients in the clubs learn how to make lifestyle changes that will improve their own management of their diseases. The policy is referred to as 'patient empowerment'. It is an excellent idea that affords the masterminds behind it lots of commendation with very little work. The day-to-day running of the clubs has been delegated to the registrars.

Each registrar is supposed to facilitate one club meeting every three months, and so this afternoon I have been scheduled to speak to the diabetic club about healthy dietary choices. They probably should have delegated the talk to someone slightly closer to his or her ideal body weight than I am to mine. A junior-school teacher once told me a tale about a young boy who was taken by his mother to see a wise man. When they reached the feet of the old man, after climbing seven hundred stairs, the mother explained to the guru that her son ate far too many sweets and that this was ruining his health. The wise man listened and nodded sagely, then told the mother and son to go back down the mountain and come back in a month's time. So the woman dragged her son down the seven hundred stairs and went home. One month later they were back at the feet of the sage. The wise man remembered the mother and son immediately and promptly told the son to stop eating sweets because they are bad for one's health. The mother, obviously expecting a more dramatic miracle, asked the guru rather irritably why he could not have told her son this on their first visit. The wise man replied that before he could tell the son to stop eating sweets, he first had to learn to give them up himself. I never did understand why the teacher singled me out to listen to the story, but it runs through my mind as I hurry across to the former nurses' hostel where I am supposed to give the talk.

The old hostel is covered in the same faded orange face-brick as the hospital. It's rumoured that the specifications for the building were given to the original architect by a dragon of a matron. The hundreds of interconnecting passages and surprise stairways are enough to have waylaid any potential lovers who were attempting to visit her young and innocent wards.

Having misplaced the timetable that gives the venues for the talks, I stop at reception to ask where I should go. The shrivelled woman behind the glass window seems to be expecting me and, before I get a chance to open my mouth, directs me down a corridor with a frail hand. I open the door at the end of the corridor and make my way into a dimly lit room that is cluttered with unused desks and broken corduroy-covered armchairs. The yellow foam filling of one of the armchairs is spilling out and the floor is covered in tiny mustard sponge balls. They could have chosen a more comfortable venue for the talk, or at least made the room look a little less like a storeroom for old and broken furniture. There are about twelve patients waiting for me, sitting in a semicircle in front of the desks.

I walk to the front of the room and introduce myself, and the patients break out in applause. This is a better reception than I had hoped for. But I am struck by the average age of the audience, which seems to be around eighty.

'I have been asked to speak to you about healthy eating and the way in which diet affects blood-sugar levels,' I tell the diabetic sufferers. Three lavender-headed women nod sagely. 'Does anybody have any idea what type of diet is suitable for people with diabetes?' I ask. The nods continue and eventually a woman with a large mole on her cheek raises her hand.

'Yes?' I ask her, relieved that at least one person is responding to my attempt at interactive learning.

'Can I go to the ladies', please?'

Damn. 'Yes, sure,' I say. I wait for her to leave but she doesn't move. 'You can go to the toilet,' I tell her, more loudly and exaggerating my lip movements. It seems to work. She gets up from her chair and wanders slowly to the door of the lecture room. I wait until she has left before continuing.

'Let's go back to what diet is suitable for diabetics,' I suggest, but the response, or lack of it, is disappointing. I decide that perhaps I need to start at the beginning.

'Does anybody know what diabetes is? Have you had

a talk on this yet?' I know that they were supposed to have had this lecture two weeks ago. I remember seeing it scheduled on the timetable that has since disappeared. One of the women in front of me smiles and nods more vigorously. I presume her nod means yes.

'Then you know that in diabetes, one's blood-sugar level is too high.' I'm now ad libbing, dropping the standard of the lecture that I had prepared. 'Do you think, then, that it's a good idea to eat sugary foods?' I realise that what I am mistaking for nods are more likely Parkinsonian head tremors. I wonder whether the registrar scheduled to give the previous talk on diabetes decided that going to the beach was a better option.

'Do you think that it is a good idea to eat lots of sugar if you have diabetes?' I target an old man who seems more interested in extricating his leftover breakfast from his remaining two front teeth than in listening to my lecture.

'A good idea to eat sugar,' he repeats.

'Do you think that, if you have high blood sugar, you should eat lots of sugar?'

'You should eat lots of sugar.' He nods and smiles.

How did this man make it to the diabetic lecture without getting lost? Oh shit, the woman with the mole who went to the toilet has not returned. I hope that she hasn't had a heart attack in the ladies' room. I imagine some inquisitive cleaner stumbling across her decomposing skeleton in a locked toilet cubicle in three years' time. The old man has turned his attention back to his leftover breakfast.

I decide that learner participation is not going to work and revert to didactic teaching methods.

'People with diabetes should not eat foods with a high sugar content,' I say. 'Often we forget that certain things contain lots of sugar. Coke is an example.' One of the

1

1

lavender ladies raises her arm and I feel that at last I am getting somewhere.

'Are we having Coke?' she asks.

'No, people with diabetes should avoid Coke because it contains a lot of sugar. Instead they should drink something like Coke Lite which does not contain sugar.'

'My husband likes Coke,' she tells me, as though divulging a secret. She raises a painted eyebrow and I expect her to tell me that her husband also gambles, smokes joints and is having an affair with a sixteen-year-old.

I have entered my own hell. I have died and this is the punishment for all my sins. An eternity of trying to educate mentally challenged geriatric diabetics stretches out before me. Just as I am about to start a bargaining process with God and explain that there were extenuating circumstances in most cases of my misbehaviour, the door opens. A young woman carrying a box of puzzles walks into the room and I wonder if she is God's envoy.

'You have no idea how glad I am to see you here,' she says to me as she puts the box of puzzles on one of the desks. 'I got caught in an awful traffic jam and was so worried that they would be left here on their own. I presume that you are one of the final-year students.' She stretches out her arm to shake my hand. I register her white blouse and green slacks and it dawns on me that she is wearing an occupational therapist's uniform and not some heavenly garb.

'Are you an occupational therapist?' I ask

'Of course. Aren't you one of the fourth-year students?'

'No, I'm a doctor. I was asked to give a talk on healthy eating today.'

'That's strange. Nobody told me anything about that. Most of the patients are in homes anyway, so they don't have much choice about what they eat.'

'In homes? For diabetes?' I wonder if the occupational therapist is just a new dimension of my hell.

'No, for Alzheimer's.'

'So this isn't the diabetic club?'

'No, that's in room A115. This is the Alzheimer's support group. I work with them once a week, try to motivate them a bit. The homes are good but the patients don't get much stimulation. There are too few staff, you see. Often they end up just sitting in front of a television.'

Marvellous. I have just spent the last thirty minutes trying to teach a group of Alzheimer's patients about a diabetic diet. I wonder what the diabetics are thinking about the puzzles that the fourth-year occupational therapy student is probably trying to get them to do.

I had completely forgotten about the woman who went to the toilet until I walk out of the nurses' hostel and see her outside. She is sitting on a bench, her face turned to the sun, so that the hairs sprouting from her mole glint as they catch the light. I take her hand and lead her back inside to join the rest of the group. She follows me without complaining and I wonder if she is thinking that at least she managed to wrangle half an hour of freedom.

# A guilty goodbye

It is Friday, and Justine's last day with me. I realise during the morning, when it is too late, that I probably should have organised a goodbye tea for her. I should have bought a cherry-decked chocolate cake and a platter of greasy miniature sausage rolls on toothpicks and a litre of

Coke Lite. I should have set everything up in the sisters' tearoom, asked one of the sisters to call Justine, and then shouted 'Surprise!' when she walked unsuspecting into the room. But I have done none of this, so instead I offer to buy her some coffee and a slice of cake as a goodbye token.

We walk down to the cafeteria together and I order two cups of coffee, a slice of cheesecake for me and a bran muffin for her. I wish that I had prepared something to say, a little goodbye speech to inspire her for the rest of her medical career. Instead I just tell her how much I have appreciated her help over the past few months and that I know she will do well in the future. Both are true.

She pulls out a cerise-pink packet from her bag and hands it to me.

'This is to say thank you', she says, 'for all that you've done for me. I don't think I would have survived Cape Town if it weren't for your support. I was so lonely here and you were really my only friend.'

I wonder if she is being sarcastic, if there is a snake or some other horrible surprise in the packet. A jack-in-the-box waiting to slap me in the face.

'Thanks, Justine,' I mumble. How did I miss her loneliness? Or, even worse, did I choose to ignore it? 'I'm sorry I didn't spend more time with you. If I'd known that things were so bad, I would have made more of an effort.'

'No, you were great. You're one of the best doctors I've worked with. You're always so calm and collected and hardly ever get emotional.' I want to interrupt her and tell her that it's not true, that it is all a façade that I put on to convince myself, most of all, that I am coping. I want to tell her that the reason I don't get emotional is because of weakness and not strength, but she carries on talking. 'I learnt so much from you. I was privileged to have you as my registrar.'

Donald's arrival at our table banishes my mounting tears and momentarily displaces my guilt.

'Hello, beautiful,' he says, giving me a kiss. 'May I join you?' He doesn't wait for an answer but pulls another chair up to the table and sits down. 'Who's your friend?' he asks, indicating Justine.

I introduce them and watch as Donald's eyes linger on her. For a moment I am jealous of her manicured nails and her beanpole Coke Lite figure. Donald asks Justine how her year has been and which rotation she is doing next, and I notice a blush behind her tan as she tells him that she is moving to surgery.

Instinctively I want to flirt with Donald and reclaim his attention. I know that I can. But just as I am about to lean over the table and squeeze up my cleavage, a cerise-pink flash of conscience stops me. It is, after all, only my vanity at stake.

'I am going to have to leave you two. Justine, thanks again for the present and for all your help over the past few months. I couldn't have asked for a more diligent intern.' I leave quickly, before I can change my mind.

I open the packet when I get home. The present inside is carefully wrapped and decorated with straw-coloured raffia, dried chillies and miniature guinea-fowl feathers. There is a thank-you note from Justine dangling from one of the raffia bows. She has given me a blouse, a designer-labelled top with a plunging neckline and an open back that must have cost a quarter of her salary and that will never fit me. I hope that my leaving her with Donald will somehow substitute as a gift from me.

# Chapter Twelve

## The other side of Julian

I am early for my date with Julian. We have arranged to meet at seven o'clock at a pub at the Waterfront, but I arrive at a quarter to seven. I sit down at the quayside bar and order a gin and tonic while I wait for him. It is dark already, a reminder that we are closer to winter than to summer, and the light thrown from the shops and restaurants reflects off the harbour water, scattering only when an unexpected breeze disturbs the otherwise still surface. The pub fills up quickly, mostly with tourists, so for a moment I imagine that I am alone in a foreign country. There is a rudimentary stage next to the bar, nothing more than a raised wooden platform, upon which a man has appeared. He has a guitar in his hands and he balances himself uncomfortably on a bar stool that has been moved onto the stage. He starts picking at the guitar strings until an instrumental madrigal emerges and the notes drop into the buzz of conversation, eavesdropping for a moment before drifting out to sea. It is only once the piece is finished that I remember that I am waiting for Julian. I check my watch: it is a quarter past seven. I turn around to look for him, wondering if I have been stood up, but then I see him waving to me from the end of the bar.

'What were you doing?' I ask him as he walks over and takes the seat next to me.

'Watching you.'

'For how long?' I am suddenly self-conscious. I feel as though by watching me observing the musician he has uncovered thoughts not meant to be made public.

'Only for a minute or two. You looked too engrossed to disturb. You've got a lovely profile, especially when you're concentrating. You get this little frown and your eyes crinkle up. It's very endearing.' He pulls his face into an expression that I hope is not at all similar to the way that I look when concentrating.

Julian orders a beer for each of us and then turns his attention back to me. 'I'm sorry I haven't spoken to you for so long but I've been incredibly busy at work. One of the guys went on leave and the other one was sick, so I ended up doing five calls in twelve days.'

'That's ridiculous. How did you cope?'

'Not well. I still feel like I'm sleepwalking. I think I'm going to spend the whole of this weekend in bed.'

'I know how you feel. I wish I could spend the weekend in bed but unfortunately I'm on call tomorrow night. Oh, shit!'

'What?'

'I forgot about my call tomorrow night and I arranged to meet Gina for coffee. Please remind me to phone her later to cancel.'

'Sure. Is Gina the crazy one?'

'She's not crazy, just a bit misdirected on a baseline of hypomania. I'm worried about her, though. She's drinking too much and I think she has a bit of a drug problem as well. I feel so helpless in the whole situation. I can't just book her into a rehab clinic and drag her there.'

'Maybe you should take her to see a psychiatrist.'

'I've suggested it but she's in denial. She refuses to see anyone. It's weird to think that I'm not even thirty yet and

I have a friend who's an alcoholic. It scares me. Sometimes I think that you reach a point in your life where you make the decision about which direction your behaviour is going to follow: whether it's going to mature or whether it's going to regress. I'm so scared that I've made the wrong decision, or not even that, just that I haven't made any decision.'

'Oops, perhaps you shouldn't be with me tonight.'

'Why?'

'Because I'm tired and stressed and have had a week from hell and know I'm going to drink too much.'

'Okay, let's suspend all decision-making for tonight. If I drink enough, I won't remember your behaviour tonight anyway.'

He orders a plate of hot chips and we pick at them. Soon my fingers are stained red from cheap tomato sauce and smell of vinegar. Julian is drinking quickly, has drunk more in the last hour than I think he has drunk on all of our previous dates combined. How stressed is he?

'Hey, do you play pool?' he asks.

'I haven't played pool since standard eight and pool halls were the only places that served alcohol to underage kids.'

'Well then, it's high time that you rediscovered the joy of the game.'

After the ice-skating fiasco I'm reluctant to revive another youthful pastime, but Julian doesn't give me much choice. I hope that he has drunk enough not to notice what an atrocious snooker player I am.

We find a pool hall somewhere in town, a dark, smoky bar populated with Hell's Angels and their leather-wearing girlfriends. Jukebox tunes blare out from blown speakers. We start playing pool and order shooters for the loser, which is always me, but Julian matches me drink for drink anyway. At two o'clock in the morning they kick us out. We have outlasted the chrome-and-leather gang.

We walk arm in arm down the pavement. As we pass under a street light, I notice that Julian's eyes are wide with alcohol, puppy-dog eyes under floppy hair, and I kiss him. I can taste the whisky and lime that he has been drinking. We stumble to a twenty-four-hour burger place and wolf down greasy day-old cheeseburgers and cups of burnt black coffee that are supposed to sober us up. I decide that I like Julian drunk. I decide that I like Julian.

* * *

I wake up ten minutes late for my call on Saturday morning and curse Julian for diverting me from my path to maturity. I hope that my quick shower and a touch of soap is enough to wash off my rum-scented sweat. I rush to the hospital swearing that I will never drink again. An hour into my call, the bacteria that previously colonised last night's cheeseburger establish their new home in my gut. I develop diarrhoea and have to run to the toilet between patients.

I see a woman who is complaining about heart palpitations and the sister whispers to me that she thinks that the patient has been drinking because she can smell alcohol. I agree fervently with her, look disgusted at the patient's lack of morality and pray that it is not my breath that the sister can smell. As soon as I have a break I run down to the cafeteria and buy myself two packets of chewing gum.

By midway through the call I'm convinced I am dying. I tell the sister that I have gastro, which is only a partial lie, and ask her to put up a drip on me. One litre of rehydration fluid later I am feeling well enough to feel guilty about being this hung-over while I am supposed to

ROSAMUND KENDAL

be working. I wish that my job involved something less risky than people's lives, something like packing shelves or admitting people to the gym. That I could handle; I could even smile while swiping them through the turnstile.

The paramedics bring in an unconscious man. They were called to the house by his girlfriend, who found him lying on his bed in a coma. The senior paramedic tells me that there was a packet of sleeping tablets and an empty brandy bottle next to the bed. The man still has a heartbeat and is breathing spontaneously, but he has no gag reflex to protect his airway. I need to intubate him to prevent him from aspirating his vomit and oral secretions. I check that the bulb of the laryngoscope is working, get the correct size of endotracheal tube ready and move to the head of the bed behind the patient. I tilt his head back and lift his tongue with the blade of the laryngoscope to visualise the vocal cords. The sister hands me the endotracheal tube and I smear the end with KY jelly, then introduce the tube through the cords. As the tube enters the trachea the man vomits up half a bottle of brandy stained powder-white with partially digested sleeping tablets. The smell is enough to turn my stomach even without the influence of my own alcohol poisoning. I stand holding the tube in place and concentrate on keeping the contents of my stomach from coming up.

It takes supreme effort and will-power for me to make it to the end of my twenty-four-hour call. As I walk past the sisters' office on my way out of casualty I hear one of the sisters saying my name. I slow down to listen to their conversation, petrified that they are going to report me to the medical superintendent for arriving at work in such a deplorable state. But it turns out they are discussing how diligent I am to have come to work with such a bad gastro. They could see that I was so sick, that I was almost green, but that I just carried on seeing patients. Somehow hearing this is even worse than if they were threatening to report me.

* * *

As I crawl into bed, I realise that I have forgotten to cancel my date with Gina. For the fiftieth time in the last twenty-four hours I swear that I will never touch alcohol again. I wonder how long Gina sat at the coffee shop waiting for me to arrive. I call her to apologise but her phone is off. So I leave a message on her voicemail, pleading forgiveness. How can I possibly be at the same time the most useless doctor and the worst friend ever? I would do something about my deplorable self immediately if only I could think of something other than how rotten I feel.

## A global gift

I'm still suffering from the after-effects of the cheeseburger on Monday morning. I do not have a new intern yet and I miss Justine. I miss being able to delegate drawing bloods to her, and I miss her neat green folder with its endless supply of X-ray request forms and discharge summaries. The students are in a lecture until half past ten so I struggle alone through two hours of ward work. At eleven o'clock they finally arrive and I notice that Matthew is with them. This is his first day back at work, and the first time I have seen him since his pancreatitis. I know that by now he should have got back the result of the initial follow-up HIV test, but I cannot ask him about it because the information is confidential. Most of me is too scared to want to know the result, anyway. But I do ask him how he is feeling.

'Much better, thanks. The doctor that you sent me to changed the antiretroviral medications that I was on. He thinks that I had a reaction to one of them which caused the hepatitis and pancreatitis. The nausea and vomiting has cleared up. I just can't eat greasy foods or drink any alcohol.'

I know the feeling.

'Oh,' he adds, 'the first HIV test results came back clear.'

I want to run over to him and hug him, kiss his fat cheeks. But such a move could lead to a sexual harassment case, so I just put my hand on his shoulder and tell him that I am very glad and that he must let me know if there is anything else I can do for him. I hope that he doesn't ask me to rewind time and draw the bloods on the prisoner myself. If only I could.

I go to outpatients once I have finished the work in the wards. There is a man waiting for me when I get there and, because he does not look like a patient, I wonder what he wants from me.

'Doctor!' he greets me, smiling with a familiarity that suggests I should recognise him. His skin is very dark, and in the dim light of the corridor all that I can make out clearly are his shiny white teeth.

'Doctor, hello.' He speaks with an accent that I cannot initially place.

'Can I help you?' I ask.

'Mr Mohammed,' he prompts.

As soon as he has said his name, I recognise him – the malaria patient from Somalia. He's wearing smart trousers, incongruous with his open leather sandals, and a long-sleeved linen shirt, not tucked in and hanging loose on his lanky frame. He looks very different out of his hospital gown.

'You can speak English?' I ask.

'Small English, small English.' He smiles. 'Gift for thank you for Doctor,' he says and hands me a small globe. It is a perfectly scaled-down replica of the world revolving on its axis. And so unexpected that I am lost for words.

'How are you feeling now?' I resort to being the doctor again, because it is familiar. I am not used to patients coming back to thank me and I don't know how to react. He tells me that he is studying now. He received a bursary for the University of the Western Cape and he is doing a Bachelor of Commerce degree. He tells me that he already has a degree but he must also get one here, from a South African university, so that he can get a job. He is one of the lucky ones, he says, because he managed to get a bursary. Most of his friends, some of them even better qualified than him, cannot get jobs or bursaries. Most of them are still working as car guards. It makes me wonder how many university-qualified car guards I have tipped.

I play with the globe when I get home. He has written his name, followed by his degree in brackets, in green pen on a little piece of paper that is pasted to the base of the globe. I spin the sphere around and guess the capital cities of countries: Hungary, Budapest; Peru, Lima; Sri Lanka, Colombo. I swing it to Africa and look for Somalia. Somalia, Mogadishu. It is infinitely far from Cape Town, a distance greater than can be measured in kilometres. I can't conceive of having to travel it, can't comprehend the immensity of the longing for another place. I do not want to imagine what the conditions were that forced Mr Mohammed to leave his home to come to Cape Town. He is thirty-four. Isn't that too old to have to start life over again?

I keep the globe on my desk, not only because it is, relatively speaking, one of the most valuable gifts I have ever received, but because it reminds me that sometimes I actually do make a difference.

## The engagement party

Leah has organised a belated engagement party for Thursday night, which means that I will have to miss my philosophy lecture. She couldn't have the party any sooner because she was waiting for her parents, who live in Port Elizabeth, to come to Cape Town. In a way, I'm glad that I will be missing the philosophy class because I still haven't come to terms with the goodness of mankind and I don't feel it's fair for me to force my cynicism on Carol. I hope that by next week either a miracle will have happened to change my view on humanity or Mrs De Marigny will have moved on to a different topic.

I have taken the next step in my relationship with Julian and invited him to the engagement party. Consequently I am as nervous as Leah is about the evening. Introductions imply a permanency that I have not been ready for until now. The guests are supposed to arrive at half past seven, and from six o'clock onwards Leah and I wander around the house rearranging cushions and straightening trays of eats that are already straight. I pour us glasses of champagne and we have finished a bottle and are far more relaxed by the time that the first guests arrive.

I am speaking to Leah's elderly Aunt Mary when Julian arrives. If I lean to the side and look past Aunt Mary's large girth, I can see him standing at the doorway scanning the room for me. But every time that I try to escape from the aunt's company, she thinks of another very pressing medical concern about which she needs my advice. We rush through mercury poisoning, which I guarantee her is far less common than the media suggest;

malaria, which I assure her she is unlikely to have picked up at the airport; and her constipation, which I suggest she change her diet to improve. By now I am panicking that Julian is going to leave. Eventually I give up being polite and run to the door to rescue him, leaving Aunt Mary explaining her incontinence to a rather baffled colleague of Leah's. Julian has brought Leah a bottle of wine from his father's farm, which I can see makes a good impression on her, and I start to relax. I go to the kitchen to pour a glass of champagne for Julian, and by the time I get back to the lounge Gina has cornered him.

I can see immediately that there is something wrong with her. Her pupils are dilated, big black discs floating in her blue eyes. She is jittery and plays with the plaited silver ring on her middle finger. It falls to the ground and she bends down to pick it up, flashing a pink G-string from below the hem of her tiny miniskirt.

'Gina, did you get my message about Saturday? I'm so sorry, I feel awful about it,' I say as I walk up to her. She ignores me. 'This is Julian, the doctor from Paarl Hospital. The one that I told you about.' I try again to make conversation but she shifts to her right so that I am excluded from her and Julian's little circle. She is standing too close to him.

'I know, we've met,' she says and her tone of voice makes my stomach tighten. 'I always make a point of introducing myself to the most gorgeous man at a party.' Julian blushes and looks down. At least he has the decency to pretend he is uncomfortable with Gina's attention. 'Sue, won't you be an absolute darling and get me another drink?' Gina shoves her empty glass into my hand.

I don't want to get her another drink. I want to tell her to get away from Julian and to grow up. But I don't, because I still feel guilty about letting her down on Saturday night. I leave, not to get her a drink but to escape. I stand no chance with Julian if Gina has made up her mind to charm him. I don't know if she is behaving as she is because she's pissed off with me or because she is doped up or both. I watch her from across the room. She touches Julian at every opportunity. Twice he moves away from her and she follows him, sticking out her chest to show off her pert, expensive breasts. I sit down on the arm of the couch and down the glass of wine that was supposed to be for Gina. It gives me heartburn and I suddenly feel old. Leah is talking to one of her friends and fragments of their conversation filter into my consciousness.

'The wedding is planned for the end of December but we still need to finalise a date,' Leah says.

'And will you move into John's place then?' the friend asks.

'Well, we're planning to buy a new place together. We've been looking but we haven't seen anything that we like or can afford yet.'

And for the first time, the full implications of Leah's engagement dawn on me. By the end of the year I will no longer have a housemate. I will be left alone in our little semi-detached house. I will be forced to buy a cat for company, and before I know it I will have become the proverbial spinster with her cat. Scenes from my future flash before me. I see myself babysitting Leah and John's children. I have become Aunty Sue. I see Gina and Julian's wedding. I am not invited. I see myself knitting little yellow jerseys for my cat.

I have drunk too much. I run to the bathroom and lock the door, splash cold water on my face and take deep breaths to stop myself from crying. I cannot make a scene now, not on Leah's special night. The cold water has made my mascara run and I grab a piece of toilet paper to wipe

THE KARMA SUTURE

the black streaks off my cheeks. I manage only to smear them even more so that they start to resemble Maori warpaint. Someone knocks on the door.

'Busy!' I shout.

'Sue, are you okay?'

Oh God, it's Julian. Why couldn't it have been incontinent Aunt Mary knocking at the door?

'I'm fine. I'll be out in a moment.' I try to control the tremble in my voice.

'Please come out. I need to talk to you.'

'I said I'm coming.' I flush the toilet and open the door, look down so that Julian won't notice my blotchy face and puffy eyes.

'Thanks for just disappearing and leaving me with that crazy friend of yours. I couldn't get away from her,' he says.

'She's not crazy, just high.'

'I thought she was going to try and kiss me. She couldn't keep her hands to herself.'

'Most men wouldn't complain.' The tremble has reappeared.

'Look up, Sue, I can't hear what you're saying.' He gently lifts my chin, forcing me to expose my puffy eyes and warpaint mascara.

'Leah is leaving and Gina is so thin and beautiful that you're going to fall in love with her and I'm going to end up growing old with just a cat with yellow jerseys to keep me company.' I listen to myself snivelling and want to run into the bathroom and lock the door and never come out. I wonder if other almost-thirty-year-old women also have outbursts of teenage behaviour.

Julian puts his arms around me and kisses the top of my head. 'Don't be silly,' he says. 'I ended up telling Gina that I have scabies so that she'd leave me alone. I don't even know if she knows what scabies is but it seemed to work.'

I can't help giggling and Julian starts laughing and then I am laughing and crying and I lose track of which tears are from laughter and which are from sadness.

'Come, let's go somewhere else,' he says, grabbing my hand and leading me to the door. 'There's a really nice coffee shop that I know of in Observatory that plays wonderfully depressing jazz from scratched LPs and serves espressos until three o'clock in the morning. It's just what you need, I promise. I'm sure your friends won't even notice that you've gone. Anyway, who wants an old spinster hanging around at their party?'

# Chapter Thirteen

## The chirping of Cape sparrows

Stellenbosch Hospital is one of my favourite hospitals to work in, purely because of its architectural beauty. It is an old building, with wooden sash windows and high beamed ceilings. Built in an era in which people still believed in the healing power of nature, when things like sanatoriums were popular, the wards all open out onto long, sun-facing balconies. The gardens were once landscaped but are even more magical now that they are wild and overgrown, bearing only a hint of their previous order. The doctors' room is on the ground floor and opens out onto a small veranda. I am standing on the veranda, trying not to get drunk on the night-time scent of lavender and fiddlewood, when a sister calls me to the resuscitation room.

Thus far it has been strangely quiet for a Friday night. I reach the resuscitation room as the paramedics wheel in the stretcher. One of them starts speaking to me.

'Twenty-year-old man involved in an MVA on the R300. High-impact collision. A guy speeding in the opposite direction lost control of his car and skidded across into oncoming traffic. He hit this guy first and then another car. The patient was unconscious on arrival. Glasgow Coma Scale score was three out of fifteen. Pupils were reacting only very sluggishly. He's bleeding from his right ear and has a large haematoma on the back of his head. Obviously we immobilised his spine. He also has an open femur fracture on the left. We couldn't find any ID on him, so we don't know if he has medical aid. We brought him here because this was the nearest hospital.'

The other paramedic interrupts the one speaking to me. 'Can we move him across, please? I need to clean the spinal board; we have another call.'

We all need to help move the patient from the stretcher to the bed because we need to keep him immobilised until we have done X-rays. Until X-rays show otherwise, we presume there is a spinal fracture. We line up at the bed and logroll the patient off the spinal board and onto the bed. Once he is positioned correctly, I start to examine him more thoroughly. Although he is breathing spontaneously, the paramedics have intubated him to protect his airway. His breathing is irregular, alternating between shallow and deep breaths and at a rate of only eight breaths a minute. I tell the sister to attach a bag to the endotracheal tube and start ventilating the patient. I quickly listen over the lungs to make sure that the tube is placed properly. The fact that the patient is not breathing normally is a bad sign, an indicator of brainstem damage. I move up from the chest to examine the head injury.

'Sister, please get a hard collar and our head blocks. The paramedics will need theirs.' The sister nods at me and fetches the hospital head blocks and a stiff collar to immobilise the neck. I stabilise the patient's head and neck while the sister removes the bright orange head blocks between which the patient's head is sandwiched. She exposes the patient's face and my heartbeat suddenly deafens me. I feel myself retching. It's Carl, one of my brother's best friends.

'Please, come and take his head!' I shout to one of the paramedics. He rushes over to me and I carefully place the patient's head in his hands, without moving the spine. I grab the side of the resuscitation bed to stop myself from falling over. All I can see are his shoulder-length blond curls matted with blood. I remember him telling me that he and my brother had made a pact to grow their hair as soon as they finished matric. The other paramedic is still talking and his voice floats past me.

'The guy that caused the accident seems to be okay. Just a few minor injuries. The other guy that he hit was DOA. I don't even want to know how fast he must have been going. I reckon probably around one-eighty. A new beemer, now a write-off. All the cars are a write-off.'

I want to ask him if there was anyone else in the car with this boy, with the patient, but I can't seem to find the right words.

'Doctor, are you all right?' the sister asks me. 'Quickly,' she turns to the staff nurse, 'she's going to faint. Hold her!'

'No, I'm fine.' I hear my voice but don't remember making a conscious effort to speak. My knuckles are aching from gripping the bedside. I turn to the paramedic.

'Was there anyone else in the car with him?' I ask urgently, almost aggressively. 'Did he have any passengers?'

'No, he was alone.'

Thank God, Joe was not in the car with him.

'Doctor, are you sure you're okay?' the sister asks me again.

'I'm fine, I'll be all right.'

I pull a light from the set mounted on the wall and check Carl's pupils. They do not react at all. He has been friends with my brother since they started high school together. He was a boarder whose family lived in Stellenbosch, and he used to spend at least one weekend a month at my parents' house. The sisters are cutting off his clothes, suctioning the tube in his throat, putting in a urine catheter. My body functions on automatic. I shout out instructions: drugs to be given, X-rays to be taken, blood and fluids to be transfused. I am glad that I am experienced enough to act mechanically because my mind is going crazy. Every time I look at Carl's face I see him playing water polo in my parents' swimming pool or watching MTV on their television or making himself peanut butter and apricot jam sandwiches in the kitchen. And then I cannot let my thoughts wander any more because my mind is flashing red lights, telling me that he is dying and I need to focus everything I have on saving his life. I know the signs. I know that when he was brought in, it was probably already too late. His injured brain has swollen too much inside the hard skull bone. It is herniating downwards, through the only opening there is, where the spinal column exits the skull. And the brainstem, the part of the brain that controls all of the vital functions, is being crushed. I give every drug that has any chance of working, phone the neurosurgeon on call at Bellville Hospital for advice, ventilate Carl with restrained tears choking me. I know that we have been resuscitating for too long, far longer than the usual thirty minutes that I give, but I cannot stop. Though I am exhausted and I can see that the sisters are waiting for me to terminate the resuscitation, I can't bring myself to say the words. I don't want to make his death real.

After an hour and a half, I know that I have to give up. There is nothing more that I can do, that anyone can do. I want to curl up in a ball on the floor and cry until there is nothing left inside me. I want to escape from the hospital and the blood and the pain. I never want to see another patient again. But I cannot run away because I still need to speak to Carl's parents. They are sleeping peacefully in bed, unaware that their son is dead. I tell the clerk Carl's surname and she looks up his parents' number in the telephone book. Nobody asks me how I know his surname. I hold back my tears because I need to be lucid when I speak to Carl's parents. I have met his mother before and I remember vaguely what she looks like: she has the same blond curls as Carl. I imagine her sleeping in bed, pyjama-clad with no make-up on, lying next to her sleeping husband. I don't want to wake them up. I want to prolong handing them this moment that will change their lives forever. I want to let them sleep peacefully a little longer.

The phone rings five times before it is answered, a man's voice, gruff from sleep. I ask the voice if he is Carl's father, tell him that his son has been involved in a car accident and that he and his wife need to get to hospital as soon as possible. I tell him that yes, it is serious, and that I cannot discuss it further with him over the telephone. I do not tell him that his son is dead.

Carl's parents arrive fifteen minutes later, jeans and jackets over their pyjamas, hair unbrushed. His mother is pale, too distraught to recognise me, and I do not remind her. There is no official mourning room, so I take them to one of the examination rooms to tell them the news. There is too little space and we squeeze uncomfortably between the bed and the desk. It is five o'clock in the morning, still dark, but the birds have already started singing outside, pre-empting the dawn. Against the background of chirping sparrows, I tell Carl's parents that their son is dead. All that I notice of their response is a kind of inward collapse, a sudden fragility, as though their son's death has made real their own mortality. The wife clings to her husband, shrinks into him, until they seem as delicate as the sparrows outside the window.

* * *

There are twenty patients waiting for me when I get back from speaking to Carl's parents. They are the usual Friday-night casualties, the targets of drunken stabbings, and all are stable enough to wait ten more minutes. I beg a cigarette from one of the sisters and go back to the veranda off the doctors' room to smoke it. I try to blot the image of blood-clotted curls from my mind, try not to think about what this weekend will be like for Carl's parents. I tell myself over and over again that I did the best that I could, that anyone could, and that there was nothing more that could be done for him. I try to get drunk on cigarette smoke and the night scent of lavender and fiddlewood.

I go straight to bed when I get home after my shift but I cannot sleep. I toss and turn and crumple my sheets until they are wrapped around me like a shroud. I know that I should speak to my brother, but every time I pick up my phone to dial his number I think of excuses not to press the green 'call' button. I don't have the strength to go through last night again, even if it is only verbally. I will not be able to handle someone else's grief on top of my own. I want to banish the images of last night from my mind, forget those few hours forever. I never want to hear sparrows chirp again.

\* \* \*

I have arranged to meet Carol for coffee on Sunday morning, and by the time I remember the arrangement, it is too late to cancel. At least she didn't know Carl, so I can pretend that Friday night never happened.

The coffee shop where we have agreed to meet is in Rondebosch, a distance compromise between our two houses. I have never been to the place before, it was Carol's suggestion, and when I walk in I am surprised to find big, comfortable couches in place of the usual hard coffee-shop chairs and tables. Mingled with the aroma of coffee are the scents of cocoa and spices – cloves and cardamom, I think. There are board games stacked on a table: Monopoly, Cluedo, Trivial Pursuit, Jenga.

Carol is already sitting on one of the couches and waves at me. I go and sit down beside her. She looks thinner than when I saw her last, more haggard, and I ask her if she is feeling all right. She assures me that she just has a cold and that the chemo is going fine. She doesn't sound convincing, but when I try to probe the issue she changes the topic.

The teenage couple next to us are hunched over a Scrabble board. I can see the girl's letters and I whisper them to Carol and we try to make words for her. I order some hot chocolate and Carol orders chai tea, which is, she tells me, the origin of the clove and cardamom scent. The girl plays a four-letter word instead of one of the three possible six-letter ones that we thought up for her and I start crying. Somewhere between the hot chocolate and the Scrabble, Carl slipped into my mind. I have the weirdest thought that he will never again drink hot chocolate or play Scrabble. It makes no sense; I don't even know if he liked hot chocolate or Scrabble. I try to hide my tears by blowing my nose because I don't want to tell Carol what I am crying about, but the more I blow, the more the tears stream down my cheeks.

'Is it normal to become more emotional as you get older?' I ask Carol as she hands me a serviette. 'I never used to cry when I was younger. Now it seems to be a daily event. I'm beginning to think there's something wrong with me.'

'I know how you feel,' she says.

'Yes, but at least you have a reason to cry.' The words are out of my mouth before I realise what I'm saying. I cringe and wait for her to join me crying. Or to get up and leave.

'I'm sure you also have good reason to be upset,' she says calmly, as though I have not just made the most insensitive comment possible. 'Do you want to talk about it?'

'No, not really.' I don't want to talk about it. Not to Carol, not to anyone. And for some reason, perhaps because of the couple sitting next to us, or perhaps because I don't know whether anyone could ever understand what I experienced on Friday night, I tell Carol about Kevin and our break-up. I explain to her how he never understood me, how he would forbid me to tell him about my day because it would upset him too much. I tell her how he couldn't comprehend that, even though I officially finished work at four o'clock, I couldn't just leave at four o'clock if there were still patients that needed my attention. I describe how he would expect me to be able to cook supper for him when I arrived home after thirty-plus hours in the hospital. I tell her how I could not get out of a call one weekend so he went to Hermanus with another girl.

'His parting words to me were that I was never there for him,' I say into the crumpled serviette. 'I suppose I wasn't, really. He broke off the engagement and moved in with the girl two weeks later. I think she was nineteen. I still loved him. A year after he left me I would probably still have taken him back if he'd asked.' And because telling her this makes me cry, I don't have to tell her the real reason that I am crying.

Carol is the first person that I have spoken to about my failed engagement. She is the first person to whom I have acknowledged the hurt that it left within me. I realise that since then I have built a wall around myself and conned myself into thinking that it can protect me. Each time I've been hurt, I've added another brick to the wall, making it stronger and more impenetrable. And in the process I have shut out not only the pain, but also the good. It dawns on me that the only way I will ever be able to find the good again is by having the courage to break down the wall.

## The decline and fall of Gina

It is already the beginning of winter, but it has been so long since it last rained in Cape Town that it takes me a moment after waking to recognise the scent of wet earth that blows in through my open window. Leah has risen early and is busy stirring a pot of oatmeal when I walk into the kitchen. It is the one dish that she can prepare to perfection. She spoons some into a bowl for me and I sit down at the kitchen table and dot the oats with sugar and butter. Rain patters loudly on the corrugated iron roof as the drizzle turns into a downpour.

'Have you decided on a wedding date yet?' I ask. The rain has made me happy; this morning I am strong enough to broach the topic.

'Most likely the ninth of December. By the way, will you be my bridesmaid?'

'Only if you promise me a gorgeous groomsman.'

'What about Julian? Don't you like him? I thought he was very nice and he's obviously besotted with you.'

'What do you mean?'

'I mean that he couldn't take his eyes off you the whole evening of my engagement party. He obviously adores you.'

'I hope so. I like him a lot too.' I am too scared to say more in case I jinx the relationship, so I tell Leah that I will be her bridesmaid and that I have to rush because I am late for work again.

\* \* \*

I still have not got an intern to replace Justine and so I have to work hard to get the ward work finished. I started Lindiwe on treatment for cryptococcal meningitis a few days ago and she has responded dramatically to the therapy. Cryptococcus is a fungal infection, not a usual cause of meningitis except in the immuno-compromised. She waves to me as I walk into the ward, lucid enough now to recognise me. The aunt is visiting and has brought the baby with her, and so far Lindiwe has not tried to eat him. I hope that I will be able to discharge her soon.

I move on to the next patient, a man I admitted a week ago with an endocarditis. I tell him that I have got his blood-culture results back.

'What's a blood culture?' he asks.

Usually I use the words 'blood culture' glibly, but something in his intonation makes me stop to think about what the words actually imply. For a moment I am disgusted. 'Do you remember that blood sample we took from you a few days ago?' I ask him. He nods. 'We took that blood and injected it into a culture medium, which is really like a bowl of nutrients, and waited for the bacteria in the blood to replicate enough for us to distinguish individual colonies. The colonies that grew are like the extended families of the bacteria colonising your heart valve. Now that we've found out which bacteria are causing the infection on your heart valves, we can treat it properly, with the correct antibiotics.'

'What bacteria was it?'

'I'll write the names down for you; they're too long to say. But don't worry about the bacteria. The important thing is that now we're able to treat the infection much more specifically and aggressively, so you'll get better sooner.'

I write the names of the bacteria on a piece of paper and give it to him. He folds the paper up carefully and stores it in the drawer next to his bed, in much the same way that I have seen surgery patients do with their gallstones. It is as though by having a concrete cause for his illness, he is better able to deal with it. For the rest of the morning the names of the bacteria run through my mind over and over until they start to sound like a children's nursery rhyme: *Kingella kingae, Cardiobacterium hominis, Acinetobacillus actinomycetemcomitans.*

At midday Donald calls me on my cellphone. He phones from a landline and I don't recognise the number; if I had, I wouldn't have answered.

'Just wondering, if you aren't too busy, if I can tempt you with lunch? On me, of course,' he says.

'Sorry, there's absolutely no chance that I'll be able to leave the hospital before five this evening.' I use the excuse of not having an intern.

'Then dinner again sometime?' he persists.

I know that I have to take the plunge and that this is the decisive moment, the right moment, the moment that if I do not take, I will later curse myself for bypassing.

'No, I don't think so. I'm kind of seeing someone.'

'Oh.' I can hear that Donald is put out. 'Anyone I know?'

'I doubt it.'

'Well, if you change your mind, you've got my number.'

I want to end things amicably. It makes working in the same hospital more pleasant. 'Thanks for the dinner and the movie,' I say. 'I enjoyed both of them. If you're ever sitting alone in the cafeteria desperate for a coffee mate, give me a shout.' I know that he won't. Donald is not the type of man who ends up sitting alone, especially not with a female-intern fan club anywhere in the vicinity.

I phone Julian after speaking to Donald. I suppose it is to reassure myself that I have done the right thing. I don't tell him about Donald. Instead, I blab on about how disgusting blood cultures actually are when you think about them properly. He tells me about an ex-girlfriend of his who was studying microbiology and grew a fungal colony from a swab that she took from her ear, and then assures me that they broke up soon after that.

'What kind of person cultivates their own fungal colonies?' I ask, laughing.

'I don't know,' he says. 'She was rather odd in many respects.'

'Do you always pick strange girlfriends?' I ask.

'Well, so far you haven't displayed too much abnormal behaviour. Any secrets that I should know about?' he asks.

I can't help smiling. He called me girlfriend.

\* \* \*

My call is busy. The change in weather is causing all the asthma and emphysema patients to get acute exacerbations and I end up nebulising every second patient that I see. Even my chest is slightly tight. By ten o'clock in the evening I have reiterated the adverse effects of smoking so many times that I think I have convinced myself never to touch a cigarette again. I get a voicemail from Julian, saying that he is at a whisky festival with some friends and that he wishes I could be there with him. Later I get an SMS from him, misspelt words hinting at the volume of whisky tasted, telling me that I am amazing and that he misses me.

My phone rings at midnight, while I am busy seeing a woman with stomach cramps, and I excuse myself and answer because I am sure that it is a drunk Julian calling me. But it is Gina. I have forgiven her for flirting with Julian because I still feel bad about missing my coffee date with her. The telephone connection is bad and I struggle to make out what she is saying.

'My dad's new girlfriend has moved in with him. I can't handle it.' I hear her blow her nose.

'I'm sorry, Gina.'

'She's four years younger than me. A real blond bimbo. She's after his money, I know. I can tell it from a mile away, but his ego is so bloody big that he believes she's actually attracted to him.' I can hear that she is drunk. Her voice always gets a nasal intonation when she has been drinking and she speaks too loudly.

'Listen Gina, I'm on call right now so it's difficult to talk. Do you want to go for coffee tomorrow night? I promise I won't forget.' My patient is rolling around on the bed, trying to get my attention.

'Sue, I just can't handle this. My life's falling apart. My mom is in a major depression and every time I go home to see her she spends the entire time sobbing. She looks awful. She's put on about twenty kilograms and has stopped colouring her hair and her roots are all grey. I've told her to see a psychologist but she refuses.'

My patient has started crying.

'Gina, I have to go. I'm on call and I've got a patient here. I'll speak to you tomorrow.'

'No, please don't go. I don't know what to do. I can't cope with this.'

She is drunk and hysterical and I know that I won't be able to reason with her. My patient is screaming and rolling around so much that I fear she will fall off the bed and then I will have to deal with her head injury as well as stomach cramps. I tell Gina to wait at home and not to do anything stupid; I will phone Leah and ask her to go spend the night with Gina. I quickly feel my patient's stomach and then send her to the toilet to collect a urine sample for me, which seems to appease her a little. Nothing like a bit of attention for good analgesia. While the patient is in the bathroom I call Leah and explain the situation to her, and by the time my patient comes back I am off the phone and waiting to test her urine.

The dipstick shows the presence of blood in the urine. I tell the patient that she most likely has kidney stones and give her an intravenous anti-spasmodic and opiate for pain. After fifteen minutes she is fast asleep and I phone Leah to find out if Gina is okay. She tells me that Gina was lying passed out in the bath with the door of her apartment open when she arrived.

\* \* \*

The Gina saga has exhausted me emotionally and I am glad that there are no more patients waiting for me. I go to the doctors' room to try to get some sleep, but as I open the door I am hit by a terrible stench. I gag, cover my nose with my jersey and turn on the light, expecting to see a dead body on the doctors' bed. The cause of the smell is not that immediately obvious, however, so I start searching. I check underneath the bed, empty the rubbish bin and remove a plastic container of half-eaten chicken from behind the fridge, but the smell remains. I decide, as one last option before giving up and forgoing sleep for the night, to try the desk drawer. It takes me a while to figure out that the green thing sticking to the bottom of the drawer was once a tuna sandwich. I fetch a pair of gloves from the unit and try to pick it up. It crumbles and the stink worsens. I try again and succeed only in smearing the mould over even more of the drawer base. It is half past three in the morning. I am tired, worried about my friend, half deaf from a patient's screaming, and on the verge of vomiting from the smell of a rotten sandwich. I dislodge the entire drawer from the desk and throw it into one of the big metal bins in the sluice room. Tomorrow it will be incinerated with the rest of the hospital waste.

* * *

I have had fifteen minutes of sleep when the sister raps at the door of the doctors' room to call me to see a new patient. It is a young woman in her early twenties. She is sitting on the edge of the bed waiting for me.

'What's the problem?' I ask her. I'm sure that it must be something serious to have brought her into hospital at four o'clock in the morning, especially since it is pouring with rain outside.

'I've got a dry mouth,' she says.

I wonder if I have heard correctly.

'You have a dry mouth?'

'Yes.'

Nothing wrong with my hearing, apparently.

'Have you got any other symptoms?'

'No, I just have a dry mouth.'

'When did the dry mouth start?'

'Two weeks ago.'

She has come in to hospital at four o'clock in the morning, in the pouring rain, for a dry mouth that she has had for two weeks. I am too baffled even to be cross.

'Why did you come in now?' I ask, trying to fathom her logic.

'Because of my dry mouth.'

'Yes, I know, but why now? Did it suddenly get drier?'

'No, it is still the same dryness.'

'So you just decided that the time to come to hospital for your dry mouth that you have had for two weeks and that has not suddenly got any worse is four o'clock in the morning?'

'Yes.' She nods.

'Good thinking,' I say. 'We all know just how dangerous a dry mouth can be at four o'clock in the morning.'

'Really?' she asks.

Perhaps my choosing this job means that I am as crazy as she is.


## An undesirable ending to a (slightly) more successful dinner date

Leah and Gina are going to watch a movie together, so I have the house to myself. I phone Julian and invite him to dinner. He accepts immediately, despite the short notice, and promises to bring a good bottle of wine.

I briefly toy with the idea of cooking a meal myself and then remember that I am post-call and therefore have a very valid excuse to buy a meal from Woolworths. At half past six in the evening I pop a pre-cooked lasagne into the oven, set the table, light some candles and walk through the house waving a stick of 'Sensual Secrets' incense like a magic wand. Once I have scented all of the rooms, I leave the incense burning on the lounge window sill. I hope that it will live up to its name.

When Julian knocks on the door at seven o'clock, I am the very image of the perfect 1950s housewife: dressed and made up, my lounge clean and a bowl of lasagne on the table. I say a silent prayer of gratitude to Woolworths for pre-cooked meals. Julian has kept his promise and I pour us each a glass of deep purple-red cabernet sauvignon.

'Wow, I'm impressed!' he says, looking around the lounge.

'Why?'

'I didn't realise that you were so domesticated.'

'The domesticity is very superficial.'

'What do you mean?'

'Well, the underwear I'm wearing is decidedly un-housewifely.' I didn't plan to advertise my sexy new underwear right at the beginning of the evening; the line just somehow popped out. I cringe and Julian blushes and for a moment I think I have ruined the evening, but then his arms are around me.

'I'll have to see for myself,' he says. The situation is saved.

We stumble over each other onto the couch. His hair smells of apple sherbet. He undoes the buttons of my shirt and kisses his way from my breasts to my navel, then down over the curve of my stomach to my hips. He slips his hand up my skirt and traces imagined patterns on the skin of my inner thigh. I push him away and wriggle out of my clothes, then lift his arms up and pull off his T-shirt. I undo his jeans and rub my hand against the hardness of his erection. I can feel blood rushing to my pelvis. I pull him closer to me. I want no space between us. I want every exposed millimetre of my skin touching his. I want him inside me, need him inside me. My chest closes up.

'I can't breathe,' I gasp.

'What?' Julian mumbles. He is on top of me, his mouth on my nipple, too distracted to have heard me. Why not with Eric Freemantle? God, I can't be too old even for sex.

'Stop! I can't breathe!' I shout. I push him off me, jump up and wheeze my way to my bedroom. I search frantically through my drawers for my asthma pump and curse 'Sensual Secrets' incense. Eventually I find the pump in the side pocket of my gym bag.

'Are you okay?' Julian is standing at my bedroom door,

naked, worried, gorgeous.

'Asthma,' I pant. I shake the pump and inhale twice and my chest opens up enough for me to string words together.

'I'm sorry, my chest closed up,' I explain. 'It hasn't happened for ages. My asthma is usually so well controlled.'

'Do you need a neb?' Julian asks and I shake my head.

'I'm all right.' All right is relative, however. I'm alive, but what should have been the most perfect night of my sorry life up to this point is a wreck.

'It wasn't something that I did, was it?' Julian asks.

'No, it was a combination of the weather and the incense, I think. So much for trying to create a romantic mood.' I take two more puffs of my inhaler. I am sure that Julian is ready to run away, that my chances with him are ruined. I have probably scared him off sex with me forever.

'Well, I like the underwear,' he says. 'Next time you can leave out the incense and just bank on the lingerie creating the mood.' Suddenly I see light at the end of the tunnel. There will be a next time.

After Julian has left, I notice that in our brief cavorting the nail polish from my toenail has rubbed off on the wall above the couch. A thin crimson streak two centimetres long. I decide not to wipe it off.

# Chapter Fourteen

## Beauty redefined

Carol arrives late for philosophy class, and when she walks into the room I notice that she has lost even more weight. She sits down on the edge of the semicircle so that the red velvet curtain forms a backdrop to her face. It makes her look as pale and fragile as a porcelain doll. I struggle to concentrate on the lecture because I keep wondering if she is okay. I go over to her as soon as the lecture is finished.

'Carol, do you want to grab a cup of coffee quickly? I know a coffee shop five minutes away.'

She hesitates for a moment before agreeing.

The coffee shop is warm, busy and loud. Under-age teenagers try to order cocktails from harassed waiters. I recognise the smell of the place from my days of waitressing: the blend of cigarette smoke, over-brewed coffee and cooking food. We sit down at a small table in the far corner of the non-smoking section, where it is relatively quiet. I order a coffee but Carol sticks to her rooibos tea.

'Coffee makes me nauseous,' she says. 'I think it's the chemo. Do you know how much I wish now that I had drunk coffee when I could? All that trying to be healthy, so silly. I would kill for a cup these days. I get so cross thinking of all the times that I refused cups of coffee. Crazy, isn't it?'

I smile. 'Well, I'm finding it more and more difficult to define crazy. Sometimes I think that crazy is entirely dependent on one's point of reference.' I take a sip of my coffee. It is lukewarm and weak but I don't complain. 'Are you okay, Carol?'

'Not really. This is the worst that I've felt since I was diagnosed. My hair is falling out in chunks. Look.' She dips her head forward and I see scalp shining through her thinning blond hair. 'I'm even losing my eyelashes. I look so ugly, like a white rat. And I'm nauseous, Sue, all the time.'

'Have you told your oncologist?'

'Yes, he gave me another set of tablets and a patch that I can wear on my arm but it doesn't help. I've got this pain in my chest too. Right here.' She points to the centre of her chest. 'It's there all the time and it's getting worse. I know that I'm probably just imagining it, but crying seems to alleviate the pain a little. Sometimes I think that it's the pain of my heart breaking. Now you must really think I'm crazy.'

'No, not at all. Has the oncologist done a chest X-ray or ECG or anything else to investigate the pain?'

'No, I haven't told him about it. I'm too scared to. I'm too scared that it will show that the cancer is back.'

'Carol, you must tell him. Please. When are you seeing him again?'

'Next week.'

'Please tell him about the pain then, or try to make an earlier appointment with him. That would be even better.' I'm scared too, of what the X-ray will show. Chemo shouldn't cause chest pain, not unless it has damaged her heart. I am worried that the lymphoma is resistant to the chemotherapy and has grown and that this is what is causing the pain. And I know that this is the same thing that Carol is afraid of. Though I have almost finished my coffee, Carol has not touched her tea. I ask her if she is too nauseous to drink it.

'No, I have to wait for it to cool down a little bit. Otherwise it burns my mouth. Look here,' she says, lifting her upper lip. Her gums are swollen and bleeding, with thick white plaques peeling off them. Severe oral candidiasis.

'Carol, how long has your mouth been like that?' I ask. My coffee is suddenly not quite as appealing, not when she is unable to drink.

'A week or so. I told the oncologist and he gave me a mouthwash and some lozenges. They haven't helped much.'

I look down, stare into my coffee. I am worried that the expression on my face will reveal my fears.

'I'm dying, Sue. I can feel it. I'm so scared. I don't want to die yet. I'm too young. There's still too much that I want to do. I want to get married and have children. I want to see the clivia I planted last year bloom. That isn't asking much, is it? I don't even know if I'll make it to September.'

'Carol, you aren't dying. It's just the chemo that's making you feel like this.' But she ignores me.

'I haven't told my fiancé. I pretend that everything is okay. I pretend to get ready for work in the morning, and then when he has left the house I crawl back into bed. I wear three layers of clothes, even to bed, so that he can't see how thin I am. I tell him that I feel too sick for sex. At least that's true. I haven't been to my spa in over a week. For all I know, it could have closed down. The worst thing is that I don't even care. Nothing seems to matter any more except the fact that I am dying. And when I try to be philosophical about my situation, instead of so self-pitying, I realise that I don't even know if I believe in an

217

afterlife. What if this is it? What if this is the end? Do you know how often I wish that I had been brought up in a religious family? At least then I would have something to look forward to.'

'I want to speak to your oncologist, Carol. I want to find out what's going on. Do you mind? I can't let you go on like this. We'll sort it out. I'm sure that these are all just side-effects of the chemo. You are going to get through this, okay? No more talk about dying. Look at you, you are far from dying. You are a beautiful, beautiful woman.'

And now I know what the philosophy lecturer was trying to tell us about beauty, because to the casual observer Carol would appear skeletal and balding with swollen, bleeding gums.

## Security checkpoint

Because I still have no intern, I am kept busy with ward work until well after lunch, and the first opportunity that I get to phone Carol's oncologist is at three o'clock. I introduce myself to him and explain that I am a friend of hers and that I am finding it difficult to support her without knowing exactly what is going on. I have had a few patients that have come to see me with doctor relatives in tow and I know how irritating it can be, so I make it clear to the oncologist that I am not questioning Carol's management but am just trying to find out how she is and what else can be done for her. He tells me that he is worried about Carol because she has not responded as well as he had hoped to the first course of chemotherapy and that he has had to put her on stronger drugs. He mentions names but they are medications that I have never heard of before and that, unless I decide to specialise in oncology, I will probably never hear of again. I tell him I think Carol is depressed and he says he will put her on antidepressants at her next visit. Eventually I pluck up the courage to ask him what her prognosis is, but he is non-committal. I don't push him for an answer, because I know that, were I in his position, I would also be vague. Medicine is far from an exact science. It is a strange feeling for me to be on the 'patient' side of the interaction. I am usually the one doing the explaining, the juggling with figures and the weighing up of possibilities. I never realised before how important the words of the explainer are, how each word carries its attached weight, its innuendo, its sentence. I resolve that I will choose my words with more deliberation in future.

I finish work reasonably early, at half past four, and decide to do some training on the punchbag before going home. As I leave the ward, Lindiwe waves goodbye to me. Her baby is lying on the bed with her. She is almost ready for discharge, but before I can release her, I need to find a translator to tell her that she is HIV-positive. I have been putting it off, justifying my delay by convincing myself that I am giving her a few more days of hope.

There is a traffic jam backing up from the exit of the hospital grounds all the way to the parking lot. After twenty minutes of waiting, my frustration at possibly forgoing gym has been replaced by a fear that I will run out of petrol waiting for the line of cars to start moving. My reserve petrol tank light has been warning me to fill up for three days already. I wonder what is causing the back-up of traffic. I wait for another fifteen minutes and move a further two hundred meters, which brings the exit within the range of my short-sightedness. At last I am able to discern the cause of the traffic jam. It's not an accident, as I had presumed, but a security check. The security guards, who usually dismiss me with no more than a cheerful wave, are stopping and searching every car as it leaves the hospital grounds. Eventually it is my turn and I get out of my car to open the boot for one of the guards.

'What are you looking for?' I ask.

'Things is getting stolen from the hospital.'

I am irritated. I want to ask him what on earth he thinks I would want to steal from the hospital. If I were going to steal anything, I would make sure that it was something valuable and useful, like a vial of morphine, that would fit very easily into my handbag, which he has not bothered to search. I am irritated that they have wasted forty-five minutes of my valuable time on such a stupid search.

'This is ridiculous, really. I'm a doctor here. I guarantee you that there is nothing in this hospital that I would want to steal.'

'Sorry, Doc, just doing my job. People will steal anything, you know. Just the other day someone stole a drawer from the desk in one of the doctors' rooms.'

My complaints are silenced.


# An altered view of the parasuicide

The trill of my cellphone shocks me out of my sleep. I think that it is my alarm waking me too early until I see 'private number' flashing on the screen. I wonder who could be calling me at one o'clock in the morning, but I answer because I hope it might be Julian.

'Is that Dr Carey?' a female voice asks.

Shit, I shouldn't have answered. It must be one of my patients.

'Yes, it is,' I say in a grossly unsympathetic tone. Whoever is calling had better have a very valid reason for waking me up in the middle of the night.

'It's Sister Travistock from Victoria Hospital casualty. We have a patient here who asked me to phone you. Her name is Gia or something. She said that you are her doctor.'

'Gina?'

'Yes, that could be it.'

In my half-asleep state I cannot think properly. I imagine Gina mangled from a car accident, on a ventilator, dead from a drug overdose.

'Is she okay? What happened?' My heartbeat threatens to deafen me.

'She's fine.' Thank heaven. 'She took an overdose of sleeping tablets and paracetamol, but she's stable. However, she's rather emotional.'

'I'll be there as soon as possible.'

'Please. Gia is a bit of a handful and we're very busy tonight.'

'Gina, her name is Gina,' I tell the sister, but she has already put down the phone. It strikes me that I never realised before now how important a name can be.

I pull on some jeans and a jersey and try to capture my curls in a hairclip with one hand while simultaneously brushing my teeth with the other.

I should have seen this coming. I should have prevented it. I should have spent more time with Gina and been firmer with her. Leah is sleeping at John's house, and I phone her to let her know what has happened and promise to keep her updated.

I drive to the hospital but my mind is far from the roads. I wonder if this would have happened if I had not forgotten my coffee date with Gina. I curse myself for not heeding the warning signs, all so obvious. I pray the whole way to the hospital that Gina will be okay.

I find Victoria Hospital easily and park my car in the parking lot. It is strange arriving at a government hospital as a visitor and not as the doctor about to start a shift. I see the people around me as other people, not as stab wounds or chest pains or gastros, not as numbers that I have to fit into the night. Gina has to be treated at a government hospital, as certain medical aids will not pay for suicide attempts unless the patient has been previously diagnosed with depression. On the few occasions that I have had suicidal tendencies, I have remembered this small but significant administrative detail and made a remarkable recovery.

I have not worked at Victoria Hospital before and so I do not know where casualty is. I ask at reception and the woman behind the desk directs me down a gently sloping corridor. Victoria Hospital is an old building, similar to Stellenbosch Hospital, with thick warped-glass window panes and wooden banisters shiny with the passage of hands.

I see Gina immediately on entering the casualty unit. She looks unfamiliar in the blue open-backed hospital gown, an outfit that I do not associate with my friends. She is sitting on the bed with her legs crossed and her head resting in her hands.

'Gina.'

She looks up at me, her eyes too big and too young for her face. She has been given activated charcoal to drink and her lips and the ridges on her teeth are stained black. 'I'm sorry about all of this,' she whispers. 'I just want to go home.' Her speech is slurred from the sleeping tablets and the alcohol, her breath sour from vomit. I ask her if she is okay and she tells me that she is tired. I help her to lie down and tuck the hospital sheet over her fragile frame. I wipe the black charcoal from the corners of her mouth and stroke her hair. Within seconds she is asleep. What I find strange is that I don't feel old tucking her up and stroking her to sleep: I feel the right age; Gina seems too young.

I read through the doctor's admission notes while Gina is sleeping. I wonder if he was irritated with her when she came in, if he shouted at her. She has taken an overdose of a few sleeping tablets and some paracetamol. She should be fine but they will keep her overnight for observation and to wait for the blood-toxicology levels. The psychiatrist will see her in the morning. Under the examination notes the doctor has written 'ETOH++++', shorthand for high alcohol levels, which I have used in relation to so many drunk patients myself. Her urine-toxicology screen showed positive for amphetamines and cocaine. It scares me to see it all written down, so real and without any excuses. Death does not have the patience to listen to justifications or apologies.

The night is long and I have too much time to indict myself. I try to quantify to what degree my negligence is to blame for Gina's breakdown. I worry that I should not have prescribed the sedatives for her. I question whether I did the right thing by backing down each time I confronted her. How much were my own insecurities determining my interactions with her? Eventually I can take it no longer and I get up and walk to the bathroom. I splash my face with cold water and rearrange my hair. I ask the sister, on my way back from the toilet, whether Gina's parents have been contacted. She says that they tried to get hold of her mother and her father but that neither was available. I want them to see Gina like this. I want her fragility and her bony limbs and her pale-blue government hospital gown to shock them out of their illusionary worlds of egotism and selfishness.

I don't like Gina's father. I went to her house once, one New Year's Eve. Her parents were having a party and I remember being impressed by the suave guests, the mountains of caviar-decked oysters and the heavy scent of imported perfumes. Her parents lived on the Atlantic seaboard and their house had a big wooden deck that looked out over the ocean. Everything, the flickering night-light reflections, the funky music, the buzz of tipsy conversation, was all so different from my parents' simple, family-orientated Greek–Irish household. I felt like I was part of a glamorous Hollywood movie until Gina's dad made a pass at me. I was fourteen at the time. I never told Gina. In fact, I never told anyone.

Now, as I sit beside Gina's curled-up skeleton, I recognise how grateful I am for my parents, even though they never threw film-star parties. For the first time, I am not jealous of Gina's beauty. It came at too high a price.

At eight o'clock I phone Bellville Hospital to advise that I will be a little late for the Saturday-morning ward round. Personal crisis, I explain. Gina wakes up as I get off the phone. 'Hey, you're still here,' she says, smiling at me.

'Of course. How are you feeling?'

'Shit, like I've been ridden over by a train. And like a real loser. I'm really sorry about this.'

I need to broach the subject of the drugs. I have thought of about twenty different opening lines during the night, but now none of them seems appropriate.

'Gina, I think that you may have a problem with drugs and alcohol,' I say eventually. I can't bring myself to use the word 'addiction'. 'Problem' sounds so much more manageable. 'I think that you need to go to a rehab clinic. The only reason I'm telling you this is because you're like a sister to me and I don't want to see you like this again. I'm not trying to lecture you or to be your doctor. Okay?'

I wait for her angry denial and her reassurances that she is fine, but perhaps the night's events have scared her because she just nods. I phone Gina's mother and explain to her what has happened, organise the number of a psychologist that does family counselling, and speak to half-a-dozen private rehabilitation clinics until I find one that will accept Gina.

At ten o'clock I leave Victoria Hospital feeling emotionally and physically exhausted. As I drive to Bellville to do my ward round, I can't help thinking that Gina is actually one of the lucky ones. She can afford to book herself into an expensive rehab clinic for as long as she needs to. Ironically, her modelling jobs and her wealthy parents have guaranteed her that. The tragedy lies in those people in similar situations who have nothing to fall back on and who get thrown out of hospital as soon as they are medically stable and have to try to find their own way back onto their feet. I wonder how many of them make it.

## HIV counselling

Miraculously, although I have been unable to get hold of a translator for the past two weeks, there is one available at Bellville Hospital this morning. Tired as I am, I know that I cannot let the opportunity pass, so I organise for her to meet me in ward D9, where Lindiwe is lying. The translator is a large Xhosa woman with orange beads plaited into her long braids. As she walks towards me I can hear the clicking of the beads knocking together.

I start by asking Lindiwe general questions through the translator: How is she feeling? Is she glad to be reunited with her baby? Does she feel ready to go home? Lindiwe answers that she is feeling much better and is definitely well enough to go home. I ask her, still via the translator, if she has heard of HIV before. She nods and the expression on her face becomes suddenly wary. I ask the translator to find out how much the patient knows about HIV. Very little, it seems. She knows that it is spread by drugs and blood and she knows that it can cause TB. She thinks that it is a sickness that makes people become very thin. I ask her if she knows that it is the same virus that causes AIDS. She shakes her head. I try to explain, in layman's terms, what HIV is and what AIDS is and the relationship between the two.

I tell Lindiwe, again through the translator, that we did an HIV test on her when she was delirious because we needed to know how best to treat her. I explain that only I know the result of the test. I ask if she wants to know the result and assure her that it will remain confidential. Lindiwe nods her head. I ask the translator to make sure that the patient understands the implications of finding out her test result and that she has someone she trusts enough to talk to about the result. The translator says something to Lindiwe in Xhosa and then tells me that the patient is ready to hear her result.

'Your test result was positive,' I say. I can see that Lindiwe has understood me without any help from the translator. She closes her eyes and cups her face in her palms. The only evidence of her crying is the shaking of her shoulders. After a while she wipes her eyes with the corner of the hospital sheet and asks me, via the translator, how she could have got HIV. I start explaining how the virus is transmitted but she interrupts me.

'She says that she has only had sex with one man, the father of the child,' the translator says. 'She says that she knows that this is true, so she cannot have HIV.'

'She does have HIV. We did two different tests and

both showed that she was positive. Does she know whether the father of the child had other girlfriends?' The translator speaks to Lindiwe and I watch her face as the implications of my words become clear.

Beneath everything that I am saying, my scientific explanations and rationalisations, I am telling her so much more. I am telling her that she is dying; I am telling her that the father of her child is dying; I am telling her that there is a chance that her child may be HIV-positive and may also be dying. The best-case scenario is that her child is negative and left with no parents.

'She wants to know if there is any way that you can treat it,' the translator tells me.

'We can give her some medication which will help her live a little longer, but it won't cure it. At the moment, there is no cure for HIV and AIDS.'

The translator speaks to Lindiwe and then says to me, 'She wants to know who will look after the baby.'

I don't know. What am I supposed to say?

'Tell her that she needs to get the baby tested so that we can start the child on antiretroviral treatment if the result is positive.'

Again the translator speaks to Lindiwe and Lindiwe responds.

'She wants to know how much longer she has got to live,' the translator says.

'Tell her that I am going to try to get her onto the list for antiretroviral drugs. If she can start on antiretroviral medication, she can have a few more years of being healthy. Probably five years, but up to ten years if she is very lucky.'

What is five years? I ask myself. What is ten years, even, when you are twenty-three? Realistically, Lindiwe will probably be dead before she is my age. I feel as though

I am lying to her because I am not telling her everything. I am not telling her how awful the disease actually is and that the five or ten years are very unlikely to be spent pleasantly. I am not telling her that the antiretrovirals can have serious, occasionally fatal, side-effects. In the First World HIV is treated as a chronic disease and patients live relatively normal lives. Unfortunately, my patient lives in the Third World. Perhaps I am acting immorally by withholding all of the facts from her, but something in her expression cautions me. She has been told enough bad news for one day.

I ask the translator to tell Lindiwe that I am going to discharge her later today and that I will give her a follow-up date at the infectious-diseases clinic. As I walk away from her bedside, I think about how much HIV has changed medicine in South Africa. It has brought with it a whole new host of illnesses and created a full dictionary of new medical terms. I wonder if anyone outside of the health profession realises the enormity of the medical, social and economic implications of the HIV pandemic. The relatively small number of people who are actually doing something about HIV is a poor reflection on human nature. Unfortunately, it normally takes personal involvement in the disease before people start believing that its threat is a reality.

## A West Coast diversion

I phone Julian and describe my awful night and morning to him and he tells me to get ready to be picked up in fifteen minutes to be taken to a surprise destination. Fifteen minutes is not long enough to shower, so I rub some foundation over the black rings encircling my eyes and drown myself in perfume to disguise the smell of hospital. Exactly seventeen minutes later, Julian is knocking on the front door.

I have never been in his old Land Rover before, and the clattering and whistling fills my ears so that I want to cover them. I can't even hear the radio and eventually I turn it off because it just adds to the din. Obviously Julian is used to the noise. He doesn't even try to speak to me, just turns his head to smile at me occasionally and squeezes my thigh with the hand resting on my leg. The luxury of the space in the vehicle, however, more than compensates for the deafening rattling. I can put my feet up on the dashboard and curl into a ball on the seat. In that position the noise somehow becomes more tolerable and I almost fall asleep.

Julian drives up the West Coast until we reach Langebaan. It is one of those winter days peculiar to the Cape, and especially the West Coast, in which the air seems clear and still enough to cut. The West Coast has a wild beauty, a beauty that, unlike the green gables and oaks of Constantia or the picturesque vineyards of Stellenbosch, is not always immediately apparent. The environment appears tortured by the elements: twisted kelp disgorged over sharp beaches, scarred rocks burned black by the sun, fynbos stunted and whipped by the wind. I try to explain this to Julian as we sit on the bonnet of the Land Rover watching waves break onto the rocky shore. He smiles and says that it is because everything about the West Coast is extreme: in summer, the wind and the heat; in winter, the bitter cold. He tells me that this is what he loves most about the West Coast. I wonder if that is why he enjoys medicine so much, because it is also filled with extremes. The emotions are never mild, not when you manage to save someone's life or when one of your patients dies, not when you have to tell a grandmother that her granddaughter has AIDS or when you give an old man his sight back after twenty years of blindness.

We stop for afternoon tea at a place called The Range that looks out over the lagoon. The division between water and sky is only just decipherable. We order scones that taste of too much baking powder and smother them in thickly whipped cream and strawberry jam. I realise, as I wipe a pinkish cream blob off my jersey, that I am happy. Happy with Julian, not because of him. I know that, even if it doesn't appear that way all the time, I do always try to do the right thing.

# Chapter Fifteen

## Coming clean

The students take turns helping me with the weekend ward rounds. Today it is Matthew's turn.

'You know what I wish most?' he asks me while I am filling in a chest X-ray form.

Probably that I will let him leave the ward round early, I figure. 'No, what?' I ask.

'That I just knew for sure I was clear.'

I put down my pen but continue staring at the X-ray form. This is the first time that Matthew has talked about his needle-stick injury with me, and I find myself unprepared for this discussion. 'It must be torture waiting,' I finally manage to say, looking up at him. 'The first test was fine, though, and that pretty much means that you're clear. The follow-up test is really just a safety net.'

'I know, but there's still that tiny chance that the test will be positive. Believe me, my mind can convince me that the smallest possibility is huge.'

'Matthew, I haven't had the chance to speak to you about this before, but I'm going to say it now because I don't want you to move on to another rotation without it ever having been said. I . . . I want to apologise for what happened. I've always felt that it was my fault. I should have drawn the bloods myself or made sure that Justine did it. You don't know how many times I've wished that I could just rewind time.'

'Oh, I do. Believe me, I do. I'll never forget any detail of what happened that morning because I've replayed it so many times in my head. Sometimes I rewind it for just a few seconds to when the prisoner knocks the needle into my finger, sometimes I rewind it to where you ask Justine to draw the blood, sometimes I rewind it all the way back to waking up that morning and wonder why I didn't decide to bunk that day.'

'I'm so, so sorry Matthew. I know that it's no consolation but I feel absolutely awful.'

'Don't, Dr Carey. I never even considered that you should have drawn the bloods. I was a bit pissed off with Justine at the beginning but then I realised, hey, shit happens and we have to deal with it.'

Shit happens.

* * *

I drive straight from the hospital to meet Carol for our usual coffee/rooibos tea. We meet in Constantia this time, because it is closer to where she lives and she is too ill now to drive far. There are oak trees outside the coffee shop and the thought passes through my mind that they will outlive both Carol and me. Looked at in that way, life is so insignificant. And yet as soon as the individual is introduced, the significance of life becomes the point of that person's existence.

Until she waves at me I don't recognise Carol, because she is wearing a wig of long black hair. I wonder why she has chosen black and not something closer to her natural blond. It is as though she doesn't want to hide the changes that are happening to her: is it an act of defiance? She has the same dream-catcher necklace around her neck that she was wearing the first time I saw her and it, in combination with her black nylon hair and hollow cheeks, makes her look unworldly. She hugs me when I get to the table. She is in a strange mood, too jovial, and I wonder if starting her on antidepressants was a mistake.

She laughs at her bald head and her new wig, laughs about all the weight she has lost, weight that she spent so many years dieting and exercising to get rid of. She laughs because now that she can finally eat whatever she wants to, she has no appetite.

'It reminds me of that advert,' she says rather loudly. The elderly couple at the table next to us glance in her direction. 'The one where a man is cutting a big, juicy orange and suddenly it squirts him in the eye. The punchline is that you never know what life is going to surprise you with next.'

Shit happens, I think. I don't recognise the advert, though, and I wonder if she has remembered it correctly. It was probably for an insurance company.

I haven't had time to eat since breakfast, which was eight hours ago, and I am starving. There is a piece of cake that I can see on the counter, directly across from me, underneath a big glass dome. I can't take my eyes from its four layers of alternating chocolate and caramel, but I feel too guilty to order it after Carol's talk about appetite. I speak to her to distract myself from the cake.

'So, are you feeling better than the last time I saw you?' I ask. 'You look a little bit better.' I'm lying, but it's justifiable, I think.

Carol says she is feeling much better and that she doesn't want to talk about the cancer. Instead she tells me about her childhood. She tells me about how she used to spend her holidays on her uncle's farm in Elgin and how she used to make miniature mud villages on the banks of the river that ran through the farm.

'Sometimes they would last for ages and the sun would bake them quite hard,' she says. 'Then suddenly, the river would rise overnight, and there would be nothing left of the village. Not a trace, as though it had never existed.'

She tells me about how she used to peel dried drops of resin off the branches of the apricot trees and how they looked like amber jewels when she held them up to the sunlight.

'Sometimes little insects, little fruit flies or mosquitoes, would get trapped in the resin. They would be perfectly preserved. You could see them, fragile black fossils in the amber,' she says.

She tells me that her aunt's rose garden was once a dump for the farm, more than a hundred years ago, and that she used to walk between the rows of roses collecting pieces of broken china to see if she could find ones that fitted together.

'The blue and white pieces were my favourite,' she says. 'Willow leaf, I think it's called. I remember once finding two pieces that fitted together. I think it was one of the most exciting discoveries of my life.'

I'm trying to figure out why she is telling me all of this. I don't know whether it is because she simply feels like reminiscing or whether it is because she believes that she is dying and she doesn't want her memories forgotten.

I try to steer the conversation back to the present. I ask her what the oncologist told her and whether he did a repeat chest X-ray, but she tells me again that she is not in the mood to talk about it and that she just wants to have a normal conversation, the type of conversation that she would have had before she fell ill. So I pretend that she is not sick and try to speak to her as I would to Leah. I tell her about a patient I saw last week who complained of chest pain. I tell her how I tried to get the patient to describe the pain to me.

'I asked him if it was a burning pain and he shook his head,' I tell her. 'I asked him if it was a stabbing pain and he shook his head. I asked him if it was like a dull ache and he shook his head. Eventually I told him that he must try to find the best way to describe the pain in his chest. He thought for a while and then he told me that it was like the pain of a '*verdwaalde poep*'. Imagine describing your chest pain like that: a fart gone astray.'

Carol laughs, and I realise that if all anyone talks to her about is her cancer, she probably doesn't get many opportunities to laugh. Nevertheless, it is difficult to act as if the cancer is not there. Not when it is so glaringly obvious.

\* \* \*

The house is empty when I get home. Leah is spending more and more time at John's house, trying to get used to living with him gradually. Contrary to what I was expecting, I'm actually enjoying the time alone. I like being able to listen to whatever music I want to whenever I want to, and to watch whichever television channel I choose. I like being able to buy crunchy peanut butter without the contents of the jar disappearing within a few days. I like being able to get out of the bath and walk to the kitchen naked to pour myself another glass of wine. And so, when I get home from coffee with Carol, I light candles and put on some New York jazz, which Leah hates, and pour myself a full glass of wine and sit on the couch and think about how lucky I am that I'm not a drug addict and that I don't have cancer.

## A case of bilious lung disease

I'm at outpatients and my first patient for the day is a man who wants a disability grant. He looks as though he is in his early forties and appears to be relatively healthy

'Why do you need a grant?' I ask him.

'It's my chest, Doctor. I'm very short of breath.'

'Do you smoke?' I ask, and he nods.

My examination of his chest finds no pathology apart from some mild emphysematous changes consistent with heavy smoking.

'I'll need to do some tests to see what the problem with the chest is. I can't make any diagnosis clinically. Everything sounds fine,' I tell him.

'But my chest is very weak. Can't you just fill in the form?'

'No, I can't. Anyway, don't you want to know what the problem with your chest is? If there is something seriously wrong, the earlier we're able to diagnose what it is, the more effectively we'll be able to treat it.'

'No, you won't be able to treat it. The other doctors all told me that my chest is too bad for treatment.'

'What other doctors?' I am abrupt because I am irritated that he is questioning my professional opinion and because he is so persistent in his desire for a grant.

'All the other doctors that saw me. They all said I needed a grant.'

So why didn't you ask one of them to fill in your disability grant form? I snarl in my head.

I send the man for full lung-function testing, the results of which are completely normal. I send him for a chest X-ray which, apart from a small, clinically insignificant bulla in the right lung apex, is normal. I tell the patient that all his results are normal and that he can still work.

He continues to insist that he qualifies for a grant. I tell him that I cannot fill in the disability grant form and he shouts that he wants an older doctor who actually knows something.

'I am your doctor, and while you are at Bellville you are stuck with me,' I reply with forced control. 'I have more than enough experience to be able to recognise a normal chest X-ray and normal lung functions. But since you are so convinced that you are sick, I will send you for an exercise test. That will give us an unequivocal answer.'

I complete the request for an exercise test and write in red capital letters on the top of the form that the patient is very uncooperative and that whoever does the exercise test will need to motivate him to exercise fully. I hand the form to the patient and explain to him how to get to the laboratory. On his way out he mumbles something about me being useless, but I don't have the energy to argue with him.

I have finished seeing the remainder of my patients by the time that the man with the shortness of breath returns from his exercise test. As I suspected, the result is completely normal. I tell the patient this and can't help adding that the results of the test have nothing whatsoever to do with my doctoring experience.

'So you aren't going to fill in the form?' he asks.

'Correct. I am not going to fill in the form. You are healthy and can carry on working.'

He storms out of my cubicle and I worry briefly that I might be ambushed on the way to my car by an irate man waving a green disability grant form.

\* \* \*

ROSAMUND KENDAL

Leah is leaving as I get home.

'Are you staying at John's house again tonight?' I ask her. I feel like company this evening.

'No, I'm going to visit Gina in that clinic you sent her to. The visiting hours are from seven onwards. Do you want to come along?'

I don't. I tell Leah to give Gina my love. I'll visit her another time, when I'm less hungry and tired. I've been seeing patients all day; I can't manage yet another one.

I call Julian to see if he wants to go to a movie but he is obviously busy because he cuts off my call. So instead I settle down with a slab of chocolate and *Tess of the D'Urbervilles*. I remember only when I get to the seventh and last part that the novel has a tragic ending. I am still busy wiping tears from my eyes when Leah gets home.

'How's Gina?' I ask.

'She looks very tired. I think she's still going through the withdrawal process. I wasn't with her the whole time; I only stayed for about half an hour and then met John for dinner. She said she wanted to sleep.'

'I don't think that trying to break free from an addiction is ever easy, but in her case I think it's even more difficult because it was an addiction to more than one thing. It doesn't help that the rest of her family is so unstable. At least she's at the clinic and seeing people who can help her.'

'Listen, Sue, there's something that I need to tell you.' Leah sits down next to me. She looks awkward and I panic. People giving you good news don't look awkward. I wonder if she is going to tell me that she and John have found a house and that she is moving out.

'I didn't know whether I should say anything, but I spoke to John about it and we decided that it was probably best that I tell you,' she continues.

I must be right. I want to interrupt her to tell her that

it's okay and that I have prepared myself for this, but she continues talking.

'Gina spoke to me about something this evening. Remember the night of my engagement party, when Gina was talking to Julian?'

Oh God, no. This has the potential to be worse than I thought. I notice my heart rate suddenly accelerate.

'Flirting is probably a more appropriate word,' I say.

Leah nods. 'Well, Julian mentioned to Gina then that he has syphilis. She wanted to tell you but she was too embarrassed to bring up the party, so she asked me to. I'm sorry.'

I am totally confused, too confused even to be upset. Julian with syphilis? I can't imagine it, but if it is true, I wonder why he hasn't just treated it. We aren't living in the eighteenth century. Syphilis is curable; all it takes is a shot of penicillin. Why on earth did he tell Gina about it? I wonder. What guy in his right mind would tell one of his girlfriend's friends that he has syphilis? And then a bell rings in the back of my mind and I start giggling and Leah's expression becomes even more worried.

'Are you sure he didn't tell Gina he has scabies?' I ask.

Leah looks puzzled. 'Gina could have got it wrong . . . I might have got it wrong . . . It was definitely something medical with an "s" that sounded bad.'

I call Julian and inform him of his new diagnosis.

\* \* \*

Matthew, Jono and Zahira have moved on to another block and a new group of students has started with me this morning. This extends my ward round by about two hours because I need to explain to them how I do ward rounds and what ward work I expect of them, and they need to get to know all of the inpatients in the ward. I ask one of the female students, a tall girl with freckles splattered across her cheeks in the pattern of a butterfly, to draw some bloods on a patient for me. She hesitates.

'You've drawn bloods before, haven't you?' I ask.

'No, not really.' She blushes.

'Not really? Does that mean yes or no?'

'I've seen it done but I haven't done it myself.'

No is what she means.

I turn to the rest of the group. 'Have any of you drawn bloods before?'

They all shake their heads. Great. I see the next two weeks suddenly becoming a whole lot longer than I anticipated.

'Right. Well, it's time to learn. Follow me.' I feel like a kindergarten teacher. 'I want you all to have drawn at least one blood and put up one drip by Friday.'

I take them to a geriatric woman I have admitted from an old-age home for a urinary tract infection. She needs bloods drawn and I suspect she is too demented to mind acting as a guinea pig. I show the students how to use a rubber glove as a tourniquet, show them how to feel, rather than look, for a good vein.

'The vein must be palpable, almost tense, underneath your fingertips. You will learn to recognise the feeling. Just be careful when you are taking blood near joints that you don't confuse tendons for veins because they can feel similar in very thin patients. Remember that veins are compressible. I think that for the first few weeks you should stick to trying to take blood from the cubital fossa because it's the easiest place to draw blood.'

The students crowd around the old woman's arm. Her skin is finely wrinkled, paper thin and tattooed with purple-red age spots. Her veins are clearly visible blue tracings that knot and branch just beneath the surface. But she is the exception. In many black and coloured patients the veins are invisible.

'Once you have found your vein,' I continue, working as I speak, 'clean the skin with an alcohol swab and then go in with the needle slightly to the side of the vein. If you go in from directly above the vein, it often slips away. If the veins are very mobile and slippery, you can anchor them with your other hand. In some patients you will actually be able to feel yourself going through the wall of the vein. Look for the flashback of blood and, as soon as you see it, stop progressing the needle. If you don't, you will go through the vein and blow it and end up with a big purple bubble beneath the skin and a very pissed-off patient.' I pull back on the syringe and draw up ten millilitres of blood. 'When you have finished, undo the rubber glove and put a piece of cotton wool over the puncture site, then withdraw the needle. If you forget to release the tourniquet you will make a huge mess and the sisters will not be impressed with you. Have you got all of that?'

They nod.

'So, are you ready to try your hands at drawing blood?' I ask.

The nods are not as forthcoming.

'I'll show you on one more patient and then you can try on your own. Remember to check with me that you have the correct blood-collection tubes before you draw the blood. Oh, and please don't go into an artery instead of a vein. Arteries pulsate.' It was a joke, meant to lighten the mood. They don't laugh.

I am busy watching the students blow patients' veins when the sister calls me to take a phone call in the office. The man on the line is the employer of the patient whose disability grant form I refused to fill in, the man with the apparently weak chest.

'I just want to check that it's safe for Mr September to be working on a construction site,' the employer says.

'Yes, of course. Why wouldn't it be?'

'Well, in your letter you said that he was on high doses of morphine. I was under the impression that morphine makes you drowsy.'

'What letter?'

'The one that you sent back with Mr September.'

'I didn't give him a letter. Could you possibly fax it to me?'

The fax shows that the letter has been written on a hospital letterhead and that my name has been signed at the bottom of the page, but neither the writing nor the signature is mine. I read through the letter. Apparently I have diagnosed Mr September *'with a rare and seveer lung disease (Bilious lung disease) that causes extreme pain and that he has to take morfene for. Because he is on very high doses of this morfene, he is unable to do any work except for extremely light jobs that do not have any activity.'*

Interesting. I know this forgery should piss me off, but the whole thing is so ridiculous that I can't help laughing. It confounds me that a healthy, albeit lazy, person would go to all the risk and effort of stealing a hospital letterhead and forging my signature just to get off work. I phone the employer and tell him that the letter is fraudulent and that the man is quite capable of working.

I know, of course, that there are greedy GPs with unsavoury practices who will complete a disability grant form with whatever diagnosis the client wishes, for a nominal fee of a few hundred rands. I wonder why the patient chose to come to me and not to one of those doctors. Perhaps he didn't have enough money.

* * *

## A declaration of love

Just before leaving the hospital, I get an SMS from Julian: *Dinner at my place at 7, no excuses, use your asthma pump before you come.* Of course I accept. How can I refuse someone who can pun in text messages?

I have never been to Julian's place before. The address he has given me leads me to a flat in a modern apartment building on the beachfront. I make my way up to the fifth floor and knock on the door. Julian answers in jeans and an apron, and I am very impressed.

'Are you actually cooking dinner yourself?' I ask.

'Of course. What did you expect? Some ready-made meal?'

'Ha, ha.'

Julian's place is small: a bachelor flat with an open-plan lounge and kitchen and a separate bedroom with en-suite bathroom. It is all cream and white with granite kitchen countertops and aluminium window frames. Simply furnished, no ornaments or decorations except for a woven Turkish saddlebag hanging on one wall and a didgeridoo leaning against the wooden bookshelf. I glance over the titles of his books; most of them are biographies of sportsmen. There is a small balcony that looks out over the sea and onto Table Mountain, and we sit there and drink champagne.

'I must just go in and check the pasta,' he says after he finishes his drink. I can hear him moving plates and banging pots in the kitchen.

'Can I help you with anything?' I shout through the open sliding door.

'No, just relax.'

I stand up and lean over the balcony railings. He comes back outside and puts his arms around my waist, kisses the top of my ear. Five floors below us, the people in the ground-floor flat are having a braai and the smoke from their fire mixes with the wet-kelp scent of the ocean. For a moment it's easy to imagine that I am camping on the beach.

Julian goes inside again but I stay where I am, my senses heightened. The air is cold on my skin and raises the hair on my arms.

'Julian, come and look!' I call to him. 'The sun's about to go down.' But he is still busy in the kitchen. He comes out again once the sun has set completely and only an orange glimmer on the clouds suggests that it was ever in the sky.

We make love after dinner and this time my chest does not close up. Julian's touch is lingering and gentle and, strangely, it leaves me feeling far more vulnerable than any of my aggressive one-night stands ever did.

'Julian, I really like you,' I say into the warmth of his neck. 'I know that this sounds stupid since I hardly know you, but I think I am falling in love with you.' I fall asleep squashed up against him. My dreams are green, like apple sherbet.

# Chapter Sixteen

## Pretty in green?

Part of the honour of being Leah's bridesmaid is that I get a dress handmade and fitted specially for me. Today is my first meeting with the dress designer. I ring the doorbell of the home salon expecting a gorgeously gay man to open the door. Instead, the dressmaker is a short, middle-aged woman with mounds of dyed black hair piled on top of her head. Leah has already chosen the fabric and the pattern so I am really just there for measurements. The dressmaker leads me to a large room cluttered with reams of fabric and half-finished wedding dresses. Veils hang from cupboard doors, replicated endlessly in the mirrors lining the walls, so that the room seems shrouded in mist.

The diminutive dressmaker stands on her tiptoes in her cork platform shoes and reaches into the top of a cupboard. She pulls down a piece of folded cerise silk.

'Is that the material?' I ask, disappointed. I was hoping for something more subtle.

'No, no.' She shakes her head and tut-tuts and reaches again into the depths of the cupboard. 'This is the material for your dress,' she says, pulling out a folded square of emerald-green satin.

I struggle to contain my horror. Throughout my life, I have been haunted by emerald green. I have never been able to understand why relatives and friends think that just because I have ginger hair and green eyes, I look good in emerald green. Or that I even like it. And why satin? For Leah, who has a plank-like stomach and mosquito-bite breasts, satin does not present a problem. She cannot know that the way light reflects off satin highlights every bump and curve.

The dressmaker frowns and tuts as she takes my measurements. I hope that it is in concentration and not consternation.

* * *

I phone Julian between the dressmaker appointment and my philosophy class. He doesn't answer and I wonder if my declaration of love has scared him. He probably thinks that I'm a completely psycho chick who falls in love with any man who pays her attention. How can I think I'm in love with him after knowing him for only a few months? I have been hurt enough before not to confuse infatuation and love. But the truth is that I do think I'm in love with him, that I want to spend every moment that I can with him, and that it scares me as much as it must scare him.

## Dripping arteries

Carol is not at philosophy class on Thursday night. The theme of the lecture is about living in the present instead of the past or the future, but I struggle to concentrate on Mrs De Marigny's words because I am worried about Carol. It is too late to phone her after the lecture, so I call her early on Friday morning. I don't realise quite how worried about her I have been until I hear her voice.

'Oh, thank heaven you're okay.' The words are out before

I have time to stop them. I am glad that she cannot see me blushing. 'I mean, are you okay?' I try to save myself.

'I'm alive, if that's what you're asking.' Carol hasn't missed the implications of my exclamation, but she is laughing. At least she still has a sense of humour.

'They admitted me yesterday. Apparently I have an infection that's out of control. I really feel miserable.'

'I'm so sorry, Carol. I'd like to come and visit you. I'm on call tonight, but do you think that I could see you tomorrow?'

She tells me which hospital and which ward she's in. After saying goodbye to her, I wonder how sick she is. I know what chemotherapy does. It kills off the cancer cells, but at the same time it kills off the rapidly replicating cells in one's own body, including those that fight infection. Chemotherapy wipes out one's immunity. It is like a drug-induced HIV except that different fighter cells are affected. Making judgements over the telephone is always difficult, but from what Carol has told me I suspect she has a neutropaenic sepsis, a medical emergency.

I want Friday and Saturday morning to be over quickly so that I can see how sick she is. I know that it's crazy because I am far from specialised in the field, but I want to check that the doctors looking after her are doing the right thing. I want to check that they are doing everything possible for her. I want to check that there is no 'Not for active management' written on the top of her prescription chart.

* * *

One of my students feels confident enough to cannulate on her own and she calls me to come and watch her. It is her first drip. The patient that needs the cannula is a fifty-year-old man who moved from England to South

Africa when he was twenty-five. He is muscular with a blue-ink tattoo on his right forearm, and he still speaks with a British accent. I make sure that the student has prepared the drip correctly by running the intravenous fluid through the drip line to get rid of the air in the tubing. I watch her tie the tourniquet and feel for a vein. I am glad that Carol is in a private hospital where there are no students. They would struggle to get drips up on her because chemotherapy destroys veins. It burns and scars the walls of the vessels until eventually they stop functioning properly.

'Dr Carey!' the student shouts, jolting me from my reverie. I look to see what has worried her. She has connected the drip to the cannula and bright red arterial blood is coursing up the drip line and into the bag of clear intravenous fluid. I can see that the student hasn't grasped what has happened. She is panicking.

'Take it out. You're in the brachial artery,' I say, leaning over the patient and closing the drip tap. The student pulls the catheter from the patient's artery and blood squirts rhythmically from the puncture site.

'Have you got some cotton wool?' I ask. She shakes her head.

'Shit.' I run off to find a ball of cotton wool. The ward seems to have run out, so I settle for the stiff tissues from the wall dispenser. By the time I get back to the patient's bed, the sheets are blood-drenched and the wall behind the bed is spray-painted red.

'Don't worry,' I reassure the patient, who has beads of sweat forming on his forehead. 'It looks like more blood than it really is.' I press down on the puncture site with the wad of tissues. Within seconds they are soaked through with blood. I tell the student to go get a bandage and some gauze so that I can apply a pressure dressing. I wonder if she will ever try to put up another drip. Wonder how long it will be before the patient self-discharges from hospital.

\* \* \*

When I get down to casualty, I discover that Lindiwe is back in hospital. This time it is not for trying to eat her baby. I can see even before examining her that she is critically ill. She is breathing quickly, struggling to get enough air into her lungs. Her whole body crunches up with the effort of each breath. I tell her to get onto a bed and I put an oxygen mask on her face immediately. I place my stethoscope against her back and listen to her lungs. Her airways are filled with fluid so that all I can hear are loud crackles. When I remove my stethoscope from her chest wall it leaves a pitted imprint of its shape on her oedematous skin. For some reason she is fluid-overloaded: either she is in cardiac failure or her kidneys are not excreting urine. I give her a diuretic and draw some bloods to check her electrolytes. She is too sick for me to wait for a porter to collect the bloods from casualty, so I run the bloods up to the lab on the ninth floor myself. The results are ready by the time that I have recovered my breath.

I check her electrolytes. The urea and creatinine are both raised more than four times normal and her potassium has risen to dangerously high levels, all of which suggest that she has developed acute renal failure. Her kidneys are not excreting urine and are failing to regulate the electrolytes in her blood. I restrict the total amount of fluid that she is allowed to drink to five hundred millilitres daily and instruct the sisters to measure any small amount of urine that she might pass. I write up drugs to lower the potassium and make a referral to the renal unit.

Her appointment at the infectious-diseases clinic is only for December, so she hasn't yet been started on her antiretroviral therapy. I'm worried that the renal failure is caused by the HIV itself: HIVAN, HIV acute nephropathy. The acronym sounds deceptively innocent, like some kind of vehicle. I order an ultrasound of the kidneys, but the only sure way to get a diagnosis is to do a renal biopsy.

\* \* \*

The next patient that I see is an elderly man, probably in his mid-seventies, wearing a brown suit with a matching waistcoat and felt hat. His shoes have been polished to a brilliant sheen. He walks into casualty leaning on a wooden cane, and at first glance he doesn't appear to be too ill. I read his name from the folder in my hand.

'Mr Paulsen, how can I help you?' I ask. He peers at me through the thick lenses of his spectacles. The plastic rim of the glasses has been bent slightly skew so that the spectacles balance unevenly on his nose.

'I went to see my house doctor,' he says, 'because I have blood coming out from, you know, from behind. He said I needed to come here because he was worried that there was something going on.'

'Oh dear,' I respond, wondering how he landed up with me and not the surgeons. Lower gastrointestinal-tract bleeding, unless it is of infectious origin, is a surgical problem.

'How long have you had the bleeding for?'

'Two days.'

'And is it fresh red blood or a dark black colour?' Blood from the upper GI tract gets digested and turns the stool black, while blood from lower down in the tract is bright red.

'It's bright red.'

'And do you have any pain with the bleeding? Any rectal pain?'

He nods and describes his pain to me.

'Do you have any other medical problems, sir?'

'I had a double ammonia two years ago.'

'I'm sorry?' Images of bath cleaner flit into my mind.

'A double ammonia, in my lung.'

'Ah, a double pneumonia?'

'Yes,' he affirms, 'a double ammonia in my right lung.'

'Anything else?'

'I also have a septic ulcer that's causing me some problems at the moment.'

I wonder where this ulcer is. Ulcers in elderly people often form on the lower legs where there is poor perfusion, especially if they are smokers or have diabetes.

'Can I see it?' I ask. I want to check that it is not infected.

The patient looks at me rather strangely.

'Could you show your ulcer to me?' I repeat myself, in case he has not understood me.

'No, no.' He shakes his head and looks worried.

'I am not going to do anything to it,' I say. 'I just want to make sure that it's not infected.'

'In my tummy?' he asks slowly.

'What?'

'My septic ulcer.'

The little light bulb above my head clicks on. 'Do you mean a peptic ulcer?' I ask him.

'Yes, a septic ulcer. I've had it for years. I take antacid for it.'

I explain to the man that I need to see where the bleeding is coming from and that this will entail a digital rectal exam. He is unusually reluctant (a moderate amount of reluctance for rectal exams among men is not uncommon, especially when I explain that it will be me doing the examination), and I wonder if the septic ulcer confusion has infringed on his confidence in my doctoring skills. I am concerned that the old man may be bleeding from a rectal cancer or a prostate cancer that has spread locally and so am glad when I pull down his underpants and see the deep purple grape-like haemorrhoids protruding from his anus. I refer him to the surgeon on call for a haemorrhoidectomy.

## Things fall apart

I get out of the hospital at eleven o'clock on Saturday morning. I have a quick shower when I get home, and then drive to see Carol. She is in a private hospital, not a government one, and as I make my way up to her ward I cannot help comparing it to the facility in which I have spent the last twenty-eight hours. The floors here are softly carpeted, in sharp contrast to the stained linoleum that graces the corridors of Bellville Hospital. The walls are painted peach with dark green trimmings and are decorated with popular kitsch reprints. No handwritten petitions to the Lord are necessary here. I walk past a trolley loaded with plates of roast chicken, rice and gravy and little bowls of jelly and custard. The food actually looks edible.

Carol is in her own room, isolated so that she doesn't pick up germs from any of the other patients. There is a bunch of flowers at her door, left outside because of the hostile bacteria that they might carry. Before I can enter her room, a sign tells me, I need to sterilise my hands and put on a mask and gown. I rub the alcohol into my skin to destroy any remaining Bellville micro-organisms. Crisp blue paper masks and gowns are folded into a bag next to the door. I take one out and wrap it around myself, then cover my mouth and nose with the mask. I wonder if I will be recognisable in my sterile disguise.

Carol is sleeping when I walk into her room. There is a jug of water and a glass on her bedside table. A television is suspended from the wall, directly across from her bed, and strains of Vivaldi filter through the air. The black wig that she was wearing the last time I saw her is hanging from the bedpost, the strands of artificial hair alive in the draft coming from the air-conditioning duct. It looks like a warning, a grisly scalping memento.

The doctors' notes and prescription chart are on a ledge at the foot of the bed and I glance through them. Everything is suggested in barely legible euphemisms. It is as I suspected: Carol has a neutropaenic sepsis. At 0.5, her white-cell count is far below 4, the lower limit of normal.

Although the doctors who are looking after her are still trying to locate the source of the infection and have not yet got back the blood-culture results, they have already started her on antibiotics that cover every possibility. She is also receiving G-CSF, or granulocyte colony stimulating factor, supposed to stimulate white-cell production and very, very expensive. The chemotherapy has been temporarily withdrawn to be resumed once her immunity has recovered.

It is strange to read someone else's notes and decisions, someone else's messily written comments. I don't know where or how I fit in. I don't know how to act on the other side of the bed.

I don't want to wake Carol so I decide to leave a note, but she opens her eyes as I am halfway through writing it. She smiles at me and pulls herself into a sitting position. Her nightgown has slipped off one shoulder and I cannot take my eyes from the bony ribs that have replaced breasts. Her skin is an odd colour, yellow without being jaundiced. Lemon yellow. Her eyebrows have thinned to almost nothing and her face looks oddly bare. I wonder why I don't notice these details on my patients. Perhaps it is because I am too busy looking at their illnesses.

'The oncologist says that if I can get through this I'll be okay,' she says. 'He's happy that the lymphoma is responding to this new chemo.'

Yes, but it is killing you, I think. I sit down on the chair next to Carol's bed and resort to pleasantries.

'I'm sorry that I didn't get you anything, but I was on call last night and came straight through. Is there anything you need?'

'Some nail-polish remover would be great. It sounds so vain but my nail polish is peeling off and it looks awful. The doctor keeps on wanting to look at my hands and every time I show them to him I get embarrassed.'

'Sure. Any other requests?'

'Not that I can think of immediately. I don't even know what I'm allowed to have in the room. Maybe the sister will confiscate the nail-polish remover. She took away the flowers from my aunt and uncle and put them outside the room where I can't even see them. Cheap decoration for the hospital, I think.' She carries on talking but my attention has been distracted. There is a photograph next to her bed that I have just noticed.

'Carol,' I interrupt her, 'can I see that photograph? Who's it of?' It's Julian, I am sure. There are three figures in the photograph: Carol, a man with his arms around Carol, and Julian. I even recognise the blue shorts he is wearing.

'It's my fiancé,' she says, handing me the photograph. 'The man next to him is his brother. But you've met him, haven't you?'

I'm too confused to answer immediately. I've mentioned Carol to Julian numerous times. How could he have forgotten to tell me that Carol is practically his sister-in-law?

Carol mistakes the meaning of my silence. 'You probably don't even remember him. His name's Julian,' she says. 'When I first met you at the philosophy workshops, you looked so understanding and approachable that I decided to ask you for some advice about my lymphoma. None of the doctors that were looking after me were female and I felt like none of them understood me. Of course, when I told my fiancé about it, he almost had a heart attack. He wanted to know where you worked, how much experience you had . . . all your credentials. All I could remember was that you worked at Bellville and sometimes did shifts at Paarl Hospital. He was so paranoid he asked Julian to check you out to make sure you knew what you were doing. I think Julian swapped a shift or something, so he was on call the same night as you. Anyway, he gave you the all-clear and my over-anxious fiancé was pacified.' She smiles. 'So much has happened since then, I'd almost forgotten about it. I don't think I ever asked you what you thought of him. Do you remember meeting him?

'Vaguely,' I lie. I need to get away. I need to be alone, away from Carol, so that I can try to make sense of what she has just told me. I say goodbye and walk quickly from the hospital building, my mind in a whirl.

I get in the car and put the key into the ignition, my hands shaking. I feel sick from the realisation that my whole relationship with Julian is a scam. He didn't come and talk to me that first time because he thought I was attractive; he came to speak to me because he wanted to make sure that I wasn't a quack doctor. The whole evening that I spent semi-flirting with him, he spent judging my medical skills. I recall all the times that I subsequently spoke to Julian about Carol, and feel like an absolute idiot. What was he thinking? Was he still checking up on the advice I was giving Carol? How I could have been so mistaken in my estimation of him? I was so sure that he was a nice guy. But nice guys don't lie to you.

By the time I get home I am furious. I'm angry with Julian and I'm angry with myself because I allowed myself to fall in love with him. I punch Julian's number into my phone. It rings long enough for me to think that I'm going to get his voicemail, but at the last minute he answers. I take a deep breath to stop myself from swearing at him.

'So, how would you rate me as a doctor, on a scale of one to ten? Do I make it? Do I pass? Or am I some crazy kook poisoning your sister-in-law's mind?'

'What are you talking about?'

'You can stop the lies, Julian. Did you just *forget* to tell me that the real reason you've been seeing me is to check out my medical proficiency?'

'No, that's not true, Sue. Let me explain.'

'Well it'd better be a fucking good explanation.'

'I admit that the reason I first introduced myself to you was to make sure you weren't a dodgy doctor, but after speaking to you for five minutes I knew my brother had nothing to worry about. Since then every time that I've seen you or spoken to you has been because I've wanted to. It's had nothing to do with my brother or Carol.'

'So why didn't you tell me?'

'I felt too embarrassed to. I'm sorry. Please don't let this ruin things between us, Sue.'

'It's a bit too late for that now.'

'Hey, come on. You're over-reacting. You know how much you mean to me.'

'No, I don't. Not after this.'

'Christ, Sue. I've pictured myself marrying you. I'm too old for superficial relationships. By the third time I asked you out, I was pretty sure that I wanted to marry you.'

'Cut the crap, Julian. Let's just leave it, okay. I knew I'd made a mistake getting into another bloody relationship. Don't bother trying to speak to me. If I want to speak to you again, I'll call you.'

'This is ridiculous, Sue. You can't end our . . .'

'Oh yes, I can,' I interrupt. 'In fact, I have. Cheers.' I slam down the phone. I knew that this would happen. I knew that I would get hurt again as soon as I allowed myself to fall in love. And Julian's betrayal could not have been worse, because my profession is the only sphere in which I feel any real confidence in my abilities.

## Meeting Carol's mother

I decide not to speak to Carol about Julian when I visit her the next day. Luckily she seems to have forgotten our conversation about him. I have bought a bottle of nail-polish remover for her and I hand it to her as I walk into the room.

'Thanks, Sue. You've got no idea how much this means to me. My nails are driving me insane. What a pity that you didn't come a few minutes earlier. My fiancé has just left. You could have met him.'

Thank heaven I did not come a few minutes earlier. 'How is your fiancé coping with all of this?' I ask quickly. I don't want to give her a chance to remember our chat about Julian.

'He comes to visit me every day, but I can see that it upsets him and then that upsets me. I can tell that he wants to leave as soon as he gets here and that he feels guilty about it. I think that he's still in denial and this reminds him too much of reality. I know it sounds awful but I almost wish that I were single. It would be so much easier for both of us.'

She turns her head towards the window. 'Sometimes I imagine that life is just a dream,' she continues. 'No one knows if it's real, there's no proof. Perhaps it's all a dream, a wonderful, wonderful dream, and when we die, we are actually waking up. Maybe I'm only just about to start living.'

'You're not going to die, Carol. I looked through the doctors' notes yesterday. They're managing you well. You're on the best medication there is.'

'I hope so. The doctors seem good enough and they're very nice to me.'

Again I have an odd feeling of misplacement. Am I one of 'the doctors'? Or am I Carol's friend?

The door of Carol's room opens and a woman walks in. She looks to be in her late fifties and has long, blow-dried blond hair and disturbingly familiar blue eyes, highlighted with thick black eyeliner. She brings the scent of cigarette smoke into the room.

'Ma,' Carol smiles, 'this is Sue, the friend of mine that I told you about from the philosophy workshops.' She turns to me. 'Sue, meet Marilee, my mother.'

'Nice to meet you.' Carol's mother stretches out her hand to shake mine. Her nails are long and beautifully manicured. 'Carol has told me so much about you,' she says. 'Now I can place a face with a name.' She speaks with the trace of an accent, vowels slightly too well-rounded and consonants articulated individually. I have heard the accent before, in Afrikaans doctors who have worked for a period in the UK.

'I brought some presents for you, my sweet,' Marilee says, turning to Carol. She digs in her crocodile-skin handbag and pulls out a brown paper packet marked with The Body Shop logo and hands it to Carol. The packet contains travel-sized tubs of body butter, hand cream, lip ice, shower gel and foot moisturiser, all in deliciously edible-sounding scents.

I had never really thought before about patients wanting toiletries, that they might need deodorant, body lotion, lip balm. Or even nail-polish remover. I'm too busy thinking about what medications they need and what investigations I must still request and how to interpret their latest blood results.

Which will mean more to Carol? I wonder. The analgesic that her doctor has written up or the strawberry-scented lip balm that she is rubbing on her cracked lips? Strawberries to disguise the rancid reek of cancer . . . Suddenly I feel exhausted. This is too much to think about.

I say goodbye to Carol and her mother and promise that I will pop in again within the next few days.

'Hopefully that won't be necessary. I'm going to be out of here soon,' Carol says. I look back as I walk out of the room. Carol's mother is leaning over her, smearing body lotion onto her arms as though Carol is a child. To her, I suppose, she is a child. To me, she is almost my age.

# *Chapter Seventeen*

## Early release

Lindiwe is crying when I reach her bedside on Monday morning. She looks sicker than she did when I admitted her. Her breathing is even more laboured and she is unable to lie down flatter than a sixty-degree angle. I check her urine output: one hundred and eighty millilitres in the past twenty-four hours. She should have passed at least a litre. I wonder how long it will be before her potassium approaches fatal levels, causing her heart to change rhythm. I ask the woman in the bed next to Lindiwe to act as translator for me and to ask Lindiwe what is wrong. In response to the question, Lindiwe lets out a mournful wail.

'Her baby died last night,' the unofficial translator tells me.

'Tell her I am so sorry. How did it happen?'

There is an exchange of Xhosa that I cannot understand and then the translator speaks to me. 'The baby was very sick, the stomach was running too much, so the aunt of this lady took the baby to the hospital. The baby died in the hospital. She has not seen her baby from the time that she came into this hospital.'

'Please tell her that I am so, so sorry.'

'She wants to know if she can go to funeral. It is tomorrow.'

I am ready to shake my head, body language that Lindiwe

will understand without the aid of a translator. She is far too sick to leave hospital, even if only for a day. Should something happen to her, I would be legally responsible. To let her go would be completely negligent. What would I say in my defence? *Well, Your Honour, since she is dying anyway, I thought that at least I could let her see her child buried. I understand, Your Honour, but I wanted to let her look at her child one last time and say a proper goodbye. I was under the impression that one is allowed to grant the dying one last request.*

'Tell her she can go, but just for the day,' I say to the translator. 'She must be back before the evening.'

Lindiwe smiles at me and I notice how dry and cracked her lips are.

## A heart-to-heart between manicured shrubs

I am so nervous that something will happen to Lindiwe while she is at her daughter's funeral that I wait at the hospital until she gets back. She arrives at five o'clock, breathless and tearful but still alive. I tell the sisters not to let her drink anything more today and rush to my car. Gina is expecting me at five thirty.

The rehabilitation clinic is a salmon-coloured building with spacious sculptured gardens. I give the receptionist Gina's name and she contacts her on her cellphone to tell her that she has a visitor waiting at reception.

'She'll be down in ten minutes,' the receptionist tells me in a well-modulated voice. 'She's just finishing her acupuncture session. Take a seat so long.' She points to a deep oxblood leather seat partially hidden by a monstrous arrangement of lilies. I collapse into the chair and pick up a magazine from the glass table next to me. The pollen from the flowers makes my nose itchy so that I continually have to rub it. I make a comment to the receptionist about how bad my hay fever is at this time of year so that she doesn't mistake me for a coke addict. The pages of the magazine are glossy and thick in my hand. They ooze class. It is a magazine for the wealthy, like the clinic.

Gina comes down the stairs wearing linen slacks and a long-sleeved linen tunic, all white. I wonder whether it is some kind of uniform, but she explains that is it her yoga outfit. She hugs me, then darts into a women's changing room to pick up a scarf, which she wraps around her head and neck, then leads me out into the gardens. Although it is not raining, it is still cold, and I pull my jacket more tightly around my chest. We walk between rows of perfectly manicured shrubs. I take a deep breath and summon up the will to tell her what's been on my mind.

'Gina, I've been meaning to phone you and apologise since the night that you were admitted, but I haven't got around to it. Maybe it's better, anyway, that I say it in person and not over the telephone.'

'Apologise for what?' She kicks a small stone off the gravel path. It rolls and skips before coming to land at the base of a rose bush shaped like a giant toffee apple.

'I should have seen all of this coming and I should have spoken to you about it sooner. I was so caught up in my work and in being a doctor and in my own insecurities that I ignored what was happening to you. I'm sorry.' This is the first time that I am voicing my guilt, even to myself. I wonder if my taking the plunge now has something to do with the distant salmon walls and the neat lawns.

'You're not to blame,' Gina replies. 'I could say that you should have done more or spoken up sooner. I've even felt that at times, but at the end of the day the choices that I made were mine.'

This is a different Gina speaking, not the Gina I know.

Is it possible to grow up in two weeks?

'I need to take ownership of the choices that I made and of my problems,' she continues. 'That is the only way that I'll be able to take control of them.' She smiles ruefully. 'At least that's what my psychologist tells me. It isn't easy, Sue. I think that I'm going to have to give up my dream of being an international model.'

'What? Why?' I can hardly believe it is Gina saying this. She has spent the last ten years of her life focused on becoming famous.

'I don't think it's possible for me to follow that career and not live the lifestyle that I was living. I'm not strong enough for that kind of pressure. Anyway, I'm far too old. All the other girls in my agency are still teenagers.'

I wonder if this is for real or if it is just another of Gina's phases.

'So, what are you going to do instead?' I ask. After leaving school, Gina spent one year training as a chef. She put on seven kilograms, then decided that the food industry was not for her. She then went to Cape Tech for a year and studied human resources management before deciding that she would rather do graphic design. I think that somewhere between giving up on graphic design and now, she did a course in astrology. How many options has she got left to try?

'I've decided to go to university. After all, I got a matric exemption. I want to study occupational therapy.'

'Really?' I have no doubt that Gina is very clever, but she has never shown any interest in studying anything seriously, or in working in the medical field.

'I've decided that I need to do something with my life. I think that if I can help other people I won't get so caught up in my own problems.' She stops in the path to finger the petals of a deep yellow rose. 'It must be incredible to make a difference in people's lives. I've been looking up on the Internet what occupational therapists do, and I think that they really can change people's lives.'

I wonder how much of this is her talking and how much is her parroting the psychologist she's been seeing. I want to tell her that you actually hardly ever do make a difference, that the problems are too many and too big. I want to tell her about the people who don't care about what you do for them and about the people who don't thank you and about the people who think that it is a prerequisite for all medical workers to be superhuman. I want to tell her about the sheer frustration and overwhelming helplessness you feel when you can't help. I want to tell her about the poor pay, the unglamorous lifestyle, and that she will have to wear flat shoes and unflattering green slacks. But something stops me. Maybe this change is for real. And, as much as I hate to admit it, on that rare occasion when you do make a difference, then it is all worth it.

## Trying to be a good doctor

It's Wednesday and I'm on call again. An overdose patient comes into casualty, a nineteen-year-old girl with a history of multiple previous suicide attempts. She also has a history of depression, for which she is on antidepressants, and freely admits to being a cocaine addict. With images of Victoria Hospital in my mind, I am infinitely patient with her. Although I have fourteen other patients waiting, I sit down and ask her why she took the overdose. She tells me that her boyfriend died two months ago from a cocaine overdose and that she wants to be with him. I make what I think are suitably sympathetic sounds and explain to her that she will have to be admitted for observation and a psychiatric evaluation. She promptly starts screaming that I am a fucking cunt and a useless doctor who thinks I know everything. But I am not so easily ruffled; Gina is fresh in my memory. I tell her that it's okay to be upset but that she does need admission.

'You fucking doctors. You think you know everything just because you studied for six years. You know shit. Do you know what it feels like to be an addict?' No, I chose not to go in that direction. 'Do you know how people die when they take a cocaine overdose? You don't have a fucking clue.' I do not tell her that it is part of my job to know how people die when they take a cocaine overdose. 'Their veins close up,' she educates me, 'and they have multiple strokes and heart attacks.' I let the error pass; the danger actually lies in the arteries that go into spasm. At least the last part of what she said is relatively true. 'Do you know what that must feel like?' she shouts. It takes immense self-control for me not to tell her that cocaine overdoses don't occur at random. I surprise myself with my patience and my voice sounds incredibly restrained as I ask her if she would like a tablet to calm her down.

'You fucking bitch. You're just trying to poison me,' she screams, getting up from the bed. I grab her arm to stop her from running away and she bites me. Her teeth leave bright red semicircles on my forearm. I let her go and yell for a security guard to restrain her and then write up a strong intramuscular sedative.

The bite has not punctured the skin. It looks oddly like a ringworm. I rub my arm to try to dull the pain and wonder why my first attempt at being a good doctor has been rewarded in this way.

The next patient that I see has been brought in by the police because he has been acting aggressively at home. According to the report that the detective hands me, he tried to stab his mother with a garden fork. Two psychiatric patients in a row. I wonder if it is full moon.

The policemen bring the patient into the unit and he sits meekly on the bed. I ask him his name and he answers me politely. He smiles at me and says he feels fine when I ask him how he is. The policemen are still standing at the foot of the bed, but their presence is obviously unnecessary. Compared to my previous patient, this man is the epitome of good behaviour. I suggest to the policemen that they most likely have much better things to do with their time, but they glance at the patient and then at each other and tell me that they will wait until I have sedated the patient. I hardly think that sedation is necessary. I ask the patient a few more questions about himself and he remains respectful and well-mannered. He even leans down to pick up my pen for me when I drop it. Then I ask him what happened with his mother and he suddenly jumps up and lunges at me. I think that it was the word 'mother' that triggered the attack. I back away and the patient rips a wooden box from its bracket on the wall and throws it at me. I manage to jump backwards so the box hits my knee and not my face. The policemen leap onto the man and two security guards join the fray. Eventually it takes five men to restrain the patient enough for me to inject him with a very strong sedative. Only once the patient is limp and his hands are tied to the bedsides do I realise that blood from my knee has soaked through my clothes. I roll up the leg of my trousers to reveal unshaved legs and a deep, three-centimetre-long gash. I curb the bleeding as much as I can and hobble to trauma. The cut will need stitches. I want to cry. My arm is sore, my leg is sore, the policemen are laughing at me, and both of my attempts at being a good, caring doctor have ended in sedation. Worst of all, Julian has not ignored my ultimatum. He hasn't called me.

# Chapter Eighteen

## Reappearance of the Camel-man yacht owner

Carol phones to tell me that she is feeling better than she has in ages and that the doctor has discharged her. I wonder how she managed to recover so quickly and whether I over-reacted when I visited her in hospital. She asks me to tell the philosophy class that she is doing much better and to thank everyone for their support. I doubt anyone in the class would even notice if I stopped coming to the workshops.

The Camel-man yacht owner has reappeared. Had I known that he would be back, I would have at least put on some make-up for the class. He has carefully cultivated stubble on his chin and looks tougher and more tanned than before. The reason that he is so tough and tanned is that he has been sailing in the Mediterranean for the last two months. He tells this to the group just before he introduces us to his new wife, whom he met during his nautical excursions. She is a Cypriot, with wild dark eyes and almost black hair and breasts that are disproportionately large for her slender frame. She doesn't speak much English. I wonder how they communicate, and then it occurs to me that when you are as beautiful as she is, it doesn't really matter. What man would want to waste time on conversation with her? I am so lost in contemplation of the foreigner's black eyes and the sailor's stubble that I almost forget Carol's message. I blurt it out as Mrs De Marigny announces that she wants to plan a group visit to see Carol in hospital.

The topic of the lecture is the same as last week: being in the present moment. We are asked to give examples from the week when we remembered to be fully 'in the now'. I rack my brains trying to think of a personal observation while everyone else spurts forth illustrations. Gilbert the builder saved a man's life because he was in the moment and caught a falling brick that would otherwise have landed on the man's head. If he had been thinking of something else, he might never have even seen the brick, he tells us. A woman stopped someone from crossing the road in front of a truck because she was in the now and saw that the truck was not going to stop. I wonder how many lives have been lost because of my daydreaming. Even the Camel-man yacht owner, who was not present at the previous lecture, has an example. He saved his beautiful wife from injury when he noticed, by being in the moment, that the kitchen counter on which she was lying was about to collapse. I picture the scenario he is describing, aware that there is only one reason for people to be lying on kitchen counters. I will myself to abort this train of thought, and volunteer that I have remembered to be in the present moment only once during the week, and that was immediately after leaving the workshop the week before. Mrs De Marigny smiles patiently and assures me that as long as I am trying, it is okay. I leave the class resolving to concentrate more on being in the now. And never to visit Cyprus.

## The HIVAN highway to the thirteenth floor

Lindiwe has had her renal biopsy and I get the results. She has an HIV acute nephropathy: renal failure caused directly by the human immunodeficiency virus. Apart from antiretroviral drugs, there isn't much that will help her. I try to explain the problem to her via a translator, but she seems listless and uninterested. Ever since she returned from her child's funeral, it is as though she has submitted herself to the idea of dying. The aunt has stopped visiting her.

For some reason, I find myself noticing the oddest things about Lindiwe. I notice that she has a red, yellow and green beaded necklace around her neck. I notice that she has bitten her nails down to expose tender, bloody nail beds. I notice that every morning she washes her dirty underwear in the bathroom and then hangs it to dry over the rail at the head of her bed. I notice that her lips are cracked and peeling.

I am learning, long after leaving medical school, that doctoring lies in the small things as much as the big. The first heart transplant was a huge achievement, the development of antibiotics marked a definitive step forward in medical history, and the discovery of fibre optics changed our way of thinking about surgery. But for the dying patient with painful, cracked lips, it is lip balm that is important.

## Holding vigil

Carol is back in hospital. She managed five days out in the world before falling sick again. This time she is more seriously ill. I phone the hospital and ask what ward she is in, and the receptionist informs me that she has been admitted to intensive care. I visit her straight after work.

Even within the intensive-care unit, Carol has been given her own room to try to limit her exposure to germs. Her mother is sitting at her bedside when I arrive, dozing with her head resting in her hand. She jolts awake as I walk into the room.

'Sue, sorry, I fell asleep.' She looks ashamed, as though by sleeping, by letting down her guard for a while, she has let Carol slip further away. She has lost weight since I saw her previously. I wonder when last she slept properly.

'They're giving her morphine,' she says. She is rolling the edge of Carol's sheet between her forefinger and thumb. 'I don't know how conscious she is, but I try to talk to her as though she is awake. There are times when she wakes up and says a few words to me, but most of the time she just sleeps.'

'I have a few hours free. Why don't you go home and shower and have something to eat? I'll stay with Carol until you get back. You can give me your cellphone number and I'll call you if anything changes.'

'Please call me if she wakes up. You understand how important that time is for me.'

I nod. 'Of course. I'll call you right away.'

Carol's condition is significantly worse than when I last visited her in hospital. I don't need to read the doctors' notes to understand how ill she is. I try to look at her as though I am looking at a patient, objectively. But I cannot; there is too much emotion involved. Her bald head is covered in scabby sores. Her skin is pulled into the dip of her temples and there are hollows below her cheekbones. The corners of her mouth are split open. I pick up her hand and it is light. It reminds me of the little fallen bird that as a child I picked up from underneath a tree and cradled in the palm of my hand, hoping I could save it. She must have painted her nails again during the time she was discharged, but already the polish is starting to peel off. I look for the polish remover and cotton wool in her bedside drawer, sit down and start wiping the layer of pink from her nails.

Julian's confession has caused me to double-check myself. I wonder if I gave Carol the right advice, now so long ago, when she first asked me if I thought she should have chemotherapy. Did I lie to her when I told her that the side-effects of chemotherapy are not as bad as they used to be? I can't help wondering if she would be this sick now if I had told her to opt for alternative treatments instead of chemo. As a doctor, I know that if she had not had chemotherapy, the lymphoma would have killed her. But as a human being, I cannot help doubting the wisdom of the professional advice I gave so confidently.

## Rock-bottom with nowhere to go

Wednesday starts off badly when I get to Lindiwe's bed and it is empty. She has died overnight. The sheets on the bed have been changed; they are clean and unrumpled, ready for the next patient. Lindiwe's few belongings have been removed from the bedside table, her name erased from the ward patient list. Her aunt stopped visiting a while ago and I wonder if she knows that her niece has died. It's as if Lindiwe never existed anywhere except in my mind. Mother and child, both a figment of my imagination. When the father of the child passes away, if he hasn't already, it will be three of them, the beginnings of a family, cut short by the ravages of AIDS. And who will be left, at the end, to mourn the dying families?

\* \* \*

I have been in outpatients for just over an hour when I notice that my cellphone is missing. I discover its disappearance when I reach into my bag to see if by chance Julian has called, a check I do wishfully every hour or so these days. I tip the contents of the bag out onto a bed: car keys, two pens, my wallet containing a twenty-rand note, a crusty lipstick without a top, some spare drip needles, no cellphone. I call my number from the telephone in the sisters' office and get my voicemail, which means that the thief has already ditched my SIM card.

I generally keep my bag on me at all times, slung over one shoulder; I leave it unattended only on the rare occasions when I am urgently called away from a patient I am busy with and leave the bag at the patient's bedside. Somehow the fact that one of my patients, someone I was trying to help, stole something from me upsets me more than the loss of the phone itself.

I go to the small police station on the lower ground floor of the hospital to report the theft. The police officer, a friendly man with a big, round face and a bumbling manner, explains that it is a waste of time for them to try to find the thief, but he will give me a case number if necessary for insurance purposes. My phone is not insured. And I want the culprit found.

I don't realise the full implications of the robbery until I want to call Leah later to tell her about the incident and can't remember her number. An awful realisation dawns on me: not only do I not know Leah's number, but I don't know Julian's either. It strikes me that I am going to lose the man I love because of a stupid ultimatum that I made and because some idiot has stolen my phone. I would probably find the situation ridiculously farcical if it involved anyone else but me.

I walk down to the cafeteria to console myself with

something to eat and try to feel grateful that at least the thief left my tuck-shop money behind. But I can't ignore the despairing realisation that, should Julian decide to ignore my ultimatum, I will never know. He could be trying to phone me at this very moment. I buy myself a cup of coffee and an extra-large slice of caramel-topped cheesecake and make my way to the only empty table in the cafeteria. Unfortunately the path to the unoccupied table passes Donald. Not only Donald, I register with horror, but Donald and Justine. As I am about to turn around and make a bolt for the cafeteria exit, he notices me and beckons me to join them. Now that they have seen me, running would only make me look more pathetic. I hesitate, and in my moment of indecision the empty table becomes occupied and I am left with no choice but to sit down at the table with them. I become acutely aware of the fact that I woke up too late to put on make-up, that I haven't washed my hair for three days and that I am carrying a monstrous slice of cheesecake that I definitely don't need.

I wonder what has happened to Justine's Johannesburg boyfriend. She is all over Donald: rubbing his leg, kissing his neck, advertising ownership. I can see that Donald loves the adoration, but what Justine doesn't realise is that Donald will never be owned. I even feel a little bit sorry for her.

I wolf down my cheesecake, feeling no obligation to share it, and get up to go back to outpatients. As I pick up my bag to leave, Donald asks me how things are going with my new boyfriend. Great, I think, every time Donald asks me about a boyfriend, things are going badly.

'Uh, we're not speaking at the moment,' I say, hoping I don't sound as sheepish as I feel. 'My cellphone got stolen and I lost his number.' I can only hope that mentioning the phone theft will distract them from the truly pathetic aspects of my situation.

'I'm so sorry,' Justine gloats, slipping her arm around Donald's waist and pecking him on the cheek.

\* \* \*

I go straight from work to a dress fitting. Leah meets me at the dressmaker's house, bridal folder under one arm. She keeps lists of all the things that she needs to do before the wedding. As I arrive, she hands me a piece of paper headed 'Sue's dress-fitting appointment dates'.

We knock on the door and the diminutive dressmaker ushers us into the veil-misted room, then hands me a carefully ironed bundle of green satin to try on. The dress looks worse than I imagined it would. Miraculously, I have managed to put on weight since the dressmaker measured me and my breasts bulge over the top of the low-cut bodice so that I look more like a woman of ill repute in an old western than a bridesmaid. The zip gets stuck three centimetres from the top, even with Leah pulling on the hem and the dressmaker standing on a chair and yanking from above. This is the last straw. I sit down on a pile of emerald-green satin surrounded by incomplete wedding dresses and start laughing. Leah looks uncomfortable and whispers something to the dressmaker, who tuts and shakes her head.

I think that my life has hit a record low: I have one friend in a rehab clinic and another dying in intensive care, I have frightened away the man I love, my cellphone has been stolen by one of my patients, I have six stitches in my knee, I don't fit into the bridesmaid's dress that I am supposed to be wearing in just over two months' time and my former object of infatuation is sleeping with my former intern. It all seems hilariously funny. Surely things cannot possibly get any worse. Leah eventually manages to entice me outside.

'What the hell is wrong with you? It's hardly funny!' she snaps at me once we are alone.

'Leah, did you see what I look like in that green satin? A fifties porn star. I'll have all your divorced uncles hitting on me.'

She starts laughing too, but I am not sure if it is at what I have said or in relief that I am not actually having a nervous breakdown.

'Okay, okay, we'll change the dress,' she says, scribbling a note in her folder. Dresses, at least, can be changed.

# Chapter Nineteen

## Susie Q

As a young child, whenever something horrible happened to upset me, I would run to my father for sympathy. He would carry me to his study and take out his record player. It was a red portable record player, the size of a small suitcase, with little grey feet. He would twist a knob here and a dial there and then reach up to his shelf of LPs. He would finger through them, pretending to be searching very hard for a particular record. Sometimes he would act as though he couldn't find what he was looking for and then, just when I was at the point of believing that this time it was not a game and that the record really had disappeared, he would whip it off the shelf.

'Goodness!' he would say. 'Can you believe it? I wonder how this got here.' And I would giggle, injustices and spiteful comments forgotten. He would wipe his arm over the sleeve of the LP, removing any dust that might have collected, and then he would reach inside the cover and hand the shiny black record to me. I would balance the vinyl carefully on the turntable and my father would flick a switch and then lower the needle onto the edge of the spinning disc. I would stare at the record cover as I waited for our song, at the four strange-looking men with shaggy hair and Abraham Lincoln beards who sang that they loved me. Eventually I would hear the opening chords and the wailing voice:

*Oh Susie Q,*
*Oh Susie Q,*
*Oh Susie Q,*
*Baby, I love you,*
*Susie Q.*

The guitar would tremble, John Fogerty's voice would crumble and then my father would grab my hands and swing me around his study. When he got tired he would put me down and we would jump-dance together across the floor.

*I like the way you walk,*
*I like the way you talk,*
*Susie Q.*

We would have a competition to see who could do the most bizarre walk or pull the most outlandish expressions while singing along. My father always won. He would crinkle up his lips to reveal his big front teeth and then waddle in circles like a duck.

I outgrew the song and my father's waddling sometime between the ages of eight and nine and only remembered them again in matric. I was working part-time then as a junior care attendant at a health club and saved up every week's wages to buy myself a compact disc player. They were expensive then, cutting-edge technology, and my purchase took pride of place on top of my bedroom bookshelf. The first CD that I bought was the *Creedence Clearwater Revival Platinum Collection*. Track nine was my song:

*Say that you'll be true*
*And never leave me blue,*
*Susie Q.*

That song still works to cheer me up. I can't help believing, every time I play it, that one day I will meet

someone who feels that way about me.
*Say that you'll be mine,*
*Baby, all the time,*
*Susie Q.*

*Oh Susie Q,*
*Oh Susie Q,*
*Oh Susie Q,*
*Baby, I love you,*
*Susie Q.*

# Reading Lewis Carroll

I visit Carol again on Thursday, before the philosophy lecture. Her mother is still at her bedside and I wonder if she has moved at all since I was last there. She smiles at me as I walk into the room, but it is an empty smile, a mere flicker of her lips. Her eyes are dull with grief and exhaustion. She gets up when I enter the room as though she has been waiting for me, as though we have some pre-arranged agreement.

'Thank you for coming, Sue,' she says, and I nod.

Carol is more restless than she was the last time I sat with her. She tosses and turns and the thin sheet covering her gets caught up around her legs. She is so wasted that I wonder how she has the energy to move. She moans occasionally and the sound is unfamiliar, more like the cry of an animal than a noise a human would make. The monitor above her bed displays her blood pressure, pulse rate, arterial pulse pressure and a single-lead ECG tracing. The volume of the alarm has been turned down but there is a continuous muffled beeping in the room. Don't forget that you are dying, it says over and over again. I wonder if

Carol can hear the monitor. I wonder what her reality is, what landscape the morphine is creating for her.

Carol once told me that her favourite story as a child was *Alice in Wonderland*. Today, before coming to the hospital to visit her, I had searched through the brown cardboard box of my childhood books that my mother packed for me when I left home. In standard five I won the prize for most promising pupil, a copy of *The Complete Works of Lewis Carroll*. Now, seated at Carol's bedside, I take the book from my bag and open it up to *Alice in Wonderland*. The pages are yellow and brittle with disuse and bear the faint tracings of petals where I pressed dried flowers between them.

'*Alice was beginning to get very tired of sitting by her sister on the bank, and of having nothing to do,*' I start reading. '*Once or twice she had peeped into the book her sister was reading, but it had no pictures or conversations in it, "and what is the use of a book," thought Alice, "without pictures or conversations?"*'

I don't know if Carol can hear me through the morphine, but I read anyway, just in case she can. I don't hear Carol's mother returning and, when I take a break from reading and look up, I see her standing in the doorway listening to me.

'Do you think it's because of my smoking?' she asks me, unexpectedly. 'Do you think it's because when she was younger I smoked around her?'

'No, I don't think so. I don't think that your smoking has anything to do with Carol's illness.' My response is not entirely true. I really don't know the answer to her question, but I am sure there is little point in making her feel guilty now.

## Answering questions

I arrive late at philosophy class. When I walk in, I tell the group that Carol is critically ill. I explain to them that she has a very bad infection that her immune system cannot fight and that because of the sepsis her body is unable to maintain its normal functions. I describe how her arterial pressure is falling, how her blood has lost its ability to clot properly, how her liver and kidneys are showing early signs of failure. I can't bring myself to say aloud the simpler and truer words: Carol is dying.

I wonder what the philosophy workshops meant to her. To me, they are an exotic, fairy-tale escape from reality, recharging sessions that give me the energy to go back to the harsh injustices of what I am faced with daily. But I suspect that to Carol they meant more than that. She started the course with the knowledge that she had a potentially fatal disease. She must have been looking for answers. She is not a loud person but she always joined in the arguments and discussions. Unlike me, she wasn't content just to listen. She always wanted to know more and to probe deeper, and I hope, more than I hope for anything, that she found some answers in the lectures.

This evening's talk is on the nature of love but there is little discussion. The group seems subdued by my news. A moth flutters around the light on Mrs De Marigny's side table and throws exaggerated shadows against the walls. I wait for the hiss of it hitting the burning bulb. Somewhere in the neighbourhood, a car alarm goes off. The window is open and the wind causes the red velvet curtains to billow inwards. It's a chilly wind, a winter wind, bringing a bitter inevitability with it. I cross my arms over my chest to keep it out.

Mrs De Marigny delivers her lecture almost

uninterrupted by questions. I close my eyes and listen. She describes the different forms of love, tells us that the ancient Greeks had different names for what we clump together under the label of 'love' and asks us to think of examples in our own lives of the different forms of love. And then she asks us to consider whether in their truest forms, their essences, the different forms of love are not the same. The exercise for the week is to open our hearts. That is all the direction that we get: open your hearts. But I think that Carol has already taught me this lesson.

## Alternative medicine

Perhaps because of Carol, I actually remember the philosophy class exercise over the course of the week. I try to open my heart. I listen properly to my patients and to their families, as much to what they don't say as to what they do say. As a background to each admission, I imagine grieving mothers, lonely partners, distraught friends. I think of opportunities lost and dreams destroyed. Clivias flowering unseen. This is the first time in my medical career that I have actually allowed myself to explore such possibilities and to think beyond what medications and interventions will help my patients.

I always worried that if I allowed myself to think these thoughts, I would not cope. Strangely, the opposite happens. For the first time I feel as though I am making a difference. I pay attention to the small details that are so often forgotten in the race to get patients better and discharged. Little things that count: counselling a patient behind the privacy of closed curtains, answering a relative's questions fully, putting a glass of water next to the bed, treating medically insignificant inconveniences like dry eyes and constipation. Lip balm.

It was fear that kept my heart closed, fear of giving too much and in the process losing myself, but I realise now that it was the closed heart that made me feel a failure as a good doctor. Being a doctor requires knowing how to treat patients, what medication to give when, which interventions are necessary and which superfluous; it is about knowing which drugs interact well and which are toxic together, about eliciting signs, interpreting ECGs, X-rays and scans; it is about knowing when to initiate treatment and when to withdraw it. But being a good doctor is doing all of these things with an open heart.

## Changing houses

As a compromise, Leah and I are choosing the new material for the bridesmaid's dress together. After looking through five fabric shops we eventually find something that we agree on: a simple silver-grey voile.

'John and I have found a place,' Leah says to me as we walk out of the shop. Her announcement is unexpected. I had forgotten that they were looking.

'Oh, that's nice. Where is it?' I ask, trying to keep my voice level. While I knew that this would happen sooner or later, hearing Leah's news makes me feel as if I have swallowed a slightly off oyster.

'It's in Wynberg. We can go past the house now, if you want to see it. It's a stunning semi-detached cottage with wooden floors and sash windows and the cutest little garden at the back. It's got the most beautiful front door: wood with stained-glass insets.'

'So when are you moving in?' I try to sound cheerful, happy for her.

'The beginning of next month.'

That is so soon. From next month I will be alone in

the house. No more Leah. No more burnt meals. No more smooth peanut butter. No more rainbow figure paintings on the fridge. I suppose that I could advertise for a new housemate, but I don't know if I will. If I budget well I can afford the rent, and perhaps now it is time for me to be on my own.

'Let's go past it,' I say. 'I'd love to see it.'

## An avoidable tragedy

I have a patient in ICU, a forty-five-year-old woman who was beaten up by her boyfriend. I know her from a previous admission. I saw her about a year ago when I was working a trauma shift at another hospital. She came into the trauma unit drunk, with big purple bruises over her back, buttocks and inner thighs and three stab wounds on her left leg. Her clothes were bloodstained and, when I removed them, I noticed that her G-string was dirty and torn. I spoke to her as I stitched up her lacerations. I asked her whether she had been raped and she denied it and refused my suggestion that I do a crime kit on her. I asked her whether her boyfriend had beaten her up before and she assured me that this was the first time. I asked her whether she was going to leave him, and she convinced me that she would kick him out that night since it was her house anyway. I asked her if she was going to make a case against him and she said she didn't think so but that she would consider it. Later that evening, I spoke to her thirty-year-old son, who had brought her in, and he told me that it was not the first time that she had been beaten up, that it happened on a regular basis. I urged him to persuade his mother to make a case against the man. He said that he already had and that they had got a court interdict against the man, but his mother had forgiven her boyfriend and allowed him to move back in with her.

I didn't think about the woman again until she was admitted to the hospital three days ago. I recognised her immediately on walking into casualty. Her hair was longer and dirtier than it was the first time I saw her, with grey streaks showing in the blond, and she had put on about ten kilograms, but the rest of her was unchanged. She was referred to hospital with an infection and renal failure, but I discovered soon after admitting her that her problems were far more complicated. She was seriously ill with a florid sepsis and she was passing almost no urine. She was confused and semi-comatose with a Glasgow Coma Scale score of ten out of fifteen. Because of the bruises on the rest of her body, I sent her for a brain CT scan to exclude a head injury. The brain scan was normal. My examination did not reveal any source of infection that could be causing the sepsis. She had no neck stiffness to suggest meningitis. Apart from two broken ribs, her chest exam was normal. The few millilitres of urine that she was passing showed no infection and the only abnormality on abdominal exam was slight tenderness supra-pubically. None of her haematomas seemed to be infected, and there were no sores or ulcers on her skin that could be causing the sepsis. The only finding of note was an offensive vaginal discharge, for which I started her on the relevant antibiotics. And yet her condition continued to deteriorate so rapidly that she needed to be transferred to intensive care.

When I get to her bed today, she is in overt septic shock and her GCS has dropped to six. I have to intubate her to protect her airway and give her an adrenaline infusion to sustain her blood pressure at acceptable levels. She is on three different kinds of intravenous antibiotics to cover all possible organisms and yet she is not getting any better. I send her for a repeat brain scan just in case the initial one was done too early to pick up pathology. It is normal. I request a mobile abdominal ultrasound but, because she is a large woman with most of her body fat on her middle, the result is equivocal. All that the radiologists are able to pick up is some fluid in the pelvis.

This leaves me with two possibilities that I can think of. The one is that she has a fungal infection, for which we have not started her on empiric therapy because the drug used to treat fungal infections is nephrotoxic and she is already in renal failure; the other possibility is that the source of the infection is still present and we are missing it. I draw blood for another blood culture and decide to examine her thoroughly once again in case I have missed something. I listen to her chest but it is still clear. I search her skin for any infection and find nothing. I feel her abdomen and notice that it is tenser than before. When I palpate the lower abdomen, she contracts her abdominal wall muscles, a reflexive guarding, which she was not doing before and which is indicative of abdominal pathology. I pull down the sheet covering her lower body in order to palpate her groin for nodes or a strangulated hernia and notice the smell. It almost makes me gag. I open the patient's legs slightly and the smell gets worse. I can feel beads of sweat forming on my forehead and blood rushes to my face. I start retching from what is probably the vilest, foullest stench that I have ever encountered. At least I now know the origin of the infection.

I take a tiny jar of Tiger Balm from my bag and shove the Vaseline-like cream up my nostrils and around my nose. The menthol and eucalyptus scent burns and makes my eyes water, but it disguises the reek. I get a pair of gloves and some KY jelly and call the sister to stand with me while I do a vaginal exam.

ROSAMUND KENDAL

The source of infection is a blue-handled pair of scissors, the kind used in primary-school classrooms. It has eroded through the vaginal wall and penetrated the rectum. If I had done an abdominal X-ray I would have picked it up immediately. Although I remove the pair of scissors, the patient is still critically ill. She may not make it, and if she doesn't, I will be partially to blame. I should have done a vaginal exam sooner, when I first noticed the offensive discharge. I should have done an abdominal X-ray and not just an ultrasound. I should have remembered what I ignored the last time that I saw her.

Why did she stay with the man? Why didn't she get out when she could, when her injuries were minor? Why was her boyfriend not locked away the first time that he abused her? I try to put the blame onto someone else. Should she die, I will find it very difficult to live with her death on my conscience.

Perhaps the philosophy lectures are right about beauty and about opening the heart, but I am not so sure that they make a correct assessment of the nature of mankind.


## Rites of passage

I visit Gina again in her salmon-coloured haven. We walk in the topiary garden where small-leaved bushes have been clipped into balls and squares. Our feet step in and out of geometric shadows. Gina is happy. I hope that her happiness will last outside this place of quiet order.

'I've got a response from the University of Cape Town,' she tells me. 'I can apply for the occupational therapy degree at the end of the month.'

'So you really want to go through with this?'

'Yes, I do. I know that you probably think this is just another one of my bright ideas and that I'll lose interest

286

soon, but it isn't,' she says. 'I don't think you understand what an awful place I was in before I landed up here.' She is speaking in psychologists' terms again. 'I felt like I was spinning out of control. Did you ever play that game as a young child, where you spin around and around, faster and faster, until you fall?' I shake my head. 'Well, I did. I used to spin until I got so dizzy I would throw up. And until I actually threw up, the spinning was worth it because I felt like I was flying.'

We walk in silence again and I notice that even the distant hum of traffic seems muffled here.

'And your parents?' I ask eventually.

'They need to sort out their own shit. They need to grow up.' Her tone is harsh, driven, I think, by anger. 'I have my own life to get on with.'

'Well, if you need to borrow any medical textbooks, please let me know. I think I still have all of mine hidden away somewhere.'

'Thanks.' She smiles. I have sanctioned her decision.

Gina is four years away from thirty and Leah and I are two years away, and only now do I feel like we are entering the realm of adulthood. The Xhosa have initiation rites that have to be passed before one is considered an adult. We haven't had to paint our faces or stay in isolated mud huts for weeks, but I think that all of us, in our individual ways, have managed to pass the tests set for us.

## Continuing the story

I take *Alice in Wonderland* with me every time I visit Carol. I have an unexplained urgency to finish reading it to her before she dies. She is still barely conscious, fluttering in and out of awareness. She has developed something called adult respiratory distress syndrome secondary to the sepsis and she has been put onto a ventilator. The deep, measured sighs of the ventilator and the background beeping of the monitors form the soundtrack to my reading.

At times I am convinced that she knows that I am sitting with her and that she can hear Lewis Carroll's magic. At other times, I wonder if she has left her body already and I am reading to an abandoned vehicle. Her mother and I have become silent, ghost-like friends: she gives me a smile before she slips from the room and squeezes my hand when she returns, damp-haired and smoky, a few hours later.

I have met Carol's father. He is a taciturn man who wears outdated spectacles balanced on the bridge of his hawk-like nose. He stands at her bedside, his agile hands restless. They are vet's hands, hands used to solving problems, and so he rearranges her sheets, fills the glass of water that now only her mother drinks from, neatens the pile of doctors' notes. And when there is nothing left for him to do, he escapes with a gruff farewell.

* * *

I continue reading: '*Alice noticed, with some surprise, that the pebbles were all turning into little cakes as they lay on the floor, and a bright idea came into her head.*' Carol stirs, and for a moment I feel an irrational hope. I lean over the edge of the bedside and grasp her fledgling-like hand, but the stir was an involuntary movement, a physiological spinal reflex.

I put down the book and stare at her body. It is a shell driven by automated machinery, not Carol. Where is she, I wonder? I want to shout her name, shout and shout until she hears me and incarnates the empty husk on the bed. I want her to smile at me. I want to hear her comforting chocolate voice. I want to go ice-skating with her, even if it means ten years in a plaster cast. I want to share sticky syrup pancakes with her.

I wonder if she saw her clivia bloom in those few days that she had at home. I have an absurd desire to pick some clivia for her. It doesn't matter if the flowers aren't from her garden. Any clivia will do, just as long as she gets to see the flowers. I run from her room down to the hospital grounds and search frantically for a flash of orange, but I find only pink and white roses, purple-misted lavender bushes and white mayflowers that are already starting to turn brown. I sit down on the neatly mown lawn, in the dappled shade of a plane tree, and call Carol's name. Loudly at first and then more and more softly, until it becomes a mantra chanted in time to the swaying of my torso.

I have left my book in Carol's room, on her bedside table, and I run up to ICU to fetch it before leaving. Her door is partially closed and I can hear a man weeping inside the room. I hesitate, unwilling to disturb the man's mourning. I know, instinctively, that it is Carol's fiancé in the room with her. I pull the door closed gently and ask the nursing sister to put the book with Carol's other personal belongings once her fiancé has left.

## Risk-taking

I don't know what makes me decide to risk contacting Julian, but I think that perhaps it is the memory of the sound of weeping from behind Carol's half-closed door. In the lament I heard grief in its purest form, the sound of absolute loss. I want to love someone that much; I want to love someone despite or because of the possibility of that much heartache.

Besides, I miss Julian.

I wonder if, when I got cross with Julian, I was subconsciously looking for an escape from a relationship that was threatening to erode my little wall of protection. Am I such a coward that I would rather lose Julian than risk failure? What a miserly way to live: never to try anything because the cost might be too high. In fact, that isn't living at all. Living is acknowledging that sometimes the returns are so great that it's worth taking all the risks. I dial the number of Paarl Hospital switchboard and ask the operator to page Julian.

'Julian, it's Sue,' I say quietly when I hear him answer. 'I want to apologise . . . I just wanted to explain the way I behaved because I was scared . . . I'm sorry, I'm not making sense. I miss you.'

'You took bloody long enough to call.' I can tell from the tone of his voice that he is smiling.

'I know. I'm sorry.'

'I miss you too.'

We arrange to meet at the Waterfront in half an hour, at the same place that we met before. Julian is already sitting at the bar waiting for me when I arrive. He doesn't notice my entrance immediately and I stop for a moment and watch him from a distance. I know the way his floppy blond hair falls forward as he reaches for his glass of beer. I know the tiny scar beneath his right eye where the fin of his surfboard cut him. I know, without having to see them, the ginger freckles on the skin between his right thumb and forefinger. I know the feeling of his cheek stubble beneath my lips. I can't help smiling. I know that, when I reach him, he will smell like apple sherbet.